FINDING *Kate*

A NOVEL OF THE TAMING OF THE SHREW

MARYANNE FANTALIS

CITY OWL
PRESS

FINDING KATE
A Novel of The Taming of the Shrew

CITY OWL PRESS
www.cityowlpress.com

Cover Design by Olivia at MiblArt. All stock photos licensed appropriately.

Edited by Amanda Roberts.

For information on subsidiary rights, please contact the publisher at info@cityowlpress.com.

Print Edition ISBN: 978-1-944728-15-1

Digital Edition ISBN: 978-1-944728-22-9

Printed in the United States of America

For Jeff

PART ONE

Whitelock Town

Chapter One

Sunday

I f you asked my father, he'd tell you I got my husband thanks to his clever plans. If you asked my husband, he'd say he won me over with his wit and his charm. But really, it all started with a horse, a horse that stopped me in my tracks and changed my life.

A flash of bright color in the corner of my vision made me turn my head. Two men were leading an enormous blood-red horse out through the door of the inn's stable and onto the pounded dirt of the adjacent yard. I halted, my breath rushing out in astonishment. The beast was the approximate size and color of St. George's dragon, or so it seemed to me, and it moved with the same sinuous, menacing grace. When it snorted, I jumped, half expecting gouts of flame to burst forth. The tread of each massive hoof raised a cloud of dust in the yard and seemed enough to shake the world, or at least the whole of England. I had some experience of the world, of course. I had seen large horses before, plowing the serfs' fields outside of town or drawing Father's heavy wagons full of merchandise, but this creature with flames in its eyes and cinders in its lungs was a thing apart.

The horse came to a stop, gleaming in the sun, and the men stepped away. One of them I recognized: Tom Smith, the town's farrier and blacksmith. He moved toward the horse's flank as the other, a stranger, grasped the stallion's headstall, reaching under his chin. He looked the beast in the eye, seeming to engage him in a silent conversation, and then nodded to Tom. The smith crouched beside the giant animal, running his hand down a foreleg like a tree trunk and lifting one of the massive hooves. He rested it in his lap, cradling it firmly between his thighs while he inspected the shoe and the underside of the hoof. The stranger stood over him, throwing one arm across the horse's neck and leaning into its bulk. The horse barely flinched at the man's weight, even on three legs, as though he were no more burden than a fly. Though I quivered at the fire I sensed barely restrained within the animal, neither man seemed concerned.

Even from this distance, I was arrested by the newcomer. His face was carved in pure angles: a straight nose, strong cheekbones, a level brow, a lean mouth that curved, even at rest, toward a smile. His hair, of a color somewhere between gold and brown, was short—a warrior's cut—and standing up a little over his forehead. My fingers twitched, longing to smooth it down.

I wondered what color his eyes were.

He looked up at just that moment and spied me staring. He smiled, a wise smile, a knowing smile.

My skin flushed hot from my scalp to my toes. I drew in a breath that was thick with horse stench and, choking, hurried to catch up with my father and sister, neither of whom, of course, had noticed a thing. Falling in step behind them, I kept my eyes cast down at the cobbles, another lifelong habit, to avoid the glances of the other townsfolk also on their way to church on a Sunday morning. Instead of nodding to neighbors, I watched my shadow where it stretched out thin before me, tripping on the heels of my father and younger sister. The two of them walked arm in arm, their golden heads close together, whispering—about what, I could not tell, which suited me well enough. In a few strides, we were past the inn and in the village square, and from there the church was only a few steps across the lush green.

"In nomine Patri, et Filii, et Spiritus Sancti...."

Ordinarily, I would entertain myself during Mass by picking apart the priest's errors in Latin. He fumbled his words at least a dozen times every Sunday, and I endured the tedium of Mass by placing bets with myself as to which of the sacred words he would destroy this week. Would he say *"terror"* instead of *"terram"* as he did last week? Or would he have corrected for that, only to make a disaster out of the *"Confiteor"*? Meager entertainment, but better than nothing.

Yet this Sunday, my thoughts wandered out of the church like errant children, back to the sunny morning and the stable yard of the Brewer's inn. Questions arose and floated through my mind, elusive as soap bubbles. Who was he? Where was he from? Was he just passing through, asking the smith to check his horse before he rode away again? Or would he stay? And if he did stay, would I see him again?

With a start, I came back to the present and realized I was alone in the church. Everyone had left. *They should not have.... They should have....* Gripping the edges of the bench I sat upon, I drove my nails into the wood. No. In Whitelock it did not matter what should or should not have happened. Father behaved as he liked and everyone followed his lead. It had always been so, sure as the sun shined or the rain fell.

Drawing a deep breath, I released my fingers one by one and stood. I took my time getting to the rear of the church and paused in the doorway, looking out at the folk of the town in the square. About a hundred souls, more or less, gathered in little groups around the thick grass of the green, formed where the roads out of town knotted together. The packed turf of Church Street ran north and south and cobbled High Street ran east to west. Directly across from the church, a clutch of sturdy little wattle-and-daub buildings squatted like chickens at roost, their little shops quiet on a Sunday. The sooty planks of the shed around the forge leaned against the Smiths' house and buckets of sand assembled like soldiers just outside the wide door. I looked for, but did not see, the giant red horse being fitted for new shoes there.

I stepped down from the church's stone lintel and crossed the rutted dirt onto the green. None of the groups opened to invite me, which disturbed me not at all as I did not seek to join any of them. Instead, I stopped and shaded my eyes, looking along the two roads. When the man with the blood-red horse left town, which way would he go? Up Church Street, past the fancier shops—the dressmaker and the chandler, the glover and the mercer—to take the great King's Road to Leicester or Nottingham? Or would he head south, toward Coventry? Would he travel west past the church, toward Shrewsbury and Wales? Or continue east, past Father's house, going all the way to

London?

Or, I thought with a chill despite the warmth of the summer morning, had he already gone?

I frowned, lowering my hand. If only I had a horse of my own... nay, more: had I a man's rights, his freedoms....

Were I a man, I would mount up and never look back.

Two farmers ambled past, relishing their morning off, their stained and wrinkled shirts exuding an odor of earth and sweat that simply would not wash out. One of them removed his cap and scratched at his tanned brow. Squinting up at the sky, he said, "Rain tomorrow, you think?"

The man beside him peered upward. "Nah. Not for a day or more."

A sigh escaped me. This same conversation, about the chances of rain or snow or the return of fair weather, was repeated outside the church every single Sunday. Did they never grow weary of it?

A clutch of matrons had gathered in the shade of a crabapple tree to one side of the church, cackling and gabbing in their Sunday finery. "Did you hear?" said one. "Elizabeth Darrow is with child again."

"Are those new sleeves, Eleanor?" another said, ignoring the first.

"Again?" said the next. "My goodness, what is that, their eighth? Bless them, they are as abundant as rabbits."

"Did you like it? It's the rosemary that makes all the difference."

To my ears, their voices were like wind over empty jars: all cacophony, no music. I tried to shut out the sound, wishing again that I could leave like the knight on his horse or at the least sneak away home, like the children I spied slinking around corners to play at games forbidden on the Sabbath. But Father was on the far side of the green, holding conference with the other elders of the town, and my sister Blanche stood like a queen surrounded by her courtiers under an ancient oak, and neither of them would even begin to entertain the thought of leaving yet. Even now, Blanche's laughter rang out, a beacon no less imperative than the church bell had been, pulling all eyes to her, even mine, though for me to look at her was tantamount to staring into the sun. The other young folk of Whitelock surrounded her, hanging on her every word, pale shadows around her dazzling crimson silks and expensive lace. No, Blanche was happy to stay and would complain at being made to go home.

It was I, forgotten at best and scorned at worst, who suffered from Father's dictates. Aye, if I had a man's freedom, I'd be long gone from here. There had to be a place where wit was valued over beauty. Where I, and not Blanche, would be favored. And maybe even loved.

I glanced at Father and his circle of somber men. Would he notice if I walked away? What would he do if I did?

By now, the matrons had noticed me. They swept me up and down with sharp eyes like needles on my skin. I shuddered and clenched my hands into fists, enjoying the feeling of my nails driving into the skin of my palms. I began to walk with determination toward no particular destination. All I knew was that I had to get away from the women and their scathing eyes, their piercing judgments, their unspoken condemnation: *There she goes, the shrew, the old maid.*

I made it as far as the lustrous clutch of holly bushes just west of the Brewer's inn before I was brought up short by a man saying, quite loudly, "But have you ever seen a woman so perfect?"

I froze, looking around for the speaker. He sounded so close, as if he were right at my elbow. But there was no man in sight, only the thick leaves of the holly all around me.

"I'll grant you, she is beautiful," another man replied, "but must we tarry a week entire?"

For the flutter of a heartbeat, I thought perhaps they were talking about me. My face flushed and my hands trembled as I pressed them to my mouth to keep from gasping aloud. But then the truth collapsed upon me like a pile of rotten timber: no, not Kathryn the shrew, Kathryn the unmarriageable, Kathryn the unlovely. I knew I should walk away and not listen to their conversation any further; gossip was a sin, and so was eavesdropping. But in that moment, I could not have made my feet move if my dress had been on fire.

"Your father will be mightily displeased," went on the second voice.

"What of it?" the first man said, all impatience and command. "It's just a few days. I'll still get to Warwick and deal with his affairs before he gets there, and he'll be none the wiser. And in the meantime, I'll spend my time with her. A girl like that is a treasure rarely to be found. So lovely, she would tempt Jove himself down from Olympus."

A treasure? Jove? Heavens above, did anyone outside of poetry speak thus?

"If you're determined to do this, you need to know the obstacles you face," said the other man, clearly the more practical of the two. "I am given to understand that there is an older sister yet unmarried, and the father will not permit anyone to court the younger sister until the elder is respectably attached."

"What of it? You'll step in and court the elder so I may have the younger."

I stiffened, grinding my teeth. There was now no mistaking who they were talking about. The beauty for whom Jove would descend from Olympus was Blanche, the younger sister, and the unmarried elder sister was me. With nails again drilling into palms, I leaned in closer to hear their words.

"No, no. You misunderstand," the second fellow replied. "As I have heard tell, the elder is a shrew of notorious harshness. No man of good sense would risk kissing her hand for fear she'd smite his head off as he bent before her. That's why she remains unmarried."

If the truth had been a hard fall before, it was more painful now. I closed my eyes and remembered why my heart was always bitter. Even these men—even strangers who had never met me—called me shrew.

The first man fell silent, resentment pouring off him even through the thick foliage. "There must be some way to get to her," he said at last, urgency in his every word. "We can go to her father, sell him something, meet her that way."

"Your father has all the wares and all the authority," the other man replied. "You have nothing to sell."

There was a thud and a yelp as a blow was thrown and landed. "You needn't remind me," said the first fellow. "If you're so smart, *you* think of something. What does a rich man need?"

I could tell him what my father needed. He needed to unload his unwanted older daughter. I opened my eyes and for a wild moment I contemplated pushing my way through the holly and taking out all my frustrations on these unfeeling young men.

"Kathryn!"

The voice of Ellen Brewer cut through my nascent thoughts of violence and pulled me away from the holly thicket. Reluctantly, I dragged my feet the short distance to where Ellen stood by the ancient rowan tree in front of her parents' inn. The stout, solid place had been maintained with pride by her family since brave King Henry, fifth of that name, took his armies blazing through France and brought home a queen some seventy years ago. It had bedchambers for six guests but was mostly frequented by visitors to the common room below where her father served two kinds of ale and his famous hard cider. The inn—my steps grew decidedly less reluctant as I remembered the giant war horse and its handsome owner. Perhaps Ellen knew something of him if he was a guest.

"Good morrow, Ellen," I said, trying to make my voice as friendly as possible and shake off the lingering bitterness from overhearing the two men.

Ellen quirked a half smile that showed more of relief than real pleasure. "I thought surely you'd be caught spying on those two men," she said. "What were you thinking?"

I drew breath to snap back at Ellen in my own defense, then thought the better of it. In this town of some one hundred souls, Ellen was the only one whom I could count as a friend.

"I was strolling by myself. I can't help it if they choose to have a conversation out in the open where anyone can hear," I replied.

She swallowed a sound and I knew she wanted to scold me. But meek, timorous Ellen also had few friends in town and so we were always careful of what we said to each other. Any moment, the sharp-eyed, sharp-tongued matrons would spy us together and launch their word-arrows at our backs.

And they called *me* "shrew."

"What news, Ellen?" I asked, trying to deflect the stream of my thoughts.

"Have you heard about the visitors at our inn?"

"Visitors? More than one?"

Ellen gave a sly smile. "Indeed. Two wealthy gentlemen arrived last night and paid for a week's stay."

"Wealthy gentlemen?" If she was implying something about their eligibility, that was the kind of gossip that delighted Blanche, not me. Still, the man with the massive red horse.... "Merchants come through our town all the time on their way to bigger and better places. Why do these men matter more than any of them?"

"The gentlemen are unmarried."

Ah. Unmarried, and staying for a week in our town. Suddenly the conspiracy behind the holly bushes began to make sense. One of these wealthy fellows wanted to court Blanche without his father's interference and didn't want to heed his friend's sensible advice.

I gave a little toss of my head. "Let everyone get in a dither about it, but the news can make no matter to me."

"I would not be so sure," she said, her tone dark.

"What can you mean?" I demanded.

She opened her mouth to speak but snapped it shut and shook her head. Instead, she grabbed hold of my arm and pushed me forward. "Kathryn!" she hissed urgently in my ear. I turned toward her, my eyes demanding an explanation. "Your father," she whispered.

From across the green, my father's gaze upon me rang like a blacksmith's hammer, sharp and fierce. He made a small movement with one hand, summoning me to his side. I stamped my foot in frustration. I had not had a chance yet to ask Ellen about the man with the red horse. "Later, Ellen, we must continue this conversation."

She nodded but was already slipping away. No one wanted to be between me and my father's anger.

I hurried to Father's side and dipped him a curtsy.

"Kathryn," he said, his teeth tight. "Please, join us."

The men exchanged a glance as dismal as their garb. Master Hover, a white-haired wisp, picked up the dropped thread of their conversation. "As I was saying, I thought the quality of strawberries Old Ballard brought to market last week was not up to his usual standard."

The others nodded gravely.

"There is talk," another man put in, "that a certain merchant on Church Street is putting his finger on the balances." He raised his eyebrows significantly, and they all harrumphed. For this, Father had summoned me from my friend?

The men and their strawberries. The women and their sleeves. Babies and balances.

Oh, it was exhausting, and there was no respite in sight. But rather than let loose the howl of frustration that welled inside of me, I chose the only outlet I ever had in this company: words.

"*Taedēre,*" I said brightly. Latin. *Taedēre*: Infinitive. To be weary.

Of course none of them understood me. "*Taedeō, taeduī.*" I am weary, I was weary. I smiled around the circle of befuddled men, having a little more fun with the Latin conjugation. This bores me: "*Taedet mē.*"

Father turned his face toward me, his eyes flashing with anger. He took a firm hold of my elbow, squeezing so hard my fingers tingled. "What did you say?"

"I was just thinking, Father," I lied, "of a book I have been reading at home. Would you be terribly unhappy if I went home to fetch it? It is one of Madame Christine de Pisan's books, very edifying for a young woman to read...."

Before he could answer, portly Master Horton, a merchant whose balding pate made him look older than his nine-and-twenty years, waddled over to join our group. I shifted as far as my father's restraining hand would allow, to avoid the odor of unwashed skin that preceded him.

"Good morrow, Master Mulleyn," Master Horton said, bowing low before my father. Father nodded to him, a king acknowledging a subject. Thankfully, his grip eased with the movement. "I come to offer you news of some import, which I hope and trust will please you."

I rolled my eyes.

"What is it, Master Horton?"

Before he could speak, another wealthy merchant shouldered his way into the group. Tall and slender as a birch tree and with wits just as hard, Master Greenwood was a wool merchant whose graying temples showed that his age was closer to my father's than to mine. He had been sniffing at Blanche's skirts since she came of age, but Father did not shoo him away because of his great wealth.

"Master Mulleyn, good morrow," he said in his slow, sonorous way.

"Excuse me, Master Greenwood," Master Horton said, his mouth pursed like he was eating lemons. "I was speaking with Master Mulleyn."

The other aldermen murmured to each other and bowed themselves away.

Father preened and waved a hand at them. "I pray you, do speak, Master Horton. Share your news. I am sure it will be of interest to Master Greenwood as well."

Master Greenwood raised his thick, silvery eyebrows, like caterpillars crawling up into his hair. "News? Perhaps it is the same news I wish to impart."

"I was here first, Master Greenwood, so you will do me the courtesy—"

"Oh for heaven's sake, just speak!"

Three pairs of eyes turned upon me. Master Horton gaped like a fish, opening his mouth once, twice. Father renewed his grip on my elbow but said nothing. I shook my head and looked down at the ground.

Master Horton spoke at last. "News. Yes, the news is that there are two gentlemen lodging at the inn since last night."

There was silence, and I looked up.

Father was glaring down at Master Horton. "While this is, of course, interesting, why would you think this would be of particular interest to me, Master Horton?"

Master Greenwood smirked, well satisfied that he had not, after all, been the one to deliver the news.

"B-B-Because they are *young* gentlemen, Master Mulleyn, and unmarried." He looked significantly at me.

"What are you suggesting, sir?" I leaned forward, heedless of my father's fingers digging into me, skin and bone.

"Why, nothing out of turn, I assure you," he said, giving a nervous smile and half bow to my father. As if he did not owe the courtesy, and the apology, to me.

"What Master Horton may have intended to convey," Master Greenwood said, dragging his words out by the scruffs of their necks, "is that these fine, upstanding gentlemen, newly arrived, do not know what prizes Whitelock, and Master Mulleyn's home in particular, have to offer to a man who is seeking a wife. Thus may your family expect to receive happy offers in the near future. This, at least, was the message I was bringing to you, Master Mulleyn."

Father frowned slightly, trying to parse his meaning. "You gentlemen both understand that I will entertain no offers of marriage for Blanche until Kathryn is married. I will not do her that dishonor."

My cheeks blazed. I was standing beside him, and he would speak of me this way!

"Of course, of course." Master Horton was quick to agree, then glanced across the green at the inn. "But *they* do not."

A slow, vulpine smile spread on my father's face, chilling my blood. Oh, what was he thinking? "Indeed, indeed, Master Horton. And are you not looking for a bride?"

His eyes darted from my father's face to mine. He licked his lips. "Oh, aye, but one of a mild and gentle temper. Not...." He scanned me up and down, just as the matrons had earlier, from the modest lace veil over my hair to the wooden pattens covering my silk slippers. "Not one such as this."

Chilled I may have been a moment before, but Horton roused me to instant fury. I wrenched my arm from my father's grasp. "A man like you will be lucky to get *any* woman, much less *a woman such as me*, but any woman so cursed as to have you for a husband would be wise to treat you like the fool you are and dress you in motley and make you dance for her!"

Horton gasped and staggered backward as though I had struck him in the face, which, nails digging into palms, I sorely wished to do. "Harpy!" he sputtered. "She-devil!"

Father took hold of my arm and jerked me away from the men. Master Greenwood once again looked pleased with the turn events had taken.

"Kathryn," Father said, "perhaps you had best go home."

I was panting, drawing in quick, sharp breaths that felt like sobs. There was no escape, no matter how I longed for it. Like God's own kingdom, this was how it always had been, always was, and ever would be, world without end, amen.

Nay, it would not be forever.

Father would lose patience, Blanche would marry, and I would be humiliated.

I would live and die an old maid.

I would always be alone.

On my way home from church, I strode with arms swinging, blazing with fury at Master Horton. Of all the unfeeling, ill-mannered, rude, insufferable.... And *I* was the one they called a shrew! I was the one they looked down upon for speaking out of turn? For speaking the truth, more like! I nearly walked out of my pattens, so quickly was I flying down the street.

A rowdy group of scrawny boys dashed past me through potholes and cart tracks in pursuit of an equally scrawny dog, their feet throwing up mud and manure onto my skirt. "Oh fie," I cried. "Watch where you go!" They laughed and jeered, and one lad, saucier than the rest, called over his shoulder, "She-devil!" which set them off into renewed jollity at my expense. I muttered a few choice words at their retreating backs and knelt to consider the damage to my dress.

"Excuse me," said a voice as I tried in vain to rub out the wettest of the muck.

"What?" I snapped, in no mood to treat with anyone.

"You are in the street."

I paused in my rubbing, surprised by the audacity. I looked up, but the sun was behind him like a halo. All I could tell was that he was tall, for I was looking up a long way, and fair, for the sun painted his hair gold like a field of barley. It stuck up in front like barley straw too.

I flung my arm out to the side. "This is a broad thoroughfare, sir. There is plenty of room for you to pass me by."

And I bent back to scrubbing at my skirt.

The well-made but well-worn boots I could see just at the edge of my vision did not move. "My lady," he said, "forgive me, but you appear to be in some distress."

"Now why would you say that?"

"My lady." Hands on mine, stilling them. I jumped, almost jerking back; it was so strange, so unaccustomed. I raised my eyes, my insides all a-jumble. He had knelt before me and was peering at my face. Like a blow to the gut, his face, this close, knocked the breath out of me. He was handsome, the finest man I'd ever seen. My heart began to pound and I couldn't stop my smile. He returned it.

With gentle pressure on my hands, he lifted me from my crouch and helped me to rearrange my skirts. My fingers, released from his, felt empty. Flustered, I tried to stop him, our hands bumping together until at last we faced each other—me red-faced and staring, him grinning—in the street.

I fought for something to say, but all words seemed to have fled from my tongue.

He bowed low, one leg extended and arms wide, as if I were a fine lady at the royal court and not a merchant's daughter in a bedraggled dress.

I returned my best curtsy: back straight, head bowed, and knees bent deep.

In the midst of the rutted, filthy street, with mud puddles and piles of horse manure all around.

Chapter Two

At home, I headed upstairs toward my bedchamber. On the second landing, I paused outside the big bedroom, listening with one ear to the door and trying to decide whether the heavy breathing meant that Blanche's enormous mother was still asleep or merely lying abed. Our ladies' maid Margaret came down the stairs, humming under her breath. When she started to greet me, I held a finger to my lips to silence her. I didn't want her to rouse the Mountain—for so I called Blanche's mother, in my mind if not out loud—if indeed she still slept. Margaret nodded and pointed to the mess on my skirt. I rolled my eyes and gestured her to precede me back up the stairs to change.

Margaret took her time lacing up the new kirtle, pretending she could not find the matching pale blue sleeves, letting me fume all the while about the filth on the gray one I had worn to church that morning, refusing to respond to my complaints that Mistress Blanche had a dozen fine kirtles or more to choose from, sweeping the veil from my hair and replacing it with a small cap more suitable for at home…. Thanks to Margaret, I had calmed down considerably by the time Father and Blanche returned home, looking satisfied as well-fed hogs.

Father's manservant Andrew closed the thick double doors behind them, shutting out the midsummer heat. Blanche sighed as the cooler air struck her skin, sliding into the nearest chair. Despite having been outside in wilting heat, she looked as fresh as a flower at dawn. How did she manage it?

"Andrew, small beer," she said, waving a hand at him.

"At once, mistress," he said, disappearing through the archway at the back of what Father pompously liked to call the "great hall," the large central room of our main level. Immense tapestries lined the walls, woven with scenes of beautifully dressed folk engaged in noble pursuits like hunting and dancing. Furniture filled every empty space, tables and sideboards and cabinets carved from rich, dark wood, and every flat surface was adorned with ornaments and serving pieces of silver, pewter, and glass. At the far end of the hall was a fireplace of imported marble. Nothing was too expensive—or ostentatious—for my father. He was the wealthiest man in town and wanted to be sure everyone knew it.

My sister, in her kirtle of crimson brocade trimmed in golden silk ribbons and frothy lace, was his most precious ornament.

Leaving my book on a chair, I attempted to creep back up the front stairs without being seen.

"Ah, Kathryn, I'm glad you are here. I must speak with you."

Too late.

"Yes, Father?" I went and stood before him, the dutiful daughter with hands clasped in front of me, eyes downcast. The rich nap of his velvet doublet gleamed in the sun slanting down through high windows.

"All your life," he said, "you have run wild, giving voice to your thoughts without restraint."

"I speak my mind, Father. There is no wrong in that."

"There is, when the world calls you a shrew and a she-devil."

I could no longer keep my head down. "The world is full of fools like Master Horton. I cannot control what they call me."

"Kathryn!"

Blanche could scarcely contain her snort of amusement. In her seat behind his left elbow, she smiled at me, shaking her head in mock pity.

I dragged my eyes from her and returned my stare to the tips of Father's soft, pointed-toe shoes. He drew a deep breath, pulling his thoughts back to what he had prepared to say.

"Until now," he said at last, "your reputation has harmed no one but yourself, for you have shown no interest in marriage and Blanche has been too young for me to consider it."

I gaped at him. I showed no interest...? "Of course I want to get married! I won't marry a fool and I won't marry because I must, but, Father, I am not unnatural. I want—" My cheeks heated and I covered them with my hands. I was not going to stand in front of them and reveal my deepest desires, what I longed for in the dark of night, what I feared I would never find among the boors and buffoons that paraded through our town.

He simply spoke over me. "Everything has changed; surely you must realize that everything has changed, now that Blanche is of an age to be married. You heard what Master Horton said: there are gentlemen newly come to town, which means an opportunity for Blanche to marry soon and to marry well, and she cannot do so if you persist in your unseemly behavior."

My fists clenched at the memory. "I am well aware of what Master Horton said this morning. It is his behavior that was unseemly, and I cannot understand why you do not see that!"

Father shook his head over my words. "Nay, we are not discussing Master Horton. We are discussing you."

"All right, then. Why should my behavior be of any concern to these new suitors?" I flung out an arm toward Blanche, lounging so beautifully in the chair, sipping at the goblet Andrew had brought for her. "They will be looking only at her, never at me. It has ever been so."

"Because it would be improper for her to marry before you. The elder daughter must marry before the younger. I will not have Blanche spoken about like that young Brewer girl last year; what was her name?"

"Mary," Blanche and I said in unison, then glared at each other. Mary Brewer had been one of Blanche's gaggle of friends, the girls who followed Blanche around in rather the same way that ducklings follow their mother: because they are too stupid and helpless to do otherwise.

"Yes, Mary Brewer," Father repeated. "A pretty enough lass, I'll warrant, but married before her elder sister. And why? Why? Everyone knew why. Because she was hiding a rising belly under all those skirts."

"No one would believe that of me, Father," Blanche said, bristling.

"Of course not, my angel." He turned toward her, his voice soothing, crooning. "Everyone here in Whitelock would understand that your sister couldn't marry because of her reputation." Before I could splutter a protest, he went on, "But outside of this town, it would be different. Gossip is a vicious thing. I will not have a word spoken against you.

"And therefore…" He spun back to me, a finger pointed at my nose. "You will mark me, because I believe I can turn this situation to our advantage. I am going to get you married so that Blanche can be free."

"How nice for Blanche. Am I to have any say in this?"

Blanche smirked. "Say? You should say yes to any man who offers for you."

"You think I would make it that easy for you?"

"Kathryn!" Father grabbed my shoulders. "Blanche offers you sisterly advice in a spirit of Christian charity and this is how you thank her?" He gave me a shake, hard enough to rattle my teeth in my head, then released me. I had to take a step to catch my balance.

He stepped away from me to regain his composure, turning his back on both of us. Blanche stuck her tongue out at me and I rolled my eyes.

Still turned away, Father said, "Now, daughter, will you listen to me or no?"

I shifted so I no longer had to look at Blanche. "I will listen." What choice did I have?

"Good." He faced me once more. "As I have said, you must marry before Blanche. However, you have offended and outraged every decent, God-fearing, eligible man in this town—"

"There are—" I bit off my words. I decided not to say what I was thinking: that there were no decent men in this town, only men who lust after Blanche. "Please, do go on with what you were saying."

He looked at me askance through narrowed eyes, then continued. "As I say, no man from Whitelock will have you, but though a lesser man might despair of ever getting rid of you, I plan to take advantage of the good fortune that has fallen upon our village."

"To get rid of me."

His glare deepened. "Aye."

I began to suspect his plan, and ice gathered in my belly. "How is this good fortune for me?"

He put a finger under my chin, crushing my teeth together and tipping my face up toward his. "It is good fortune in that neither of them know aught of you. If we can keep you away from them and quiet for a few days, we may have a chance."

I took a step backward, away from his dominating presence, and collided with Blanche's chair. She shoved me forward again, setting me stumbling. As I steadied myself to face Father again, I shuddered to think of his plan: the merchant in him wanted to sell me, sight unseen, to a stranger we knew nothing of. And he expected me to be happy about it? "A chance?"

He shook his head as though I were a little child who misunderstood. "Yes, Kathryn, this may well be your only chance. With my wealth and their ignorance of your nature, we may strike a deal."

"You're talking about a deal, Father. I'm talking about my life." I struggled to calm myself. "Will you keep them from talking to the neighbors as well?"

He smiled grimly. "With the dowry I mean to offer, a canny fellow will put the neighbors' talk down to jealous gossip."

I could hardly swallow against the rock in my throat. "I see you have thought of everything."

"I have. And to that end, I have decided that you and your sister must stay at home for the time being and not see anyone at all."

Blanche leaped from her chair, toppling it with a heavy thud. "What do you mean, *we* must stay at home and see no one? No one at all? Not even the new gentlemen?" She flew to Father and clung to his arm.

He patted her hand. "Yes, my dearest child, you must stay at home for a few days, but you must understand that it is the only hope we have of convincing one of these men to marry Kathryn."

She tipped her head to one side, considering. "True. A man would only marry her if he didn't know her."

I clenched my hands into fists. "Really, must I stand here and listen to this? I'd much rather go drive needles into my eyes."

"Kathryn, please," Father protested. "We are only being truthful.

I am very sorry it is hard to hear, but there it is."

"Please allow me to understand you," I said. "You are going to keep us at home whilst these gentlemen are here in town, and of course they will hear through the local gossips that you are a very wealthy man and that my dowry will be substantial, and that, all by itself, will convince one of them to marry me without ever speaking to me once?"

He gave me a look that said I was a dolt. "No, of course not. He may wish to speak to you, of course, but we will hope that will only be once the deal is done. In the meantime, you *will* stay at home, and you *will* behave yourself. And you will resume your lessons again."

Blanche made a whining noise in her throat like a puppy but otherwise did not complain, which surprised me. She had moaned and moped through all of our years of lessons, be they mathematics, rhetoric, or languages.

"I don't understand," I said.

Father rocked on his feet, heel to toe and back again, looking smugly satisfied. "One of the young gentlemen approached me in the square just now and asked if he could do me the honor of calling on me later today. Obviously, he wants to ingratiate himself to me, and through me, to you girls." Blanche smiled up at him. "I started to put him off, but he was persistent, a quality I greatly admire in a man, as well you know."

"Though not in your daughter," I muttered, not intending him to hear.

"He offered to bring me a gift, and I could not nay-say him. The gift," he said, with a finger pointed at each of us in turn, "is a tutor."

"Father," I said, striving to remain calm. "We do not need tutors. We know more Latin than the priest does."

"Well I know it," Father said. "But do you not see the beauty of it?"

"I do," I said with a sigh. "Does Blanche?"

"Of course I do," she said. "I know you think I'm a fool, but I'm not." She sniffed, offended. "This gentleman will bring us a tutor. And we shall stay at home, and see no one. And then...." She blinked several times and looked to Father for help. Clearly, the beauty of it escaped her.

I put the two pieces together for her. "This gentleman has impressed Father with his wealth and education by providing us with a tutor. He has also found a way into our house, even though we are supposed to be remaining quietly at home away from any contact with others." The blankness of her eyes told me she still did not understand. "The tutor will provide a reason for the gentleman to spend time at this house with Father, where you will be having your lessons with the tutor provided by this gentleman. And of course, there will be occasion for the tutor to find himself in a situation that brings you and his true employer—the young gentleman—together from time to time." Never mind that I was going to have to endure this torment myself. What mattered, of course, was Blanche.

"Oh," she said, perking up. "That's good, then."

"But Father," I said, turning back to him, "are we truly to believe that this young gentleman is traveling through our town on business and he just happens to have a tutor with him?"

Father grinned, that same feral grin he had shown to Master Horton earlier. "Now why would I question such a thing, Kathryn? I choose to take the young man at his word, and so should you."

I shook my head. "And I suppose every bachelor in the county will soon be at our doorstep with a tutor."

"One can only wait and see," Father said.

"But will I actually be obliged to have lessons?" Blanche demanded, hands on hips.

Father patted her cheek. "Let us see what we shall see, all right, my dove? It will not be for long."

"All right, Father," she said. "But only if you promise me that this will get a husband for Kathryn."

Father glanced at me. "I promise, dear one. I promise. Both of you."

I threw up my hands.

Father waved his hands at us in dismissal. "You need to be on your way upstairs, girls, because the young gentleman said he would call on me almost directly after church."

"Now?" Blanche squealed. "He's coming here now?"

"Yes, even now."

Blanche stamped her foot in a pretty protest. "Oh, but Father, do not send me away! He is bringing a tutor for me; surely I should be here to meet them!"

"Not at all, dearest. It would not be appropriate. Gentlemen only. I must insist you go upstairs with your sister."

She was working herself into tears. I intervened, for I could not deny that I was curious myself.

"Father, if it please you, perhaps Blanche and I could stay out of sight and only listen."

"What would be the reason for that?"

Blanche turned on me. "Yes, what would be the good of that?"

I stared at her hard. "If we remain in the serving hall, there in the back, we can hear—and perhaps see a little—and learn something of this gentleman who has come to town. For if indeed he has a matrimonial inclination, I should think you would understand that we are curious to know him, Father."

Father looked at me through narrowed eyes, trying to ascertain if I had some deeper reason for wanting to spy upon him and the young man. I prayed he would not realize I had done this many times before.

"Well," he mused, "so long as you stay out of sight and make no sound, I suppose there can be no harm. But mind you," he cautioned as Blanche jumped up and down, clapping her hands, "not a peep out of you!"

I grabbed Blanche by the arm and dragged her toward the rear of the hall. "Not a sound, Father. We swear it."

For once Blanche did not protest rough treatment at my hands but followed me out the wide archway into the short corridor at the back of the hall. A door opposite led outside; a narrower arch to the right opened into the kitchen. I positioned Blanche on one side of the big arch and spun into place on the other just as a pounding on the front door summoned Andrew, who looked at us askance as he went past to answer it.

Blanche did not realize that I had kept the better vantage point for myself. I was so well concealed that I would be able to peer out and see Father's chair and perhaps the person next to him. Blanche could see nothing of the chairs, only the hall. I smirked at her from across the opening. This was the advantage of having spied here many times before.

Father had established himself in his favorite seat near the massive hearth at this end of the hall. In this warm season, the collection of other fine chairs—carved wood, tooled leather, crushed velvet—were arranged in a circle with Father's seat, rather than the fire, as the focal point. Andrew escorted the arrivals down the length of the hall to present them to Father.

The gentleman was pleasant-looking but unremarkable, with hair that fell in dark waves to brush his broad shoulders. His doublet, though made of fine-quality materials, was ill-fitting, its orange hue contrasting badly with the blue of his hose, and his gown too short for him. The overall impression was of a man wearing clothes that had been made for someone else. But perhaps they had; perhaps he had just come into an inheritance. Or perhaps he had borrowed finery to come courting.

A step behind the gentleman was a man who had to be the tutor, and Blanche, on the other side of the arch, could not contain a gasp. I glared at her. Were we to be discovered.... Yet, I could not truly blame her. He was as beautiful as one of the carved angels in Leicester Cathedral, his golden, curly hair framing his face like a halo. Because he was slight and lithe of build, his drab homespun clothes hung on him like sacks, but it hardly mattered, for all one could look at was that face. Too bad for Blanche that *he* was not one of the gentlemen coming to court her.

The gentleman and his servant bowed in unison as Andrew announced them: "Master Lawry, of Leicester, sir."

"You are well come, Master Lawry," Father said, gesturing to the chairs. Master Lawry bowed again and moved in that direction, hesitating before he selected a seat next to my father and waving the tutor to the bench for servants set alongside the hearth. Blanche craned her neck to watch the handsome young man for as long as possible, sighing.

"And so," Father prompted, "you wish to continue our conversation of this morning?"

"I do," Master Lawry said, "I do." He sounded ill at ease and cleared his throat. "Forgive my impertinence, Master Mulleyn. I know I am a stranger here, both in your home and in your town. Yet since my arrival yesterday, I have had an opportunity to become aware of…." He hesitated. "You have a daughter."

Father held up two fingers. "I have two."

"Indeed, indeed. But we—I have heard tell—in fact, this very morning, I have seen for myself the beauty and delicacy of your younger daughter."

Andrew leaned between them, offering goblets of ale on a gilt tray. Father took one, the larger and finer goblet, leaving the other for his guest. "And…?"

The gentleman flushed. "My father sent—that is, I am traveling ahead of my father, to conduct some business on his behalf at Warwick before he arrives." He certainly flustered easily, and I noticed him glancing toward the servants' bench by the fireplace. That puzzled me.

Father chuckled, taking a sip of his ale. "You are not in Warwick, young master."

Master Lawry responded with vehemence, "No, surely not, but what man would willingly leave heaven once he has found it? Who could part from the place where an angel walks on solid ground?" All his hesitation, all his stammering fled as he warmed to his subject. "Once I beheld your daughter's beauty, her grace, her loveliness, how, Master Mulleyn, how could I depart without calling upon you to seek the honor of paying court to her?"

Father sat up a bit straighter in his chair. "I have told you, sir, that I have two daughters, and you speak of the younger. While my daughter Blanche is everything you have said of her and more, I will permit no man to pay court to her at this time."

A pounding at the front door cut off any answer the young fellow might have made. Andrew went to answer it. Blanche and I exchanged a look. *Who could this be?*

Again Andrew returned, walking the length of the hall with several visitors, and amid the noise of their arrival, Blanche and I risked peeking out.

Father rose—he rose!— and bowed as the men approached. Andrew announced, perhaps unnecessarily, as Father clearly knew who this was, "Sir William Pendaran of Bitterbrook Keep."

Across the archway, Blanche was clearly startled. I could see the thoughts flitting across her face: money, property, command of others. She leaned back into the opening to try to catch a look at his face.

But I had no need to look. I knew. Of course, it made perfect sense. The massive horse, the way he called me "my lady," his courtly bow in the street—he was a knight. My heart skipped a beat. Not only had he not left town, he was here in my house. He had a name: Sir William. It echoed with the rushing of my blood, blocking out all other sounds.

I fought to still my face. It would not do to let Blanche see my reaction.

Andrew announced the others, the mayor of our town and his eldest son, and departed to fetch refreshments, striding past us with another disapproving look. Father took a step to the side and gestured to his own chair. "Please, Sir William, allow me to offer you my seat."

My jaw dropped. Never before had I seen Father give up his comfortable armchair to anyone.

The knight demurred, shaking his head, but Father insisted. The contrast between them was marked: Father's clothes—the carefully shaped and padded doublet of wine-colored velvet had slashed sleeves that revealed a bright yellow silk shirt underneath, the black hose and shoes, the fur-trimmed black gown, its hems sharply edged like knives—reflected his wealth and fashion sense. But the newcomer's clothes, though also of the finest quality, were far simpler in design and color. More pointedly, my father, a merchant who now earned his living from home while others undertook the labor for him, needed fashion's artifice to conceal his shape, whereas the knight's limbs were long and muscular, his shoulders and chest broad without the need for padding.

Blanche heaved a sigh, and I would have thrown a punch had we been closer. If we were heard, we were lost. But the men were occupied with introductions and settling themselves in the seats around Father's chair, where the knight now sat, and Andrew passed us again, returning from the buttery with a tray of goblets and a pitcher of ale.

Once everyone had been served, Father sat back in his chair, now next to the knight where Master Lawry had been sitting. One hand draped contentedly over his ample stomach, the other dangled off the chair arm, gently spinning the ale in his cup. "Well, gentlemen, your visit this morning is entirely unexpected," he said. I barely contained a snort of derision. Surely no one was fooled by his words. "This young gentleman, Master Lawry, arrived earlier to offer me the services of a tutor, isn't that so, Master Lawry?"

Master Lawry had been shifted down several places by the new arrivals and looked unhappy about this development. "Yes, that's correct, Master Mulleyn."

"A tutor of...." Father left it dangling for him.

"Languages, Master Mulleyn," the young man said quickly. "He is called Master Cameron, a man of skill and wisdom, well versed in all the languages ancient and modern that you would wish your daughters to know."

"There," Father said, gesturing toward him. "Master Lawry has brought a language tutor for my daughters. To what do I owe the pleasure of your company, Sir William?"

The knight sat easily in Father's big chair, clearly accustomed to wealth and comfort, though the strength of his form showed no signs of idleness. His large eyes—I cursed myself for not marking their color when we had met earlier in the street—took in the room around him, and I wondered how this house compared to his home. Bitterbrook Keep. It sounded impressive. Imposing. He must be used to the finest of everything.

My racing heart slowed as plain truth washed over me. I pulled back from the open archway and fell back against the wall. Whoever this knight was, he was a person of rank and importance, the likes of which our town had never seen before. And if he was indeed seeking a wife, then it stood to reason that he would choose the most desirable partner—Blanche—for himself, leaving the others to fight over what—over whom—was left.

Me.

I swallowed bile and closed my eyes. I heard words, voices, but could not make out what was being said.

For truly, who would choose the shrew over the gentle, lovely Blanche?

Sounds began to cleave together again into words. "You were acquainted with my father, Sir Humphrey, I believe," the newcomer was saying.

"Indeed, sir, an excellent man," my father replied in jovial tones. "You are most welcome for his sake. How is your father?"

The knight paused before speaking. "My father is dead these many weeks."

The other men made sounds of sympathy. "An excellent man," Father repeated, regretfully now.

"I am just now returning from Westminster where I did homage to King Richard," the knight continued. "I thought I would stop here in Whitelock on my way home and visit some of my father's connections, such as yourself."

My ears pricked up. Westminster! Then perhaps he had news. The last we had heard—or to be more precise, the last Father had permitted me to hear—out of London was the news of Queen Anne's death in the spring. Just over a year ago there had been an attempt to overthrow King Richard and put his rival Henry Tudor on the throne instead, but I only knew that from eavesdropping as I was now. If I hadn't spent time listening in on his conversations with the men who moved his merchandise, I wouldn't know anything about what was going on in the wider world. Perhaps I could find out something from this knight.

"Well," Father said, "I do hope you will find such things here in Whitelock as will help you to shake off your sadness."

"I have no doubt," the knight murmured. Then he shifted in his seat, bending to the floor to retrieve something. "If it please you, Master Mulleyn, I would offer a gift to you and your daughters...." I peeked around the archway to get a look as the knight passed my father a stack of three or four books. Books! Whether hand lettered or from Master Caxton's printing press recently set up in London— or so we had heard, none of us having ever journeyed so far—books were rare and costly things. I could imagine Father's face, something between distaste and disinterest, as he weighed them in his hands for a moment before holding them out toward the beautiful Master Cameron.

"And you, Master Holloway," Father said, turning to the other gentleman. "What brings you to my door today?"

"As you know, Master Mulleyn," the mayor said in his most obsequious tones, "I have always held you in the highest regard, and when I heard you were once again looking for tutors for your lovely daughters, I thought to myself, 'Master Holloway, surely you can be of service to such an excellent friend and neighbor, such a stalwart member of the Whitelock community—'"

I could almost feel Father preening his feathers. Blanche was delighting in the praise as well, smiling to herself. I rolled my eyes at them both. No sense between the two of them.

"—and so I have come to offer you the services of this good musician, Master Lucas, with whom I have been in contact many times over the years. He has served me well, and I trust he will do the same for you."

"A musician, eh?" Father mused.

"Ah, yes," Master Holloway went on. "He travels this way frequently and is well reputed from Westminster to Ludlow, but he has agreed to bide awhile with your family and teach your daughters to play and sing."

From the royal court in London to the Prince of Wales' household: quite a claim to fame. I doubted every word of it.

There was a stirring along the wall next to the fireplace, and a man came forward to bow to my father. I caught only a glimpse of him, but he was short and portly, dressed in colorful, loose-fitting robes, like a monk who had fallen into a dying vat and come out motley. His clean-shaven skin was darkly tanned, and one ear was pierced with a large, dangling pearl. Atop it all, he wore a liripipe hat—a long cone of fabric that wrapped repeatedly around and around his head and then draped down over one shoulder. It was meant to look jaunty and attractive, and on a more fashionable man it might have, but on him, it only looked ridiculous.

"He can teach them to play?" Father asked.

"Oh indeed, he is quite gifted in all types of musical instruments," Master Holloway said confidently. The music master bowed again, but I thought I saw concern flicker across his face.

"Harp?" Father queried as Master Holloway nodded vigorously. "Lute? Pipe?"

"Virginal?" prompted the knight. Was he making a joke? I peered around the archway, but he held his expression perfectly neutral and I could not tell.

Another pounding on the front doors set Andrew into motion. Conversation halted as the men waited to see who else would join them. I glanced across at Blanche, who was positively beaming. I marveled that the gentlemen could not see the glow of her emanating from behind the wall. She looked like a child who had been allowed to eat her fill of sweets. She caught me looking at her and smiled. "You see," she whispered, "it is working."

"Master Greenwood," Andrew announced.

Blanche made a disgusted face and looked away. The gentlemen greeted him, a less than enthusiastic greeting from those who knew him, and he joined the circle.

"Where," he said almost immediately, "is Master Horton?"

Now that his name was mentioned, I realized that his absence from this group of gentlemen was notable. Of all the men in town, he and Master Greenwood were Blanche's most determined pursuers.

There was a moment of silence, and then Master Holloway said, "I do believe Master Horton was called away on business."

Father cocked his head to the side. "So suddenly? Did I not see him at church this morning?"

Master Holloway cleared his throat and repeated, "Business, yes, or perhaps it was his family. An illness. I don't claim to know Master Horton's doings, so pray, do not question me further."

How unfortunate for Master Horton that he happened to be called away, whatever the reason, when two such impressive new persons had arrived to woo Blanche. He would never forgive himself.

Master Greenwood harrumphed and sat heavily in a chair, seeming aggrieved at having arrived so late.

"So what have you come to offer me, Master Greenwood?" Father asked. He was enjoying this.

"I have brought…." He paused, and I imagined he was sipping his ale, looking around at the other men who had so clearly staked a claim to the courtship of Blanche. I could imagine his thoughts: How had the field of battle become so crowded? Why had this happened, when he had been so diligent, so careful all these years, to position himself as a suitor?

I stifled a wicked laugh in my sleeve.

"I have brought a gift for you, Master Mulleyn, or rather for your daughters," he finally continued in his slow, sonorous voice, "in the hope that it will be of benefit to them in their lessons with their tutors. As I understand that they will be engaging in lessons once again. With tutors."

"Indeed, Master Greenwood, I am pleased to provide the best for my daughters." Father's voice was sharp. He clearly intended for Master Greenwood to stop insinuating that this was all a sham, as it was.

All of this playacting, all this falsehood, and for what?

So that none of them had to court me outright.

"A gift," Master Greenwood said, thinking past Father's cutting remark. "Yes, I have brought a gift for your daughters. A lute. A token of the honor in which I hold you—"

"Ah, yes, thank you, Master Greenwood," Father said, opening the lute case on his lap and half lifting the instrument. From my vantage point, I could just see the inlaid wood and lapis that ornamented it, the mother-of-pearl on the tuning sticks.

"Well," Father said, snapping the case closed and passing it across to the new music tutor. "This has been an afternoon of great surprises. I am humbled by your generosity, gentlemen, truly I am. But I must stress to you, as I was saying earlier to Master Lawry, that regardless of gifts or fancy speeches, I will permit no man to court my daughter Blanche at this time."

I released a breath I hadn't realized I was holding. In saying it so bluntly, in the presence of these men, my father was binding himself publicly.

"But why, Master Mulleyn?" Master Lawry burst out, almost desperate. "It seems to me a terrible thing, that so lovely a flower should be shielded from the admiration of the world. That such a beautiful dove should be caged and not fly free...."

Blanche sighed. Master Greenwood harrumphed. The knight coughed, though it might have begun as a chuckle; it was hard to know for certes.

Father shook his head. "Nay, Master Lawry, your pretty words will not sway me. For Blanche is the younger sister, and I will not have her married before the elder."

Master Greenwood chimed in. "Quite right, Master Mulleyn. Against all tradition." Master Holloway hurried to agree. His son had yet to utter a sound.

I ignored Blanche's pointed glare.

My father smiled and spread his hands in an open, friendly gesture. His tone became congenial. "However, if one of you gentlemen would care to address my quandary...."

Utter silence fell. I could imagine them all looking at one another: the local men wary, shifty; the newcomers perplexed. "Surely you would not expect one of us newcomers to make an offer without meeting her, Master Mulleyn; without even seeing her," Sir William said, his tone light.

"I assure you, Sir William, my elder daughter is..." Father paused, weighting his words with meaning. "...As endowed with other assets as my younger daughter is with beauty."

My gut boiled. It took all my self-control not to surge into the room and scream in fury at him. Here was a master merchant at work, and the chattel for sale was his own daughter.

Across the archway, Blanche's smile was ugly with gloating.

Father rose, forcing the other men to rise with him. "Well, gentlemen, I do appreciate your calling upon me today. Perhaps you will call upon me again tomorrow and my daughters can commence their lessons then."

The gentlemen remained deep in convivial conversation as they crossed the hall. Walking behind them, the language tutor kept his hands clasped behind his back and his head down while the music tutor strummed the lute, one ear bent close to the instrument. Andrew opened the great doors and Father shook hands with the men, bidding them farewell.

Once they were at the other end of the hall, Blanche rushed to me, pulling me into the archway. Her skin was flushed a delicate pink, her blue eyes alight with a greedy glee like a beggar who had just been invited to partake of a lord's feast. I could see she was thinking hard and fast, inasmuch as that was possible for her. "All right," she said, "which of my suitors do you want?"

"What?"

"You need to take one of them, and do it now. This knight is for me; you must see that."

"I see no such thing. Why must I see that?" Of course, I had already resigned myself to that idea, but there was no reason *she* had to know that.

"Let us consider," Blanche mused, ignoring my words. "How would Horton do for you? Too bad he is not here to claim you."

"Horton is a fool and a buffoon, a more fit companion for you than me," I fired back.

Why was I fighting so hard? The knight would soon hear tales of my tongue. He would be given choice words for me. Harpy. She-devil. Shrew. Compared to the sweet-tempered, gentle Blanche, why would he think of me, even for a moment? Everyone in this damned town, even the boys in the street, had a litany of curses for me and nothing but compliments for my beautiful sister, though they knew nothing of the real Blanche, and nothing of the real me.

"Perhaps Greenwood could be convinced to take you," Blanche continued as though I had not spoken. "He is rich and old. You wouldn't have to be married for long, only a few years till he's dead."

"That would please you more than me. The wealthy young widow? A perfect role for you to play. You're the one who fancies riches, Blanche, not I." I clenched my fists and squeezed my eyes shut, trying not to be drawn into this fight. "It matters not what you think, Blanche. The gentlemen do have a say in these choices."

She gave a snorting, dismissive laugh. "Who wins the prize at the fair, Kathryn? Do they give the cup to the last or the least? Nay, the reward goes to the best and the strongest and the fairest." She pointed a finger right at me, jabbing at my breast. "I will have him. The best for the best. You will clear out of my way."

I raised a hand to slap her finger away but something held me back. The touch of eyes.

I looked toward the door, expecting to see Father's disapproving glare. But Father had his back to us, saying his farewells to the final visitor.

It was the knight, his eyes dark and heavy as a night storm, who watched us. What had he seen?

He bowed to my father and turned away. I watched him go, my cheeks aflame, but knowing—*knowing*—that as always, he had not been looking at me. Could not have been. Because no one ever looked at me when there was Blanche.

Chapter Three

Monday

On Monday morning, the lessons began. I awoke quite early, just after dawn, and lay steeped in anticipatory misery of what the day would bring. Hours of useless lessons with unnecessary tutors; Father cutting bargains with the gentlemen for his daughters, body and soul, never thinking to ask what might make us happy; Blanche simpering and smiling, playing along with the charade in the hopes of drawing the eyes of men to her. I thought my skull would explode with the prospect.

My wallowing was interrupted by the high whine of Blanche's voice across the hall, like a mosquito just out of reach. I went across the landing to her bedchamber to find her in a dither, fussing with Margaret over the choice of chemise, kirtle, hair ornaments, perfume....

"Blanche," I said, leaning against the doorframe, "we are not meant to see the gentlemen today. We will only be with the tutors."

She sniffed at me, tossing a silk chemise to the floor. Aghast, Margaret dived for it and shook it out before it became crushed among the dozens of other items of clothing Blanche had already discarded. "What if you are wrong?" Blanche demanded. "What if the gentlemen return today? Even if I do not speak with them, they will see me, and I want to look my best." She held up a pair of ruby earrings, then flung them back down on her dressing table. Margaret let out a tiny squeak as one bounced off and rattled around on the floor. "One must always be prepared, Kathryn."

I couldn't bear to watch. "Margaret, when you get a chance...."

Margaret squeaked again as she replaced the ruby ornament on the table, then bent to chase down a hairbrush that had landed with a thud on the floor. "Yes, Mistress Kathryn, as soon as I may...." Her voice trailed after me as I left Blanche's room.

I managed to dress myself almost entirely without Margaret's assistance; I had so few choices, after all. Margaret brushed and fixed my hair, adorning it with jeweled pins. She scarcely breathed the entire time, but I could feel the desire to scream pent up within her. Poor thing. I knew exactly how she felt.

The hall was already abuzz with voices when I stepped off the stairs. The tutors were clustered in one corner while their masters took their ease in the chairs by the hearth. Blanche, in one of her many fine kirtles, was enshrined in Father's big chair, enjoying the attention of Master Lawry.

Sir William leaned against the wall nearby, listening but not taking part in their conversation.

My toe caught on the edge of a flagstone and I stopped still, arrested somehow by the mere sight of him, leaning. Then, clenching my fists, I forced myself to move on.

The sideboard was covered with a rich, red cloth and set with shining silver platters and bowls. I couldn't see what was in them, however, because of the men standing around, helping themselves to my father's food. Today, it seemed that even more well-to-do local bachelors were determined not to be left out, though they had not contributed to the sham of our education. The eldest son of the candlemaker was filling a plate and chatting with the last unmarried son of Alderman Blaine, and young Master Holloway, the mayor's son, had returned without his father and had brought his best friend, a fellow of French lineage named Ormond, for support.

My hunger fled and I turned away. My father may have promised he would not allow Blanche to marry before me, but he had not promised he would not force me to marry someone I detested. And there was no man in this room I would ever consider...not even the one who trapped me with his gaze and made breathing a chore I had to think about.

Father, deep in conversation with Master Greenwood, spied me and clapped his hands. When the assembled company had quieted, he smiled benevolently upon them all and said, "Gentlemen, shall we begin? I believe that with the weather so fine, the girls can have their first lesson out in the courtyard today."

Blanche, who had been preening under the men's glances the entire time, smiled and dipped a pretty curtsy to Father. I mimicked her action a bit less gracefully, a bit more sullenly.

Together, we crossed the hall and left through the rear doors, pretending not to notice the men, pretending not to notice them watching us.

The courtyard was half in sunlight, half in shade from the bulk of neighboring houses. I sat down on one of the two stone benches under the apple tree. Blanche, however, chose to stroll in the sunlight near the fountain, trailing a long strand of grass in the water. She made an undeniably lovely picture, but it struck me as unnecessary, as only the teachers would see her, not the gentlemen.

As though my thought summoned them, they emerged from the house. The odd, fat music master stepped onto the threshold and blinked regretfully at the sunlight. Then he half fell forward onto the path, making me think the language teacher might have given him a shove. Bravo for him! I smiled. This might yet be amusing.

Both of them, naturally, headed straight for Blanche, elbows jarring one another as they fought for possession of the narrow path. She feigned not to notice their approach, spying something of great interest in the water. I harrumphed a little on my bench.

"Mistress Blanche," the handsome language master said, reaching her first and sweeping a low, beautiful bow. Naturally.

She turned, just so, favoring him with a gradual view of her— profile, then angle, then full-on smile—that had melted lesser men in their tracks. If she weren't so horribly manipulative, I would have to admire her.

The music master, puffing under his hat, drew up behind him. His bow was rather like the perilous teetering of a vase at the edge of a table. "Mistress Blanche," he said, pleading a bit.

She looked them over, like peaches in a bin at the summer

market. Which would she choose?

As though there was ever a question.

"Master Cameron," she purred, fluttering her lashes just a little at that angelic face. "I do believe I am in need of help with my languages. No matter how I try, my tongue trips me up." To prove her point, she played the tip of her tongue along the edge of her top teeth.

Did the music master groan? How was the man still upright?

"Ah, perhaps," he stammered in a squeaky, unmusical voice, "my lesson for today can be simply to provide a demonstration of the qualities of this beautiful instrument. To accompany your lesson, Master Cameron."

The language master wanted to refuse. The way his rigid back blocked Master Lucas on the path made it clear he wanted no part of the portly fellow, but he knew well it would appear ungracious for him to send him away. So he turned, beaming a false smile that lit his beautiful face, and sat beside Blanche on the edge of the fountain with his pile of books. The music master stood over them, making a show of tuning his instrument.

They took no notice of me, which entirely suited me. I rose from the bench and strode to the gate set in the rear wall of the courtyard.

I moved quickly through the stinking alley, skipping between seeping piles of refuse, jumping away from anything that slithered or squeaked. I had no intent of going far, only around to the front of the house, where I could slip unnoticed back inside, and thence up to my room. I had no need, no desire to participate in this ridiculous playacting.

I was looking back over my shoulder, glancing along the street to be sure I was not seen, else I would not have walked right into him.

The knight stood in the doorway. My doorway, the door to *my* house, leaning against the jamb with one arm stretched across to the other side, entirely blocking my passage.

I gave him a thunderous look.

He smiled, a wealth of knowing in it.

"No lessons for you today, mistress?"

His tone, I thought, was overly genial, considering the circumstances. We were not formally acquainted, after all. And why should my presence here, instead of at my lessons, amuse him?

"What could I possibly learn from them?" I asked dismissively, trying to duck under his arm.

He shifted to block my way. "Indeed, what could a man of the world possibly have to offer to a fine young lady of a village such as this?"

I became uncomfortably aware of the closeness of our bodies: the heat of him, on such a warm day. I straightened up and took a deliberate step away.

"Do you mock me, sir?" I demanded.

"Do I?" he replied.

I bit back the words that sprang to my lips—he was a gentleman, and I was supposed to be trying to make a favorable impression—and instead dipped my head and curtsied quickly. "If you will pardon me, sir...."

He waited a moment, just to show me he could, before dropping his arm. There was barely enough room for me to slip by, with him standing in the doorway, and the fabric of my kirtle whispered as it brushed against his legs. That sound resonated all the way to my toes as I scurried by him, a mouse past an indulgent tomcat, and rushed up the stairs.

As I reached the landing, my head wanted to turn back, but I held it straight and continued on up the stairs. The sensation of his eyes upon me itched on the back of my neck, and the thought he might be watching me thrilled like sparkling wine in my stomach. But I dared not risk knowing for certes that he was not.

I sat on my bed, then moved to the chair by the window, then returned to the bed, but I could not remain still. I kept hearing the whisper of my skirts against his boots, kept feeling the touch of his eyes upon me.

It was like wearing a damp wool cloak. I couldn't get it off. It clung and itched and would not leave me alone.

I crept back down the stairs, sneaking past Margaret toiling away in Blanche's room, avoiding Blanche's monstrous mother snoozing and rumbling in her lair. At the entrance to the hall, I paused, listening, but it seemed the men had departed for the morning. At least *some* business was going to get accomplished this day. Out the front door I went, pausing on the front stoop to slip into my pattens. I glanced around quickly, hoping to avoid seeing any of our neighbors, and set off down the street. High Street, on which we lived, was short, with only a handful of houses for the wealthiest of Whitelock's residents, and cobbled with flat river stones. Once I got close to the inn, however, back at the center of town, the paving stones gave way to dirt scarred by the hooves of horses and cattle, rutted with the wheels of carts, and pocked with mysterious holes that appeared for reasons no one could name. And of course, one had to dodge the piles of filth that had been tossed from upper-story windows.

In front of the inn was a little patch of grass where two trestle tables stood for use on fine days in spring and summer. When it rained, the tables and benches could be quickly taken apart and leaned under the eaves of the building until the weather cleared. As I approached, Ellen emerged from the front door in her drab gown and broad apron, shaking out a large rag. Not looking up, she leaned over one of the tables and began wiping it down, a lock of fair hair escaping her cap and falling across her brow.

"Good morrow, Ellen," I said, walking across the grass.

She looked up and spied my approach. Straightening, she raised her hand in a little wave, a half smile on her face, but at the same time, I noticed her glancing around. No doubt making sure no one else saw us talking together.

"What are you doing about?" she teased, flicking her dusting cloth at me. "Shouldn't you be at home at your lessons?"

I jerked back to avoid getting my dress dirty from the filthy rag. "Careful!" I snapped, belatedly realizing she meant to be playful. She turned away, swiping at the table with extra vigor.

I twisted my fingers together. "I-I walked out. I refuse to take part in this sham."

"That's fine, I suppose," she said. "Only...."

"Only, what?"

She straightened. "Do you mean to yield the victory to Blanche so easily?"

"I don't— What do you—? How can you say that?"

She made a noncommittal noise and walked slowly over to the other table. She worked hard, I knew, and she was making the most of her time outdoors. "I mean, you know what your father's true purpose is, and by walking away like this, you are taking yourself out of the fight."

"The fight?" It exploded out of me. She stepped back from the force of it.

"Think about it. Honestly, Kathryn, you have twenty-one years already. You have a reputation, even you have to acknowledge that, and it's not every day two unmarried gentlemen come riding into town. If you don't want to marry anyone from Whitelock, you should certainly think about marrying one of these two gentlemen. Your father is just trying to help."

"Help? You think he is trying to help? He is a merchant trying to unload goods that no one wants onto unsuspecting marks."

"Kathryn," Ellen said, riding over my rant. "You don't want to be me."

I had no answer for that. I had stood with Ellen under this very rowan tree as she wept, watching her sister get married, knowing that she would now be the butt of everyone's jokes because she had failed somehow. Because younger sisters getting married first violated the natural order of things, and so Ellen was doomed to be a spinster. A laughingstock. Almost as bad as being a shrew. I smiled, trying to ease the moment. "Perhaps you can snatch up one of the gentlemen for yourself."

"Oh, that's not very likely." She snorted a laugh. "One of them's a knight, you know."

A shiver danced up my spine at the mention. "Yes, I do know. Which means I have no chance with him. Blanche will work all her wiles to get him."

"Poor fellow."

We laughed, a dismal thing.

"You will tell me everything you learn, won't you?"

"Of course," she said as I turned away. "What good is it keeping company with the innkeeper's daughter if you don't get information from her?"

I hesitated. What did she mean by that? But I glanced back at her and she was smiling, so I raised a hand and turned back for home.

On my way home, I walked with my head down, thinking over what Ellen had said. Ought I to be thinking about my father's plan, distasteful as it was, as an opportunity? God knew, I did not want to stay in Whitelock all my life, but to leap into the arms of a stranger? Would I trade a lifetime of misery of a different sort to escape the misery I faced here? But did it stand to reason that life with Master Lawry or with Sir William would necessarily be bad? How was one to know?

Arriving home, I considered joining Blanche and the tutors in the courtyard but could not force myself to do it. I went back to my bedchamber and soon enough found cause to regret my choice. The room was hot and stuffy whereas in the yard at least there was shade and an occasional breeze, and as irritating as my sister and the others were, at least they provided some diversion. As I had not planned to sojourn in my bedchamber all day, I had nothing but a small piece of embroidery to entertain me, and it was not long before that lost its appeal. Besides the bed, my room contained nothing but a clothes chest and a small table, and there were no surprises to be uncovered among my dresses. I stared out the window at the street for some time, but on a summer day, the smell of manure and refuse that wafted up from the gutter was less than appealing.

At length, I noticed voices and masculine laughter coming from the back of the house, drifting up through the open casement in Blanche's bedchamber. I crept across the corridor to investigate, careful to tread lightly so as not to alert anyone to my presence here in the house.

Margaret had not had time to finish tidying Blanche's room apparently, for her beautiful clothes were still strewn all over the floor, ribbons and sashes and sleeves tossed over the backs of chairs, slippers kicked off to lie against the wall or upside down beside the overflowing trunks and chests, her pots of rouge and kohl uncovered and jumbled on her little enameled dressing table, the stool tipped over beside it, the sheets and silken counterpane spilling over the foot of the bed like too much frosting on a cake. What I wouldn't give for just one of the silken garments she tossed on the floor and forgot… but no one showered me with gifts.

"Swine," I muttered, stepping over the stool. "Queen of swine."

At the window, the voices were louder, the laughter ringing.

The music master, standing in the shade of the apple tree, was playing a soft, plaintive tune on his lute. The language master sat on the bench with a large book open on his lap. Blanche sat beside him, holding one side of the book delicately in her hands. Around them were gathered Father and all the gentlemen: Master Lawry, Master Greenwood, Master Holloway and his friend, and that saucy knight. Sir William.

I kneeled by the window, keeping my head down so they could not see me. Their conversation—portions of the text being read aloud, with their comments and jests flying fast—washed over me.

No one noticed I was not with them in the courtyard.

No one wanted me there.

That was fine. I didn't want to be part of it. They were only there to worship Blanche.

I listened. They talked. They laughed.

But Blanche, for all her lessons, said little. The clever remarks were all from others—the knight, mostly, and the scholar Cameron, and young Master Lawry. Master Greenwood was not quick enough, Master Holloway clearly intimidated, and Father not clever enough.

And Blanche?

Blanche was probably bored beyond all reason. But she smiled and laughed because they were men and she was the globe around which their stars danced.

Why was it impossible for anything—anyone—to dance around me?

Had I truly ruined my own prospects with my sharp tongue? Had speaking my mind, boldly and brashly, turned the whole world against me?

I felt something wet on my cheek and brushed at it impatiently.

I stood up, not caring if they saw me through the window, and went back into my room.

I lit another candle against the dark that was gathering like wool on a spindle and sank down into Father's big chair with a sigh. His desk was littered with parchments, letters, books of account. All out of place, all in need of tending. What did he do all day? How was he successful?

I snorted. He was successful because he was a charming salesman, and because he had me to keep his desk tidy and his ledgers balanced.

I shifted a pile of what appeared to be correspondence to one side and pulled the main accounting book open in front of me. Most important work first. Head down, Kathryn, and get it done.

Time passed until the columns of numbers began to swim before my eyes in the flickering light. I stood to light two more candles and was startled as Margaret entered, a steaming cup of a tisane in her hands.

"Thank you, Margaret," I said, taking the warm mug from her. "How did you know?"

She smiled and said, "Your habits are rather predictable, mistress." She glanced at the desk. "Are you nearly finished? Will you be joining the master?"

"Joining the master?" I burned the tip of my tongue on the hot liquid.

"Yes. Sir William has come to call, and Mistress Blanche is sitting with them, so I thought...." She trailed off meaningfully.

In the spaces between her words, now that I was paying attention, I could hear voices, two I knew and one unaccustomed.

"No," I said, rather sharply. "I see no reason to interrupt what I am doing."

"Very well, mistress."

I scowled at her retreating back. It was not her place to be reproving of me.

I hesitated, then dashed to the door. I pressed myself into the frame as though I were part of the very wood.

"I am so envious of your journey to Westminster, Sir William." Blanche's voice was gentle, caressing. It made me cringe, but men seemed to adore it. "I do so long to see the royal court and the city of London too. It must be marvelous. So exciting! Dancing and jousting and fabulous entertainments!" She was nearly breathless with wonder, and I could picture her leaning forward, all of her many excellent features on full display. Perhaps she was even touching his arm, very lightly, just enough.

Oh, by now he was surely lost.

There was a pause, then the gentleman said, "The court is rather subdued, as one would expect, mistress. The queen having just died in March, and with the rumors of an invasion this summer by Henry Tudor."

"Oh," Blanche said. I could imagine her, brushed back but undeterred. "Of course. But is there nothing to delight the soul?"

Again, the pause. "There was a suggestion that the king seeks to remarry."

"Well, then." Briskly. Probably leaning forward again. Reminding the knight of the marriageable bounty there before him. "That is good news. And in that happy event, should you return to court? Would you pay your respects?"

"I doubt that the king would remember me if he does, and in any event, he will want me here for the time being, in the west, defending against Tudor's possible arrival."

Ah! News! I squished myself tighter against the doorway, if such a thing were possible, and strained my ears to listen. The affairs of the wider world were rarely discussed in this house.

Blanche made a tiny noise, and Father said, "You will understand, Sir William, that I do try to shelter my daughters from the worst of the world's concerns. War, rebellion, invasion—these are not proper topics for a young girl's contemplation."

"Yes," Blanche agreed quickly, and I could imagine her nodding, her beautiful curls shining in the firelight. "I prefer not to think of such horrible things." Now I imagined a pretty little shudder running over her frame, jostling her breasts just so. "I trust that my father will make the proper decisions to keep me safe... as, someday, my husband will."

"Of course, Mistress Blanche. Forgive me for distressing you." His voice was all gracious apology, but I thought I caught an edge of impatience in it. "So tell me, mistress, what does occupy your thoughts? What do you do?"

"Do?" I could imagine Blanche's eyebrows shooting up to match her tone.

"Aye. What keeps a young lady such as yourself busy every day?"

"I have learned everything necessary to keep a household, sir."

"Admirable, to be sure. And for certes you do not neglect your devotions?"

"Of course not."

"And reading? What books have you read?"

"As you know, sir, my father has just retained tutors for my sister and me."

He scoffed lightly. "You father has generously accepted gifts from fawning fellows, but I suspect he has not neglected you up till now. Even if you have no Latin, you surely read English."

I drove my fingernails into the wood of the doorframe to keep myself from flying into the hall and throwing myself between him and Blanche, crying, "Yes, I read! I read anything I can get my hands on, and she cares nothing for it!"

"Of course I read English" was Blanche's indignant reply.

"Have you read Chaucer, then?" the knight asked.

I snorted. My father had brought home a newly printed volume of Chaucer last year. She had flipped through it, glancing at the pictures, declared it dull, and tossed it on my bed.

Blanche laughed, a musical burble. Perhaps she even shook a teasing finger at him. "Now, Sir William, don't think I don't see what you are doing. You are testing me. I have read what my tutors put before me, it is true, but what woman would do more?" Her voice slid lower, seductively. "And what man would want a woman who did?"

Sir William chuckled but did not reply to her. Instead, he asked my father for more wine. I peeled myself away from the doorframe and crept back to the desk. I tried to return my attention back to the accounts and ignore the conversation in the hall.

Half a candle later, I surrendered. The numbers would not stay in their columns, the voices impinged on my tired brain, and Blanche's laugh scraped at my skin like rough-hewn wood. I stood up to stretch my back and began to extinguish the candles, one by one.

It was that plain, methodical act that made me sit down again. A thing that had been niggling and twitching in the back of my mind as I reviewed the account book became suddenly clear—there were numbers that did not add up properly, and not merely because of my father's sloppy methods of record-keeping.

I gathered up the heavy book in my arms and went to the door. Father, seated in his own big chair near the empty hearth would not see me, but Blanche, facing him, would. I waved a hand to catch her eye. She deliberately looked away from me and turned her face toward Sir William.

I stamped my foot and waved again.

She didn't even flinch.

I walked into the hall. Seeing me, she widened her eyes and shook her head once, sharply—a warning.

I kept walking.

Father turned slightly in his chair and saw me coming. He barely suppressed his groan. "What is it, Kathryn?"

"I need to speak with you, Father." I glanced around the circle, my eyes skipping over the knight like a flat stone over a pond: touching once, then again, and again.

"Not now," he said. "Cannot you see that I have a guest?"

Sir William had risen as I approached and now bowed politely. I curtsied as well as I could with the massive account book in my arms.

"Please pardon the interruption, but Father, this is very important."

"Important?"

My cheeks went hot and red. "Yes. Important." I held the book out toward him. "I have found something in the accounts. It's a small thing, a series of small things, but when they add up...."

Father stared at the book as though I were offering him rotten meat. "Can this not wait until morning?"

I looked down at my feet, or rather, I would have looked at my feet but saw only the thick pages of the account book. Of course I could have waited. Should have waited. "Yes, Father."

He turned to Sir William. "I must apologize for my daughter's rude behavior, Sir William. She should know better than to interrupt, but as you may have heard...." He raised his hands helplessly. My flush grew hotter. What can one do about the willful Kathryn?

"Not at all, Master Mulleyn," Sir William replied. "I find Mistress Kathryn's zeal— refreshing."

I was as surprised as my father. We both looked at Sir William, astonished. He continued, "In fact, I am surprised you would apologize for Mistress Kathryn's diligence in defending your interests. You must be very proud to have such a clever daughter."

All three of us stared at him.

"Why," Father said at last, "in heaven and earth would a gentleman want a clever daughter?"

Another frozen moment, and then Sir William laughed. "Of course, of course, Master Mulleyn. I defer to your wisdom. After all, you have two daughters. Who would know better than you what virtues are best in them?"

Chapter Four

Tuesday

The next morning, the hall was even more crowded with men, if such a thing were possible. I grabbed a goblet of small beer from Andrew's tray as he passed smoothly among the visitors, and headed for the long bench beside the hearth where, on Sunday, the tutors had sat. The sour smell of the beer turned my stomach, and I set it down on the bench beside me, untouched. I noted the men greedily eyeing my father's things, judging the worth of everything in the room, including Blanche and me. I put my hands down to grip the edge of the bench.

My left hand touched something and I looked down. It was one of the books Master Lawry had brought on Sunday, forgotten in this dark corner. With a glance at the chatting groups, I lifted it carefully into my lap.

The room fell away. All the noise, all the colors. All that remained were me and the words on the page.

Sometime later, I became aware of a person standing over me. I looked up, blinking.

"What are you reading?" the knight asked.

I raised the book in one hand, revealing the printed page. "This is one of the books you gave my father. It was just left here." I could hear the disbelief in my own voice. "This one is *The Consolation of Philosophy* by Boethius."

"Heavy matter," he said.

I hefted the book in my hands. "No more heavy than a loaf of bread."

"*Scriptum est quia non in pane solo vivet homo*," he quoted.

"Indeed," I replied tartly. "Scripture does say that man does not live on bread alone, although you could not prove that by this town."

I dropped my eyes back to the book, the words gliding across the page like leaves on a stream, dancing and swirling. I willed them to stay in their places and make sense.

Sir William set my goblet aside and sat beside me on the bench.

I blinked at the page. Why had he not gone away?

The silence lengthened, stretched, became oppressive to me. "Why are you here in this quiet corner, sir?" I asked. "Are you not fascinated by Blanche's conversation?" I leaned forward as though I were listening in. "I believe she is telling Master Blaine and young Master Chandler all about her taste in jewelry."

The knight leaned back against the wall, stretching his legs out in front of him, crossing his sturdy boots at the ankles. He rubbed a hand against his thigh, and the slightly scratchy sound seemed to vibrate the hairs on my forearms. He glanced at Blanche from under half-closed eyelids. "*Taedet mē*," he said.

In trying to suppress my laughter, I made a hideous snorting sound, which only made me laugh harder. Silently, Sir William handed me the goblet of small beer and sat back again, pulling the book out of my lap and studying it as though it were the most fascinating thing he had ever seen. I sipped at the beer, trying not to choke, and my giggles devolved into hiccups. I pressed a hand to my lips and tried to still my body.

If only he knew—if only I could explain to him—why I was laughing.

After dinner, Father claimed he had business to attend to, and perhaps he did, since he had spent so much of the last day and a half entertaining the suitors. True or not, he went out, and the gentlemen were obliged to leave.

Since Father was not about to notice I was not participating in the needless lessons, I claimed a megrim and went upstairs to my bedchamber. Blanche, enjoying the attentions of the beautiful language master, waved me away without even looking up.

I fell asleep in the dull warmth of the afternoon, but I was awakened as the church bell struck *nones* by a great jumble of sound from below.

Voices, yes, but also musical instruments: the whine of strings, and the thump of drums, and the flourish of pipes.

The thud of boots: many, many boots. What on earth...?

As my feet hit the flagstone floor of the hall, I halted. I was surprised, and yet not at all surprised, to find Blanche entirely surrounded by men: our tutors, their employers, other guests from the inn, local folk, every eligible male in the parish, it seemed. Even more men than this morning. Their voices rattled the rafters, nearly drowning the halting sounds of lute, pipe, and horn warming up.

"Well, wouldn't this be a revelation to my father?" I exclaimed.

The men might have ignored me if they even heard me over their own cacophony, but Blanche's ear is as tuned to my voice as mine is to hers. "How so?" she replied, and at her words, the room quieted.

"We," I said, "are meant to be staying quietly at home, applying ourselves to our lessons."

Blanche smiled, making her radiant, but only I could see it did not light her eyes. "Am I not at home?" Someone I couldn't see tapped quickly on a drum, unleashing a ripple of stifled mirth.

I folded my arms. "What lesson are you learning, Blanche? Or are you the teacher here?"

"The fault is mine, Mistress Kathryn," said Master Lucas, the chubby, sweaty music master, stumbling to his feet. "I thought—that is, it came to me that you young ladies might benefit from a musical performance by experienced musicians. A number of musicians. More than just myself, you see." He searched the crowd, looking to someone—anyone—for support, the fat pearl swinging in his ear. The others gathered there merely gazed back at him politely. He turned back to me, then darted his eyes down to his clasped hands. "There are many gentlemen in this town—I was most pleased to discover—who have the proper training, and they were, many of them, so kind as to offer to come here today...."

All of them unmarried, I thought but did not say. Instead, I said, "Of course, you sought and received my father's approval?"

Master Lucas went red to the brim of his foolish hat. "I would have— That is, I did try—"

Blanche's lips tightened. "Father will approve when he learns of it," she said, her tone reflecting none of her irritation with me. "He will be delighted to have music in the house."

"We shall see," I said as I spun and headed for the door. Father must be about town somewhere. I would find him and for once, maybe Blanche would face the consequences of her actions.

Suddenly, a voice rang out. "Nay, but stay awhile, mistress. We would hear how *your* lessons progress."

Glancing over my left shoulder, I saw one man stand, detaching himself from the crowd. But I need not have looked. I knew it must be he.

I curtsied briefly. "I thank you for the invitation, sir knight, but I have no skill with such instruments as these."

The smile that quirked his lips told me that he would not let me go. Would that I could look away. He took a step or two closer. "Pray, then, with what instruments are you skilled?"

I showed him my teeth, a wicked grin. "Thumbscrews."

The clamor of voices had quieted during our exchange. While many of the men still spoke to one another or tuned their instruments, several had diverted their attention to Sir William and me, their eyes keen with interest.

"Those will make a man sing indeed," he said, his smile broadening. "Go and fetch them."

"Gladly, if I may apply them to you."

A man choked back a laugh. Sir William did not even bother to glance at him. He held out his hands toward me, thumbs pointing up. "I offer myself to your use."

Against my will, I took a few more steps into the hall. We stood apart only a little distance, perhaps two of the large square stones on the floor, the height of a tall man. His eyes challenged me, his smile taunted me. He waggled his thumbs in my direction. Behind him, some of the men, including our beautiful Master Cameron, were laughing behind their hands.

My skin went cold and then hot all over. He had ambushed me, exposing me in front of all the others, something I was accustomed to but had not expected after our conversation this morning in the corner on the bench.

I gritted my teeth, breathing hard, fists clenched at my side. "What will you sing for me, when I put you to the question?"

He bowed deeply, as he had when we first met in the street. "What you will. I would be your devoted subject."

Mockery. It could only be. He was toying with me for the amusement of the crowd. "Methinks you would be my sovereign and ply the screws to me."

His head jerked up and his eyes met mine, bright with mischief.

Blue. His eyes were blue. Blue like still water, blue that sparkled like rain on glass. Oh heavens, oh Lord above, stop my thoughts.

The listening men gave up the pretense of preoccupation and burst out in open guffaws. The clever drummer rolled a tattoo. Sir William opened his mouth to reply, but Blanche cut him off. "What is the subject of which you speak?"

Ah, poor Blanche. Too long had attention been paid to someone other than herself.

"The subject of subjects, mistress," replied Sir William, turning toward her.

My skin cooled as though the sun had gone behind a cloud, and my heartbeat slowed. I drew a deep breath.

"Shall we not play, Sir William?" called one of the young men, cradling a pipe in his lap. He was John Everheart, young and poor and pockmarked, and he would never have been admitted into Blanche's presence had it not been for this general gathering. By the broad smile on his face, he was enjoying himself immensely, despite his lack of prospects.

"Of course, lad." Sir William turned back to me. "Mistress, i'faith, will you not join us?"

The sun had returned. My skin flushed hot once again, and yet we were not arguing. I could not account for the sensation. "Nay, sir, I shall not."

Two or three of the players commenced a tune; someone began to sing. Blanche clapped in delight.

Sir William bowed to me—a simple, unadorned bow this time, nothing mocking in it that I could discern—and returned to the others.

My heart sank. I could have joined, but to what end? None of them truly wanted me there. The knight might have asked me to stay, but he was only mocking me, after all.

Thumbscrews. Ha!

I went to the front doors and nearly did it, I almost charged out of the house to find my father. But truly, was it conceivable that he had no knowledge of this merry gathering? Would he love me better for destroying it? For interrupting Blanche's amusement and her enjoyment of her suitors? In the end, I made no further effort to disrupt their foolish little concert. Rather, I went up the stairs, my feet dragging like anchors, unwilling to leave but unable to return.

At the first landing, I sat, elbows on knees, chin in hands, and listened.

They played a few songs together, ballads and drinking songs that the whole company knew. Blanche clapped and laughed merrily, her voice like a silver bell in the midst of all that masculinity. I put my head down on my knees. Me, they laughed at; her, they tried to make laugh. What was it that made us so different? At what point had our paths so far diverged?

With a sigh, I stood and tried to convince myself there was something terribly important I needed to do in my room. And yet, my feet remained rooted to the spot.

Someone strummed a familiar tune and I closed my eyes. A pleasant masculine voice began to sing.

My stomach leaped, recognizing the voice before my ears did. The one I had not realized I had been listening for.

But the words he sang were not the ones I knew for this tune. These were different.

"A bachelor have I been long, and had no mind to marry,

But now I find it did me wrong that I so long did tarry.

Therefore I will a-wooing ride, there's many married younger.

Where shall I go to seek a bride? I'll lie alone no longer."

Laughter and scattered applause swallowed up the chords of the lute that transitioned to the next verse. "To Whitelock!" someone called out, followed by more laughter. My body went rigid.

I could hear the smile in his voice as he continued:

"O Fate, send me a handsome lass that I can fancy well.

Her portion I'll not greatly pass though money hears the bell.

Love nowadays with gold is bought, but I'm no money-monger.

Give me a wife, though she's worth nought: I'll lie alone no longer."

Above the general amusement, one of the fellows called out: "Oh, I think you'll find the portion is fairer than the lady in this house." My cheeks flared hot and my fists curled tight, bunching around my skirts.

"Why, Master Hardinge," Blanche said, her voice all teasing pout, "how can you say such a thing?"

"A thousand pardons, Mistress Blanche," the man replied. "You know I meant no slight to your fair self."

"Of course not," she purred.

A few strums of the strings, and the knight continued to sing:

"If she should chance to prove a scold, her tongue will breed my strife:

Then I must look to be controlled and curbed by my wife.

A scold, of women, is the worst; she'll force a man to wrong her.

Therefore, I'll try all humours first, and lie alone no longer."

I knew I should flee. Now there could be no question but that he sang about me—who else was a known scold in this town, in this house?—and though I was furious, I was also ashamed, and embarrassed, and... a hundred other feelings I could not name. I had one foot on the landing above, half ready to fly to my bedchamber, and the other foot trembled with the need to run down and out the door, down the street and out of Whitelock forever.

And still the music would not cease; it went on, winding its way into my veins, wrapping itself around my very bones.

"Although my wife be none o' the best, yet I must be content:

I shall speed as well as the rest which 'bout this action went.

I am not first that matched ill, therefore it is no wonder:

I'll keep my resolution still and lie alone no longer.

I trust I shall with one be sped that doth deserve my love:

If I with such a woman wed, I swear by mighty Jove,

That ere she any thing should want, I'll suffer cold and hunger:

Though she had scant clothes to flaunt, I'd lie alone no longer."

I shuddered through the last lines and the amusement that followed. I could hear the scraping of stools and chairs as his fellows got up to pound him on the back and shake his hand. Oh, yes. A triumph for him. Mocking the shrew, who was not there to defend herself.

A woman "that doth deserve my love." He'd have to keep looking.

I turned about to continue on up the stairs. There was no escape for me out the doors. Never had been, and well I knew it. But before I passed fully onto the landing and around the curve of the stairs, I saw a movement down at the bottom. I flinched, wanting and not wanting to look, wanting and not wanting to see who it was.

I took a step back.

Sir William stood there, a foot on the first riser, his arms on the walls of the stairwell, not for balance but as though he meant to block my flight, as though he sensed I had wanted to run. I froze, gazing down at him, studying his face. I waited for the *coup de grace*, the final stroke of arrogant mockery, but it did not come. There was no smirk, no sparkle of teasing wit in his eyes, only patience. Waiting.

What did he think? That I would laugh, like the others? That I was amused by his song?

I turned my back on him and raced up the stairs.

I refused to go to supper that evening. I considered refusing to play along with the entire charade any longer. In the long shadows of the dying light, I went out into the courtyard for the first cool, fresh air I'd breathed all day. Water splashed in the basin, the mere sound refreshing as a drink from a mountain spring.

Defiance filled me, fueled by anger. I kicked off my slippers, hiked up my skirts, and climbed up on the fountain's edge as I had not done since I was just past childhood, perhaps eleven or twelve. The gray stone was slick beneath my feet, still retaining much of the day's heat, while the water that danced and played in the deep bowl was cool, splashing up onto my toes.

I walked the edge of the fountain once, and then, as my body remembered its balance, I spun and hopped and kicked, a water dance of my own creation.

"Remarkable," a man's voice said, just on the other side of the plume of water. "Very like a dolphin, indeed."

I crashed awkwardly onto the granite ledge, wobbling, flailing my arms to keep from falling into the water. Flushed with embarrassment, I turned sideways, in profile to him, keeping the carved dolphin of the fountain spout between us. I could still hear his song throbbing along with my every heartbeat. I wanted nothing more than for him to go away or, if he would not, then to flee myself.

He did not go away but walked around the fountain, coming toward me. I scurried away, one mincing foot in front of the other, keeping the distance between us, until he stopped.

"You did not enjoy my performance this afternoon."

"No." I refused to face him since my cheeks were overly warm. "Did you think I would?"

"It was an amusing song. It was meant to entertain. I'd hoped you might see the humor in it."

"I did not."

"Ah."

He walked the other way around the fountain, so I was obliged to spin in place and scuttle away from him again. My feet were wet and as the evening was getting on, they were becoming cold, pressed against the hard, cooling stone of the fountain. I bent and curled my toes to try to warm them.

Still behind me, he spoke again. "How long have you been keeping your father's records for him?"

"I don't know." I took another step and made a noncommittal gesture. "A few years." Since I was ten, but he didn't need to know that. Not precisely.

He made a noise deep in his throat. "Why are you playing along with this pretense? Why would you tolerate sitting with these tutors when I saw you this morning reading Boethius?"

I half turned and gave him a stiff smile. "Why do you care what I do?"

His look was brazen, a challenge. "I'd like to know."

"I do what I'm told."

"Ha! I don't even know you and I know that's not true."

I bristled and danced backward a few steps. "Why do you ask so many questions?"

He moved forward, closing the distance. "Because no one else does. Because your father seems determined to foist you off on one of us—and believe me, the inducement offered is quite tempting—and yet despite being expected to marry you, no one ever talks to you."

My hands curled into fists at my side. "Because they know what they will get. A tongue-lashing or a scratched face, if they get too close."

He laughed.

"You mock me?" I growled. "You think I won't?" My hands twitched, but for all my talk, for all my reputation, I had never struck anyone aside from Blanche.

"I think you'd try." His words, so calm, so reasonable, and the sight of him, with that smug smile, were infuriating. But he was right. He was a trained knight, I was a well-brought-up town girl. What could I do against him?

Still. "Don't tempt me."

"Why so fierce?"

"I am the shrew, remember?"

He shook his head. "Nay. You are Kate."

My mouth twisted. "I know we are but briefly acquainted, sir, but surely you are aware that my name is Kathryn."

"Not so," he said, shaking his head. "You are plain Kate, though some may call you worse." Shrew. The epithet lurked underneath, a dark echo of my own words, whispering in the fall of the water, sliding on the evening breeze, shivering over my skin.

He seemed to sense it.

"I misspoke," he said. "Not plain Kate but bonny Kate, the prettiest Kate in all of England, Kate of charm and grace, Kate of all loveliness, Kate the fair, Kate the wise, Kate the great."

I stood staring at him like a fool, head cocked to one side. How long could he prattle on, spouting such words? Charm and grace? Fair and lovely? I had lived long enough alongside my sister to know that none of those virtues belonged to me.

"You don't know me, sir," I said stiffly.

He became serious, the smile gone from his face. "Perhaps not. Perhaps you are right." I had a strange, unsettling feeling, as though he was trying to say something more. As though by agreeing with me, he was in fact disagreeing entirely. "Perhaps," he murmured, almost to himself, "this is how it must be."

I shook off the moment like an insect that landed on my skin. "Why are you even here?" I asked. "Why didn't you marry some rich and beautiful court lady in London?"

He smiled wryly. "That is an excellent question. Perhaps someday you will learn the answer."

With that, he bowed and turned away. I suddenly found I didn't want him to go. My hand reached out of its own accord and I took a step in his direction. I had to raise my voice over the rushing water to ask my question, a challenge, the only thing I could think of that might bring him back. "Were you not grand enough for them, or were they not grand enough for you?"

He paused and looked over his shoulder at me, the ghost of a smile on his lips. "I'll never tell."

"Oh, I think you will."

He bowed again, a short, mocking little bow. "So you say."

I moved quickly around the fountain's edge. It was suddenly much darker, in the way that summer nights are, and I could hardly make out his shape moving away from me. The sound of the tiny white pebbles of the path crunching under his boots told me he was walking slowly, but walking. Leaving.

Zounds.

Why did I care? I didn't care.

I kicked at the water, which I could scarcely see beneath me, sending a long sheet of it pelting over the dolphin.

"Kathryn!" My father's outraged voice boomed from the door of the house.

I froze midkick, my leg in the air, teetering on one foot. My damp skirts pulled at me, yanking me off my balance, and my kicking foot slammed down on the granite. But the edge was slick with water, and my toes were numb and wouldn't grip, wouldn't hold. I found myself falling backward.

Not far.

One of Sir William's arms wrapped around my waist while the other scooped up my legs, and he swung me away from the fountain. His face was inches from mine, those rainwater eyes, that unruly hair. He held me for a moment, and another. I could count my heartbeats under my skin. Then, ever so slowly, he set me down, my feet touching the rough gravel path. He kept his arm on my waist to steady me, and then he waited, watching, as I collected my slippers from beside the fountain.

"Kathryn!" my father bellowed again, and I fled into the house.

Chapter Five

Wednesday

The next morning, the locusts descended on my father's house again, swarming around the sideboard for food and talking much too loudly. This time, I elbowed my way through to the board, reaching between them for a slice of bread, a chunk of hard cheese and a handful of ripe berries before retreating. Andrew handed me a cup of small beer, and I looked around for a quiet corner in which to eat.

The knight had settled in the same spot I had taken yesterday, the quiet bench alongside the hearth, the dark copy of Boethius on his lap. After yesterday, I had no desire to be sociable, but after all, he *was* in my spot.

I slipped onto the bench not quite next to him. He did not look up. I noticed he did not trace the lines of text with his finger, or form the words silently with his lips, as my father did. No, reading for him was easy, even in Latin, and clearly enjoyable, since he did it now when he could be doing other things. Talking. Laughing.

"Are you going to sit there staring at me, or are you going to say 'good morrow'?"

I jumped at the sound of his voice though it was neither loud nor sharp. "Good morrow," I sputtered. I looked at the book, searching for something to say. "Have you not read this before? When it belonged to you?"

He glanced down, running a careful finger along the crease between the pages of the book. "These books were given to me by the king. I barely had a chance to look at them before I handed them off to your father as a gift. An offering, if you will."

"You would have done better to save them for yourself. My father will put them on a shelf in his study and never open them."

"But you will, I think," he said, looking directly at me.

The blue of those eyes. My stomach did its little leap and fall again, a diver from a cliff.

I shook my head slightly to collect myself, and in response to his confused look, I said, "I shall, for certes. I am the only one who will."

He nodded, as though I had confirmed something for him, and turned his attention back to the text. I wanted to turn his attention back to me, make him look, make him speak again. It was altogether an unfamiliar, unwelcome feeling. I'd spent my life deflecting the attention of others. "The king," I began, faltering over words to express what I was thinking, which was, indeed, formless.

He looked up, patient but perhaps annoyed at the interruption.

I nearly fled with my questions unanswered, but managed, "You have been at court. You have seen the king."

"Yes," he replied drily, "but I am afraid I am ill-suited to report on the latest fashions."

"That is not—" I bit off the words in my mouth, restarted with more polite ones. "My father does not believe his daughters should concern themselves with such subjects as the current state of the kingdom or what is occurring in Parliament."

His eyes slid away, searching the room for my father. "I gather he does not wish his daughters to worry about things that are beyond their ken and control."

I squeezed my lips together, deciding not to say exactly what was and was not beyond my ken, knowing that if I argued with him, I was not likely to get any information. Instead, I said as calmly as I could, "You mentioned there is talk of the king marrying again. Surely that is not an inappropriate topic for young women."

He picked an infinitesimal speck of fluff from his doublet and flicked it away, watching it fall. "Rumors, nothing but rumors and gossip. It feels... dishonest to repeat them."

"Oh," I said. Rubbing my suddenly clammy hands on my skirts, I began to stand. Clearly, he had no interest in discussing these things with me, and I was cold with embarrassment that I had approached him at all.

His fingers curled around my wrist, sending a tremor through my whole body. I looked down and he let go, leaving my skin tingling. "Wait," he said. "Don't go."

I lowered myself back onto the bench, doubting myself even as I did so.

"What do you want to know?"

I was silent for a moment, watching my sister move with ease around the room. "The king," I said finally. "What is he like?"

"Troubled," he replied. "Alone at the center of a busy court. He has as many enemies as friends and sees conspiracies everywhere."

"Is he right?"

His eyes darted to me and away. "Perhaps. The attempt to put him off the throne may have failed, but that doesn't mean another will not be made."

I had been born a few years after King Richard's elder brother, King Edward IV, seized the crown for himself, and throughout my life the throne had been a trophy that changed hands repeatedly. In 1470, when I was young, supporters of the former king, Henry VI, had briefly restored him to the throne, but King Edward, a skilled, resourceful warrior and popular monarch had proved impossible to depose for long; then, at King Edward's death only two years ago, in 1483, his young son should have been crowned, but within a few short months, the boy's uncle Richard had suddenly "discovered" that King Edward had been secretly married as a young man and therefore his marriage to the queen was invalid, making the children thereof illegitimate. Richard took the throne for himself, but there were others who wanted to take it from him to restore either the young king or his little brother—both now rumored to be dead—or on behalf of another rival named Henry Tudor, a cousin of the old king Henry VI, who lurked in the shadows on the Continent.

"If King Richard did indeed kill the princes, he should expect the very angels to rise up against him," I said.

"Oh, indeed. And yet it is hard to imagine such a thing of a man, especially after meeting him."

"Why? I should think a man might do anything to remain king."

"King Richard appears to be a pious man, thoughtful, wise,

lawful, and caring of all his people, great and small. The boys were his nephews, his brother's sons." He shook his head. "He mourns his wife and his own little boy who died last year. I can't imagine a man in that state ordering the deaths of two children of his own flesh and blood."

His words were a vital essence, filling an empty place within me. No one ever spoke to me this way, as though I were his equal in understanding, inviting my opinion on the matter.

"But if they are not dead at his command," I said, "why does he not bring them forth? Reveal them to the people?"

"What if they are dead, but not at his command?" the knight countered. "Who would believe the king did not order it? Since they were in his care, he will be held responsible for their deaths even if he did not do it himself." He raised his hands, a gesture of giving up. "For most people, I fear, this conversation is not worth the trouble. It is easier to assume the king's guilt and to see his wife's and son's deaths as a sign of God's displeasure than to probe further into what truly happened. Perhaps the king understands that any proof he provided would, at this point, not be believed."

"Men are fools," I growled.

"Not all men, I hope," he said over a chuckle.

"All men in my experience."

He served up that knowing smile again, the one that suggested he knew more about me than I did, and I couldn't help glaring at him.

"Oh look," he said. "I believe your tutors are ready to begin," and then he laughed at the look on my face.

The gentlemen continued to enjoy each other's company—did none of them have any useful employment?—and Blanche dragged the handsome language master up the stairs to the solar. The music master took one look at me and cringed, escaping rapidly out the back to the courtyard, apparently indifferent to whether or not I followed.

Good. Perfect. I headed out to my favorite place in town. The bakery.

It was always warm, even in the harshest of winters. Every surface of it was covered in a fine layer of white flour dust, no matter how faithfully Mistress Baker cleaned. And the smells! Yeast and grain, salt and pepper, honey and cinnamon, clove and ginger and mint.

I ate the first of the sweet, sticky rolls before I even left the shop, the bread still warm in my hands. The remaining three I wrapped in a cloth to carry with me.

When Mistress Baker's pointed stares told me I had overstayed my welcome, I went back home with my eyes cast down and ahead, keeping careful watch for refuse in the street and hoping to avoid trouble as I had had with those boys on Sunday.

Odd, really, that I did not relish a fight, considering what the situation at home had done to my mood.

I hesitated, halting before a mangy dog snoozing in the road.

What I wanted—I realized, probing my inward thoughts like a half-healed wound—was not to be seen fighting in the street.

I stepped carefully around the dog and passed it by. At least it would not call me names. Shrew. She-devil. Damn Master Horton. Damn them all.

As I approached my father's house, I was surprised and pleased to see Ellen Brewer lingering on the cobbles out front. She caught sight of me while I was still some distance off and walked toward me so we could stroll back to my house together.

"Here," I said, holding out the napkin. "I bought some sweet rolls. Would you like one?"

"Yes, I would love one. I thank you." Her words were perfectly polite, but she grabbed at the napkin with great eagerness. We paused in the street so she could take her time in choosing which one she liked best. I tried not to huff with impatience.

As we walked on, she began to eat, pulling tiny pieces off the roll and putting them in her mouth one at a time. I waited for her to speak, but she was too busy savoring each bite. At last, I could wait no longer. "Why have you come?" I asked.

"There is something I thought you should know, but perhaps...." She trailed off, but it was not because she was eating. I sensed she was uncomfortable speaking.

"If I should know, I should know," I said. "There is nothing to wonder about. Tell me."

"It is regarding the gentlemen, or one of them. Or two."

I rolled my eyes. "Speak plain. Which gentlemen?"

"Master Lawry. Or he who *says* he is Master Lawry."

Her words chilled me. "Ellen, what do you mean?"

"That Master Lawry who comes courting here." Her fingers shredded the sweet roll, but she no longer ate. "He is no gentleman."

My mouth fell open. "What? How dare you say—?"

"I say it because I know it," she said, her voice rising. "When they arrived the other night, I saw the two of them, master and man. The other man was the master, not the one who calls on your father. I'm sure of it."

"How would you know that?"

"Because of the way they behaved." She responded to the scorn in my voice with heat in her own. "Because of the clothes they wore, because of what each did when they arrived and since. You don't see them when they are away from others, when they think no one is watching—"

"You must be mistaken," I insisted. What she was suggesting was not only unlikely, it was a crime.

She shook her head. "No, I am sure of it. The other one, the one that looks like an angel sent from God above, that one is the master."

I shook my head too, unwilling to believe her. "Even if you are right, why would they do such a thing, switching places?"

Ellen frowned, faltering. "I do not know. I can't imagine…." She raised her chin again. "But I know what I saw, and I am telling you, the master is now pretending to be the man. I do not claim to know why. Seems a foolish thing to do, if you ask me, but there it is."

"No, Ellen, I am sure you must be mistaken. No one would risk it. To what end?"

"I said I don't know. I'm telling you what I saw."

"And I'm telling *you*, you must be wrong."

We stood facing each other like foes in single combat.

Ellen drew in a breath and let it out. "I was only trying to help. To warn you, in case there is something untoward." She shoved the remains of the sweet roll back into my hands. "Thank you for the treat."

I stared at the mess of pastry in my hands. None of this made any sense, least of all Ellen's behavior.

"Ellen," I said as she turned to go.

She hesitated but did not come back to me.

I knew not how to plead, how to make apologies. I had no practice in such things. I felt myself leaning toward her, but I could not make my lips form words.

Fortunately, or unfortunately, Blanche turned onto our street just then, surrounded by her group of friends. The sight of them drove Ellen back to my side.

"Oh look, girls," Blanche said, her voice echoing off the nearby houses and drawing curious housewives and maids to windows. As she intended, of course. "It's the Town of Whitelock Old Maids' Guild."

What was she doing out here? Hadn't she been happily ensconced in the solar, smiling at the beautiful Master Cameron? The Master Cameron who Ellen claimed was a fraud?

I slipped my arm through Ellen's. Blanche was surrounded by her little flock: one Eleanor, two Alices, three Margarets, and two Marys. The names didn't matter really. They were all interchangeable.

"Oh look, Ellen," I said mimicking Blanche's tone precisely. "It's the *mochyn cenfaint.*"

We lived less than a hundred miles from the Welsh border, less than a hundred miles from Ludlow Castle where the old king's eldest son, the Prince of Wales, had grown up. I had picked up quite a few terms from Welsh traders. This was one of my favorites.

Blanche said nothing, just looked at me. She had never bothered to learn any Welsh. She never learned anything she did not have to.

Mochyn cenfaint. Herd of swine.

Blanche laughed.

The swine laughed.

"Truly," Blanche said, "the only right and proper thing for old maids like you to do is to commit yourselves to God." She clasped her hands together in a prayerful pose, lifting her eyes up to heaven, setting the swine to giggling again. "What else are you suited for but a convent? And you do nothing but hold the rest of us back. Do you not see there are men who want us, and you are merely stones in their path?"

I could feel Ellen trembling. She had no words to use against Blanche.

"Men," I scoffed. "You've spent more time with the tutors than the masters. And it seems to me that when you were with the masters, you could hardly put two words together to make an intelligible thought."

Blanche's perfect little mouth pursed, wrinkling the skin around her lips, and suddenly I could see what she would look like in her dotage. That alone pleased me inordinately, but when combined with the fact that she was so clearly struggling over the meaning of the word *"intelligible,"* I could not contain the laugh that bubbled forth.

"What would you know about it?" Blanche countered fiercely. "You're never with the gentlemen. You aren't invited. They aren't interested in you at all."

"That may be so," I said, still smiling, "but judging by the way they talk over your pretty little head, my guess is they aren't terribly interested in you either."

I could feel Ellen trying to pull her arm from mine, leaning away from the barbs flying between us. Did she not understand I was doing this for her too?

"Kathryn, I must go," she said, at last jerking her arm loose.

"Fare thee well, Ellen," I said cheerfully. I wanted to pretend everything was fine, even if it wasn't. I did not want Blanche to think Ellen was fleeing, even if she was.

Blanche turned to the herd. "Get you gone, my dears," she said. "I will walk home on my own from here."

While the Alices moaned and the Margarets sighed at the prospect of being separated from Blanche, I walked on alone.

The tutors met us at the door, distressed at having been given the slip. By this, I guessed that Father had discovered them idling. They shepherded us into the courtyard for lessons, glancing repeatedly over their shoulders at Father's office. The thought of spending the day retracing the path of lessons I had mastered as a child was as appealing as rolling in the filth in the alley behind the house. And all this to get Blanche a rich husband.

Which meant getting me a husband first, whether I wanted one or not.

I spent a fruitless hour with Master Cameron, in which we quickly determined that I knew more Latin than he. With a sigh, I sent him away, and he scurried away like an eager puppy to perch beside Blanche on the edge of the fountain. She exclaimed with delight to find him at her side once again, pulling the book so that it was half on her lap, half on his, and they leaned their pretty heads close together to read. Something in his demeanor, something in the way he moved near her, around her, brought Ellen's words back to me. Truly, there was an air about him that spoke of breeding and wealth, a sense of entitlement… but perhaps that was simply arrogance as a result of Blanche's constantly favoring him over the other fellow.

The portly music master heaved himself up off the fountain's edge, huffing as he waddled his way over to me. His motley robes swayed like a Bedouin's tent, and his liripipe hat perched like a massive wasps' nest on top of his head. He plopped down beside me on the bench under the apple tree, the fancy new lute cradled in his arms. I shifted to the edge of the bench farthest from him so as not to be overcome with his odor, pungent as it was fast becoming in the warm sun. He kept his eyes on Blanche as he said to me, "Now, mistress, have you ever handled a lute before?" His voice was surprisingly high-pitched and rough, not what I expected from one who excelled at music.

"I have handled many things, sir, but nay, not a lute."

He glanced at me sharply, uncertain of my jest, and I smiled innocently. He dumped the lute in my lap and went back to gazing across me at Blanche.

I wrapped my arms around the lute and ran a finger across the strings. A pretty sound, although I had no gift for music. That, like all other womanly gifts, was Blanche's part.

The sound drew his attention back to me at last. "Ah, yes. If you will permit me, you put this hand here…" He placed his hand on mine to show me. His palm was clammy and hot. "And this hand here, on the neck."

I held that position, waiting for him to tell me what to do next, feeling foolish. He was looking at her again.

"Ahem!"

He started and turned back to me. "Ah, yes. Now, these markings here, on the neck, these are the frets."

"Frets. Now that's a word."

"Mistress, please." His tone was aggrieved.

"Don't fret. Do go on."

My jest, mild as it was, was lost on him. "Well, you place your fingers upon the strings, pressing down upon the frets in patterns to create variations in the sounds. That which we call chords."

"Chords. Frets." I could enjoy myself with these words, but clearly this man did not have the wit to make it worth the effort of battering him with them.

I pressed down on a couple of the strings as he described. "I hear nothing."

He shook his head, his ridiculous liripipe hat tipping dangerously. "Press, and while pressing, strum." With one hand he shoved the pile of fabric back onto his head. "Like so." He reached out, one hand holding on to his hat, the other reaching across me to touch the strings.

"I am no fool, Master Lucas," I snapped, jerking the lute aside. Startled, he pulled back from me, eyes wide with fear and, unaccountably, hatred. The hat tipped and swayed, and while he pawed at it with both hands, it fell off entirely, unwinding in a puddle of fabric at his feet. He cried out in dismay and dove off the bench. As he scrambled to scoop up the silly thing, I caught a glimpse of paler skin around his hairline, clear evidence that he had darkened his skin with some sort of dye. I frowned down upon his balding pate. It could not be.

"Master Horton?" I said.

"Nay, of course not," the man said, plopping the shapeless mass on top of his head, his voice squeaking high, then breaking low. "Who is Master Horton? I am Master Lucas, your music master."

My fingers clenched, gripping the lute's strings, which squealed in protest. He cringed at my feet.

"How dare you!" I stood up.

He shrank lower, cowering under the hat that kept sliding from one side of his head to the other as he moved. But he glared up at me with angry, glinting eyes. "She-devil," he muttered.

I raised the lute and brought it down on his stupid, deceitful head. He howled in shock and pain.

I shrieked, wordlessly, an unmusical counterpoint.

Now I knew why Master Horton had not been among the gentlemen. He had not been called away on business or a family matter, or yielded the competition to the others. Instead, he had connived to place himself here inside our house as a tutor in the hopes of gaining Blanche's favor. It was not going to work—it would never have worked for him, even if the angelic Master Cameron hadn't descended from heaven to thwart him—but that he had the audacity to try it!

Blanche and her tutor sprang up from the edge of the fountain. Father and the other gentlemen spilled from the hall. Master Greenwood, Master Lawry, and the others, craning their necks over each other's shoulders, looked suitably horrified at my unladylike behavior. Father frowned storm clouds, his face a book that told of the exact fulfillment of his expectations. The knight, at the back of the group, looked to be hiding a smile behind one hand. I wanted to smite all of them.

Master Lucas—Master Horton, rather—was crouched half on the bench, half off, propping his hat back in place. He was hindered by the presence around his neck of the remains of the lute, its strings cutting into his throat, its neck jutting off like a third arm from his shoulders.

I stuffed my fist into my mouth. I was so close to laughing, so close to real tears.

I kicked him in one fat shin, no matter that the others were watching now.

"Kathryn!" Father's voice shook on the word. He didn't even have to say it. I was already heading inside.

All of the men scattered, clearing the path for me back to the house. Except for one.

Sir William.

I would have to stop or run straight into him. I considered it, but decided it would be best to stop.

I stared, breathing heavily, straight at his brocaded shoulder. I let my eyes slide sideways to his face and found him looking sidelong at me. Those blue eyes were laughing at me, his nose straight and pointed as an arrowhead, his jaw like the hard curve of a bow. He was smiling, just the barest curve of his lips. A storm raged in my belly, and while I wanted to beat him until he moved out of my way—anyone would do to assuage my wrath in that moment—at that same time, my fingers longed to touch him, to brush along his broad shoulders and down his muscular arms, to trace the strong line of his jaw, to finally, *finally* smooth that unruly hair. I flung my fury and confusion at him with my eyes, but his expression of gentle amusement did not change, and in a long, slow movement, he stepped aside. Just barely. Just enough for me to pass by, my hand grazing his.

I proceeded inside at a walk, but once I reached the cool, dim hall, I ran. I ran for the front stairs and up the first flight, intending to run all the way up to hide in my chamber, but before I even got to the turning, I fell to my knees, shaking with rage. I wanted to scream. I wanted to cry. I wanted to run and keep running until I was far away, so far away I never had to see this house or these people again.

I curled tight in a ball on one step, wrapping my arms around my waist and pressing hard to keep control of my breathing, my emotions, trying not to make a sound. A breeze drifted in from the window at the front of the house, soothing my fire. I dropped my head until it touched my knees.

I don't know how long I sat there. I heard voices pass in the street outside, birds chirping and fluttering in the eaves, horses clopping by on the cobbles. Ever so slowly, the pounding of my heart subsided. I stopped gulping my breaths.

The front door opened and I heard Father's voice as he bid farewell to the gentlemen who had come calling. I rose, stiff from sitting so long on the stairs, and, moving like an old woman, resumed my climb up to my bedchamber.

Then, as I passed the small window that was open to the street below, I heard someone speaking: "…your daughter, Master Mulleyn, the beautiful, wise, and virtuous Kathryn."

Was it possible? When had anyone ever put those words together with my name? Surely I had not heard correctly and he was speaking to Father about Blanche?

I skipped down three steps and pressed myself against the wall to peek out the front window. Father stood just outside the door with Sir William.

"I have a daughter named Kathryn, sir; that I will allow," Father replied.

Would it have been so hard for him to allow the compliment to me? Oh yes. He could admit that he had a daughter named Kathryn, but she was not the beautiful one, or wise or virtuous. No, everyone in Whitelock agreed on that, even the one man in the world who was supposed to see the best in me. I couldn't even bring myself to cry over it anymore.

"And what say you to my offer?" the knight went on.

Offer? My ears perked up like those of a horse offered an apple.

"I do thank you for it, sir, and you are most welcome in my home. But I fear I should say, to my great sorrow, she is not for you."

Sir William placed his hands on his hips. "Now, Master Mulleyn, it seems you mean to keep her to yourself. Or else you like me not."

Father shook his head vigorously, held up his hands in plea. "Nay, never say that, sir! Neither of those things! I only mean to spare you—she is such a headstrong, difficult girl—I would not wish to burden a great man such as yourself—"

"I think I am the one to determine what burdens I am fit to bear," Sir William said pointedly. "Good day, Master Mulleyn."

He turned on his heel and strode away. Father called after him, "Wait, good sir! There is my other daughter! You might well consider her...."

I flew down the stairs to meet Father on the doorstep as he came back in.

"What have you done?" I cried, grabbing his gown in my fists. He threw up his hands to ward me off, and I slapped at them. "What have you done?"

"What?" he said. "What mean you by this, Kathryn?"

"I see it now!" I shouted. "You mean never to allow me to marry at all. Blanche is your treasure. She will have all, and I will be an old maid because you love her entirely and me not at all!"

"Not marry? Kathryn, I would like nothing better than to have you out of my house!" He paused, glancing at the open door and from there to the stairs. "Oh, so you heard what I said to Sir William? What have I done but told the truth? What have I done but warn a man of more worth than you deserve that he would be naught but miserable shackled to a shrew like you? How could I endanger our family by marrying *you* to a man of status and power? Once he knew what you were, he would destroy us. Instead of a good alliance, it could only be bad!"

I shook my head. "It has always been thus. Blanche has all, Kathryn gets nothing."

"Tomorrow we shall see the nothing Kathryn gets," Father said ominously. "If this knight wants one of my daughters, I will see if he will have Blanche. You *will* marry, if I have to beggar myself to dower you. There must be some sum of money, some pile of coins that will induce a man, *any* man, to take you off my hands."

"Talk not to me," I said. "You are no father to me."

I flew up the stairs and into my bedchamber. I did not come out all the rest of the day, but then, I do not think I was missed.

A soft tapping drew me from sleep. I lay still, dream-cloudy, trying to identify the sound. Had that blasted woodpecker returned? Was one of the servants up early?

It came again, a dull thud against wood, and close by. Not a servant, and not the determined strike-strike-strike of a woodpecker. Almost like....

I sat up. Pulling the blanket around my shoulders, I groped my way to the window, shuttered against the night. My only guide was the faint moonlight that bled around its imperfect edges. I placed a tentative hand upon it and leaned close, listening.

The noise came again, right in my ear. I jumped back, the blanket falling from my grasp. Shivering with more than cold, I picked it up again and drew it tight around me.

Something was hitting my window.

Oh.

I frowned. It was, no doubt, one of the suitors throwing rocks, thinking he was aiming for Blanche's window. This had happened before. He was probably down there with a couple of musicians, ready to sing some execrable love song and then offer to climb up to show her how much he loved her.

After the day I had had, I grinned at the prospect of destroying his hopes.

I fumbled my way to the bedside table and struck a candle into life. Back at the window, I yanked on the shutters with one hand, hauling them open and leaning out with my candle held high.

It was not the group of men and musicians I expected. It was one man alone.

"Ah, look," he said, to no one in particular. "A light. The sun arises."

I knew that voice. Already, I knew his voice well.

"Nay, Sir William, you are mistaken. It is only a candle."

Even in the dark, the night lit only by stars and a crust-thin sliver of the moon, I could see his grin. "Nay, my lady," he echoed, his voice lilting, teasing, "I mean you." He raised both hands toward me in exaggerated pleading. "Have you never been wooed before?"

No. I had not.

"Of course I have," I said, pitching my voice lower, careful of waking Father and the Mountain who slept in the chamber below mine. "But never by a moon-mad fool such as you."

"O speak again, bright angel," he cried. "She speaks, and yet she says nothing."

I scowled fiercely. "I say *something*, sir! I say, begone!"

"Not without that which I came for."

I set the candle down on the windowsill and took a deep breath. Mayhap if I indulged his whim, he would depart the sooner.

"Which is?"

The flash of his grin once more. "The assurance of your love, of course."

I turned away from the window and he howled like a dog, setting off all the dogs along the street.

I flew back, nearly knocking the candle off the sill. "Hush!"

He was gone.

I craned my neck, looking up and down the street. Below me, a shutter opened, and Father's head poked out. I jumped back, blowing out the candle. House by house, the dogs settled. The shutter below creaked shut. I returned to the window. The street was empty. Disappointment was a cold stone in my stomach.

Lifting the smoking candle, I walked back to my bed, chiding myself. How could I be disappointed? There was nothing real here, nothing serious.

Something hit me square in my back. I spun. A pebble lay on the floor at my feet. I charged the window, nearly flying out.

"Fool! Have you returned?" My voice was half-whisper, half-shout.

He held up his hands again, this time shielding his face. "There is more peril in your eyes than in all the dogs of High Street, or in your father's walking stick."

I had to stifle a laugh. The idea of my paunchy, lazy father pursuing this warrior in defense of my honor was worse than ridiculous.

"Indeed," I replied. "Take care you do not gaze upon me too long, lest like Medusa I turn you into stone."

"Better I should perish here, a statue in the street, a beggar at your window, than live without your love."

The laugh burst out of me—I could not help it—but he did not seem offended. He smiled. Was that his end? Laughter? Was this all just mockery of the shrew?

I glowered down upon him, leaning farther out the window so that he might see it. "Lest you think me so easily won by false flattery, look upon me now. I tell you I love you not, though you swear you love me a thousand times." I smacked the sill beneath me. "We only met on Sunday!"

He cast his eyes appreciatively over my body and I realized how I must look, leaning out the window in my nightgown. Quickly, I straightened, and he smiled.

"Lady," he said, hand over heart, "by this blessed moon, I swear I love you."

"Nay," I said. "Swear not by the moon. She is inconstant,

changing, altering with every day. How shall I trust your love if you swear by the moon?"

"Then what shall I swear by?"

My skin broke out in gooseflesh. Was this still a joke? How was I to believe him? I did not know him at all, and all of his words felt like jests.

"Do not swear," I said, taking up the candle to end this farce. "Much as I have enjoyed your company this night, this declaration of yours is too sudden. It is like lightning, gone before one can even say, 'Look, it lightens!' Therefore, good night, and give this passion of yours time to grow before you speak of it again."

I blew him a kiss, secure in the knowledge of my victory. The breeze of it extinguished the candle, leaving me blinking in darkness.

It was silent outside, and I reached for the shutters, a little disappointed he had been so easily disposed of after all. Until, "Why did your father say me nay?"

There was nothing of humor in his voice now.

My heart fell to my feet. I felt it strike the floor and lie there, pulsing feebly. I left it there and leaned into the window frame once more. "What do you mean?"

He stood closer now, directly under my window, hands on his hips. I could hardly make him out; only the white of his shirt peeking out from under his doublet, the flash of his teeth as he spoke. "I asked for your hand in marriage. He refused me."

An arrow through me, then and now, but this arrogant man would never know. I forced lightness into my voice. "He is a merchant, sir. A merchant never accepts the first offer."

"He should, if there is little reason to expect a second."

"Oh!" I stamped my foot again. "You...." I knew I should shut the window, slam it closed on him and his wicked tongue. But my blood was like wine in my veins and I could not do it. What was this?

"Hear me," he said, more softly. "I am the only husband for you."

My skin went to ice, then fire. I tried to force scathing, scornful words from my lips, but I could not move, could not think. Without the candle, he could not see the effect his words had upon me. Could he?

"Until tomorrow, lady," he called, bowing low.

I had to extricate my fingernails from the wood of the sill one by one as he disappeared into the darkness

Chapter Six

Thursday

When we went down to the courtyard for lessons in the morning, Blanche stopped me at the door. "You realize your behavior yesterday will force me to sit with that fat music master today."

"Let me dredge up some sympathy for you." I closed my eyes and screwed up my face, straining. "No, sorry, nothing there."

She crossed her arms, frowning. "You did it on purpose, didn't you?"

"Yes, Blanche. I assaulted an innocent man and embarrassed myself in front of a group of gentlemen who are my last hope of marriage and a life outside of Whitelock, solely for the purpose of discomfiting you today. I am truly that devious."

She narrowed her eyes. "You might have done. I never understand why you do what you do."

"No," I replied, stepping out into the sun. "You wouldn't, would you?"

"What is that supposed to mean?" she demanded, her fingers grazing my shoulder as she reached for me. I shrugged her off.

"What is wrong with you?" she called at my back. "I used to think you were the smartest person in the world, but really you're more a fool than anyone."

I whirled around. "A fool? You call me a fool?"

"Yes!" Her face was more wary than angry. "How hard would it be for you to smile at a man? What would it cost you to say what they want to hear?"

"You mean like you do?" My fists rolled in on themselves. "Everything. It would cost me everything."

Fury darkened her beautiful features. "Your refusal to bend is going to cost *me* everything," she snapped. "But that's what you really want, isn't it? You don't care what happens to you, as long as you make me unhappy as well."

I turned away and marched over to the language master, leaving her standing in the doorway.

I plopped down on the bench beneath the apple tree. Master Cameron looked up from his book, startled, then nodded a greeting even as his eyes swept past me to light upon Blanche. She favored him with a smile, then turned her attention to Master Lucas—nay, the disguised Master Horton—who held a small pipe in his hands. Master Horton shot me a venomous glance and rubbed the back of his head. At least he had exchanged his foolish headgear for a cap more sober and appropriate. Together they walked to the opposite side of the fountain where their outlines could just be viewed through the dancing water. Beside me, Master Cameron kept his eyes on my sister as his fingers shuffled aimlessly through Plato.

I contemplated smacking him in the head with one of the other books piled at his feet to get his attention, but decided it was not worth the uproar that would follow. It was too hot.

"I have learned quite a bit of German," I said finally. "My father does a great deal of trading on the Continent, you see, and I have been helping him with his contracts and such."

"Hmmm," Master Cameron mused.

"Printed books came from Germany originally, as I am sure you are aware, although there is now a printshop in London. Have you ever seen a printing press, Master Cameron?"

Master Cameron tilted his head and sighed. "Her lips are of coral, and her breath does perfume the air around her."

"Master Cameron!" I brought my foot down on top of his.

He yelped. It was quite satisfactory.

"Mistress Kathryn, forgive me," he said, leaning down to rub his toes. "But have you never been in love?"

"Tell me, sir, is it possible for love to take hold so suddenly?" I allowed my voice to hold all of my scorn.

He shook his head, the sunlight turning his curls into a halo. I had to admit, he was beautiful. "Until I found it to be true," he said, "I never thought it possible, or even likely. But now...."

"One cannot love without knowing the essence of the beloved, Master Cameron."

He looked at me, his eyes wide with surprise. "She is everything sweet and maidenly and modest. Look at her!"

"I look at her every day, master, and I am the only one who sees her quite clearly."

He was not listening to me. He was gazing at her. I could hardly make out his words. "I burn, I pine, I perish if I cannot have her."

"Oh, God help me," I muttered, picking up a book from the pile at Master Cameron's feet. I dropped it in his lap. "Is there something we could read that might draw your thoughts from all your sufferings?"

He smiled weakly. "You are too kind, Mistress Kathryn." Setting aside the Plato, he selected a new book and proceeded to page through it upside down, never noticing his error because his eyes were once again fixed upon Blanche. She, seated on the fountain's edge, leaned one hand behind her as Master Horton played, and tipped her chin back to look through the cascading water at Master Cameron. Catching sight of him watching her, she bestowed upon him a shy smile, then quickly cast her eyes down again.

I stood abruptly. This was outrageous. It was not enough that the gentlemen were falling over each other to court her, now we had the serving men too? "Forgive me, Master Cameron," I said. "I am feeling unwell again. I believe I will retire."

He barely murmured any words of consolation before he scrambled up off the bench and headed for Blanche and Master Horton.

If only the apple tree were in fruit, I would have had something to throw.

As I walked toward the door to the hall, Father came out and hurried toward me. Glancing over his shoulder, he said, "Kathryn, I need you to go inside at once. This is a matter of great importance."

I started to object, but he cut me off, grasping my arms tightly and giving me a little shake.

"Kathryn, just this one time, you must listen to me! There is a man within, a man who is willing to marry you, who insists he *will* marry you—" He stopped, took a breath, shook me again. "Be courteous, Kathryn. Be kind. Be gentle and meek and reserved and all the things you are not for once in your life, for God's sake, Kathryn, please!"

I drew myself up, pulling my arms from his grasp. "Not for God's sake. For Blanche's, and for yours."

I stormed off, furious as I seemed always to be, carrying it with me to the door to the hall, where I came to an abrupt halt. Father's words echoed. *A man was waiting, a man willing to marry me.* And then the words he had spoken yesterday repeated in my mind. *There must be some pile of coins that will induce a man to take you off my hands.*

Father had sworn he'd have the knight for Blanche, so he must have convinced one of the other men, one of Blanche's suitors, to take me for a price. Master Horton was here, posing as the music tutor, and Master Greenwood and the other local fellows knew me too well to take me for any amount of coins, so it must be the other gentleman, Master Lawry, the solid fellow in ill-fitting clothes who seemed so uncomfortable among the other gentlemen and subordinate to his absent father.

My father had piled the gold on the table and sold me to a stranger. Now all that remained was for the gentleman to be sure he didn't regret his bargain once he spoke to me.

Well, I could make certain this gentleman understood exactly what that bargain had bought him.

I stalked into the hall.

A man *was* waiting. He heard my step and turned. It was neither Master Greenwood—I could give thanks for that—nor any of the dull local fellows, nor the newcomer Master Lawry, but the man who taunted and challenged me, the one who wooed me from my window.

The man who had asked for me.

That realization struck me like a bucket of cold water, dousing my fire.

For a fragile, frozen moment, we stared at each other. He took a deep breath, as though girding himself for hard work, and then he bowed, as he had in the street, sweeping his arms out like a courtier before royalty. When he rose, he was beaming. "There she is, my bride, my Kate."

Stunned, I did not stop to curtsy but went farther into the hall. After my father's words yesterday, I was so sure he would convince this knight to accept Blanche, even despite the performance under my window last night. What had passed between them today? What had been offered and promised?

What had my father given to get rid of me?

The chill lingered on my spine as I came to a stop near him, a safe distance away. I tried to recapture my anger. "Sadly, you are mistaken, sir. My father made these arrangements with you without my consent. Terribly sorry to disappoint you. Good day." I made him the barest of courtesies and swept past—or at least, I tried to sweep past him, but he grabbed hold of my arm.

"You do not seem to understand," he said in my ear. "When I was young, and your father would visit Bitterbrook Keep, he would regale us with stories of his daughters."

"Both daughters?" I asked, suspicious.

"Indeed," he replied. "And so I determined I would come and see for myself the truth of the matter. And what do I find?" He gestured with his free hand, taking in me, the hall, my whole life. "I find he greatly misrepresented your virtues, Kate. All it took was one meeting, one sight of you, for me to understand the truth of things."

"Indeed?" I mimicked him.

He was all smiles. "Oh yes. And so, what could I do? I knew that, with so many gentlemen here seeking a wife, I had to move quickly, and so I claimed you for myself."

His words the night before, his arms around me as I fell, the knowledge that he had asked for me and had not taken no for an answer.... I was dizzy, confused. I tried to pull my arm free from his grasp and failed. "Moved quickly, indeed," I replied sharply. "I wish whatever moved you here would move you away again. You are easily movable, I see." At his puzzled look, I gestured to the little footrest beside my father's chair. "Like furniture. Like that little stool."

He grinned, sliding his hand down my arm to grasp my hand while he dropped to one knee, patting the other. "That's right! Come, sit on me."

"Ha!" My voice was more steady than my stomach, which was trembling as though it were a winter's night. "Asses are made to bear, and so are you."

His grin turned sly. "Women are made to bear, and so are you."

Heat flared into a blush on my cheeks and I fired back, "Not for you, sir." How had this become a game of sniping about bedsport? This was too close to last night, and me in my nightgown!

I shook off the sensation and struck back with words. "How much did my father pay you?"

He froze, feigning a stricken look. "What? Did my words at your window mean nothing to you?"

"Indeed, nothing. I know full well no man would marry me save for my dowry." How it pained me to say it out loud. "Your words are noise and flattery. I know my reputation."

"Your reputation," he repeated, tasting the word like wine in his mouth. "You have a reputation among the men in this village?"

Monstrous, the way a lilt in a voice, a lift of an eyebrow, could suggest all sorts of things. My skin heated again, mingling anger with embarrassment. My hand shook in his. "Not for any reason you seem to imply, sir. There is nothing light about my worth. My reputation in that is all it should be."

"All it should beeee?" he scoffed, dragging out the last word. "And yet the bees do buzz."

I could feel my eyes narrow, my lips tighten. What was it about him, his words, that dragged such reactions out of me? "Foolish gossip of idle folk who know nothing. You have been here only a few days. What can you know of my—?" As I had the night before, I stamped my foot. The shock of it, here on the stone flags of the hall, rang up my leg and into my hips. "Blast you!" I cried. "If you hear a buzzing, take care you don't get stung."

"Hmm," he mused, one hand thoughtfully on his chin. "If that is the threat, my remedy then is to pluck out your sting."

"Oh yes," I shot back, "if you could find where it lies."

"Who does not know where the bee hides its sting? In its tail."

He lunged, reaching behind me.

I jumped back and he let me go. "Nay, in her tongue."

That was no good. He was looking at my mouth now.

"I know not what arrangement you may have made with my father, but I will not be bought and sold like a Moorish carpet. And so, farewell."

I headed for the front of the hall and the safety of the stairs, but his words arrested me.

"What," he said, "will you leave me with my tongue in your tail?"

I spun and he was right there behind me. *My tongue in your tail.* My face flared hot again, and something fluttered in my gut, lower....

"Listen, Kate," he murmured, "I am a gentleman—"

"I'll test that—" Spinning in his grasp, I swung my free hand around and slapped him, hard. The snap of it resounded in the empty hall. My own shock was reflected in his eyes, but he recovered more quickly than I. He grabbed my wrist, pulling it down. I cried out, more affronted than hurt, for he was surprisingly gentle. In a moment, he had twisted me around so that he held me from behind, one arm around my waist, the other holding my arm. But he didn't seem angry, as any right-minded man would be, only amused.

"I swear I'll cuff you if you strike me again," he warned, soft in my ear.

Even as frustrated as I was, I couldn't resist the pun. "So may you lose your arms. If you strike me, you are no gentleman, and if no gentleman, no coat of arms."

He chuckled, the vibration of it tingling against my spine. "Are you a herald, Kate?"

I writhed, trying to break free. Futile, of course. The man was a warrior, and my struggles only served to prove his strength. I had thought he might become embarrassed by overpowering me. He did not.

"Oh yes, a herald. Tell me, sir, what is your crest? A coxcomb?"

"A combless cock, unless Kate will be my hen."

I was blushing again. "No cock of mine. You fight like a craven."

"Fight, fight," he said, murmuring in my ear. "Why must you always fight me?"

I went rigid in his arms, all my breath lost. For that was the question, wasn't it? Why was I fighting him? Here he was, saying he loved me—oh, that was scarcely to be believed—but at the least offering me honorable marriage and an escape from this wretched family, this awful town, when no other tolerable offer was ever likely to come my way... and only yesterday I had raged at my father for rejecting his proposal. So why was I doing the same today?

Because there was a sack of gold behind his proclaimed passion for me. There had to be. Why would he take me otherwise?

He was still waiting for an answer.

"You—you are too old and wrinkled for me."

That must have surprised him for he loosened his grip just enough for me to squirm away, breathing hard to make him feel guilty for holding me so tightly. At least, that's what I hoped. It did not work, so far as I could tell.

"I? Old and wrinkled?" He put a hand to his face. My hand lifted, mirroring his, and I forced it back down.

"Aye." I looked at him, that perfectly formed face, those sparkling eyes, that trim form, and had to continue the lie. "Aye. Wrinkled and withered and dried up as a crabapple in winter."

"I am still young," he protested, "but a handful of years older than you. If my face be marred, it is with cares and worries, not with age."

A noble knight, just returning from the king's court? What cares and worries could he have?

"*I* care nothing for you," I said and made a dash for the front stairs. He was too fast for me. His arms encircled my waist again and he pulled me to him. My eyes were at his chin, my breath panting in the hollow of his neck, my hands pressed against his chest. Every inch of me, in fact, was pressed against every inch of him, a fact of which I became aware in that instant. I raised my eyes. He looked down. His eyes were so very blue, and so very amused.

I struggled to break free. He moved with me. His bawdy jokes took on new meaning. My heart began to pound. I tried to speak, failed. I tried again. "I will only make you... angry... if you hold me thus. Let me go."

"Nay," he said, drawing the syllable out. "I find this very pleasant." He gazed down at me and my muscles surrendered, melting into him. Did he feel it, my body's betrayal? I tried to pull away from him, but he held me close still. "This is the part of the proposal," he said quietly, "where the man declares his admiration and affection, and the lady confesses herself flattered. It won't do for her to make him suffer, and so she accepts."

I struggled again, halfheartedly. "Out of obligation?"

"Or compassion. There are worse reasons to marry."

"Like money," I spat.

"Do you not believe my declaration?"

"Believe you? How is such a thing possible? Have you spoken truth once since you arrived?"

Anger kindled its hot flame within my breast again, but before it could blaze forth, I was suddenly free. Released so abruptly from his embrace, I collapsed to the floor and glared up at him. "You!" I cried, rising to my full height, moving away to a safe distance so I did not have to feel his heat. "Go and order your servants about, sir, and leave me alone."

Yes, alone. Suddenly, I wanted—no, *needed*—to be alone, away from him, to stop this madness, to cease his flow of words, to calm my breath and my pounding heart. Away from him who could capture or release me at a whim, who could match me word for word, who wanted me—

No. He wanted the money my father offered up to take me on. The rest of this was just an amusement for him. What kind of life would this be, a constant struggle, pulse racing, skin tingling, day by day, moment by moment—?

"Ye—"

I bit down on the word as a sound drew his attention behind me, to the door to the courtyard. "Here comes your father," he said. He strode toward Father, leaving me standing, swaying, in the middle of the hall.

Father approached him, rubbing his hands together like a miser spying a gleaming pile of coins. "Well, Sir William, how goes it?"

Father. At exactly the wrong moment.

"Very well, Master Mulleyn. How could it not?"

Father faltered a little in his stride, giving him a quizzical look. I turned my back on them both, biting a strangled scream off in my fist.

"Well, Kathryn," Father said, coming up behind me. "What say you? Are you not happy now that I have arranged this for you?"

I spun around to face him. He shied, took a step back. ""Happy? You want me happy now? Yesterday I was not good enough for him, but today? What has changed? Oh, I know what it is. He refused Blanche, so you threw gold at him so he won't think he's getting a poor bargain."

"But he wanted you," Father cried. "He insisted!"

"You *sold* me," I spat at him. "You sold me to get me out of the way, to make Blanche happy. You gave no thought to my happiness at all. And that's how it has ever been."

Sir William came closer. I backed away. "Father," he said, addressing my father. *My* father! The audacity of the man! "Father, if you will permit me—" My father, curse him, nodded acquiescence. "I must tell you that everyone here has spoken wrongly of my fair Kate. She is not difficult but gentle as the dove. She is not hot-tempered, but mild and temperate as a spring morning."

Father stared. I stared.

Sir William took another step toward me, reaching for my hand. I retreated again. "In fact, Father, we like each other so well that we have agreed upon Sunday as the wedding day."

"What?" I burst out.

"Sunday?" Father exclaimed, either not hearing or disregarding my protest. "But this is marvelous news! A bit speedy. We'll have to procure a special license, dispense with the reading of the banns—but what is that if my Kathryn is to be married?"

"I did not—" I sputtered.

Father grabbed my hand in one of his, Sir William's in his other, and held tight. "I am speechless," he said, belying his own words, "I don't know what to say. Here, join your hands and God give you joy." He slammed our hands together. Sir William squeezed my fingers in his so I could not pull away.

"Listen well to me, Kate," Sir William said quietly. "You may not believe it now, but I am the only husband for you."

"Sir William," Father said, turning with a delighted smile to his new son, "let us go and see about those papers."

Our war of words was, apparently, finished. I felt Sir William's eyes on me, but I would not meet them. I stared at our hands clasped beneath my father's.

"I trust you will attend to all the proper legalities, Father," Sir William said. "I'm for Coventry to buy apparel, rings, and finery for my wife. Order the feast and invite the guests and I will see you on Sunday. Until then, farewell."

He raised my hand to his lips and released it. My fingers burned from the contact. He and Father embraced, Sir William bowed, and then he was gone.

The door shut behind him. Father stormed in and out of rooms, yelling for his scribe, starting to send a servant to the lawyer's house, then calling for his horse because he'd go himself. Diffident musical notes drifted in from the courtyard as Blanche continued to endure the attentions of Master Horton in disguise. But all of this was muffled and dim, noises in a fog.

Married. On Sunday. To *him*.

I wandered upstairs, my gaze fixed on the third floor where the solitude of my bedchamber lay, but the door to the solar was open. "Kathryn!" Blanche's mother barked. "Come in here!"

The Mountain was up for once, her enormous bulk ensconced in a chair that had been specially built for her. It was wide enough for Blanche and me to sit in together and sturdy enough to hold a full-grown ox. A blanket covered her lap and legs, despite the heat. One silk-wrapped foot peeked out beneath it, sausage-like. At least she was out of bed today, and dressed. She must have heard about the men come courting in the last few days. She must have heard—

"Kathryn!"

I dragged into the solar, a condemned heretic to the stake. "Yes, Mother?"

"What is all the commotion?"

I glanced at the window. The tootling of Blanche's instrument went on. "Blanche and I have been at our lessons with the new tutors."

Her eyes glowed balefully, like dim candles in a pumpkin on All Hallows' Eve. "That is not why your father is bound for the lawyer's. Why does he need legal papers?"

I shifted my weight from one foot to another. She must be told, and if I didn't tell her, Blanche would. Oh, how Blanche would love to tell her.

I raised my chin, squared my shoulders. "I am getting married."

She snorted. Mayhap it was laughter, mayhap it was disbelief.

"To whom?" she barked. "No man from this town would have you."

"There is no man in this town I would have," I retorted. "He is a knight, a man of good repute from west of here." I was still so shaken by our encounter, I could not bring myself to say his name. "Father knows more. He did not see fit to tell me anything of substance."

The Mountain licked her lips, tasting the increase in status. If I married a knight, I would become Lady Kathryn and the entire family would thus be elevated. "A knight," she repeated. "Well. This is— Well!" She shifted in her seat, threatening to rise, but I knew she would not. She would wait for Father's return, get the details from him then. "And the wedding? When is it to be?"

The word was poison in my mouth. I spat it out. "Sunday."

"Sunday? What, *this* Sunday? Three days from now? But that is outrageous!" She moved again, the mounds of her breasts and belly shuddering, the chair rocking under her. "How am I to arrange a proper wedding in three days, even for you? Outrageous! Monstrous!" She slammed her palms down on the chair's arms. "Sunday? Pah! What do men know of weddings?"

"He said he was going to Coventry, to purchase finery for the wedding," I said.

The Mountain scowled, a fearsome sight. "*He* may purchase what he likes, but still, we must provide him with a bride when he comes. You need a dress. Ah, but there is no time." She turned her squinted eyes on me. I folded my arms and glared back.

"You always did look well in green," she mused.

I was shocked she had ever noticed.

"Yes," she said, apparently deciding. "We'll get Dame Hutton to make over your green kirtle. We'll send for her today." She smacked the arms of her chair again. "Married on Sunday. Outrageous."

I will never be sure what pulled me out of my house and into town that day. I just knew I did not want to hear the Mountain howling at servants about clothes and food and preparations. I did not want to be there when Blanche learned the news. And I did not want to be alone any longer.

I wanted to see Ellen.

Of course, we had not parted on the best of terms. Though I still doubted her about Master Cameron, I could tell her about Master Horton. At least she was correct that *one* of the "tutors" was in disguise. Surely she would forgive me for being cross with her. Besides, once I shared my news, all else would be forgotten. Ellen would understand.

She must.

As I cut across the stableyard to get to the inn's rear door, I could hear voices in the stable and the drag and bang of objects being moved within. I swung open the heavy door leading to the kitchen and let myself in.

A crockery bowl smashed at my feet as the door collided with Ellen. "What on earth…?" she exclaimed, her eyes wide as they took me in.

"I am sorry, Ellen, I will pay for the bowl…"

"That you will, Mistress Kathryn Mulleyn." Dame Brewer, Ellen's mother, was a large and formidable woman, her dark hair barely restrained under a cap darkened with grease and soot from many long years in that kitchen. She frowned at me now from behind the kitchen's long, stained table, a cleaving knife in her hand. "What mean you by this, coming in the back way like a servant? 'Tis not proper for a young lady."

"I have come to speak with Ellen," I said, and grabbing her wrist, I pulled her with me into a corner of the kitchen.

"Kathryn," she protested, though she kept her voice to a whisper. "What are you doing?"

"Ellen, have you heard?"

"Heard?"

There was a toughness around her eyes that made me think she was being deliberately evasive. "About me," I insisted. "Me and this knight, this Sir William. My father and he have come to terms. He says he will marry me."

She glanced at the door, not the one through which I had come but the narrower one that led to the main room of the inn. "I know," she whispered. "He came back here speaking of nothing else. He has been buying ale for everyone who comes through the door. Father is beside himself with delight."

Dame Brewer's cleaver came down with a loud thwack and I flinched. "Ellen," she hollered. "You will clean up that mess. I don't care who demands your attention or how rich she is."

Ellen made a move toward the broken bowl, but I held her tightly by both wrists. "By now the whole town must be talking of it," I complained.

"It matters not," she said, "for he is leaving soon. His man is readying his horse and he is going away."

"He said he would go to Coventry to buy things for the wedding," I told her.

"All right, then," Ellen said, clearly anxious to get rid of me so she could do as her mother bid. "And now that you are betrothed, Blanche is free to court, so she should be less of a torment to you, so you have everything you want. Now let me go." She shook her hands, breaking loose.

"Everything I want?" I was stunned. How could she think such a thing?

I watched her on her knees picking up the broken crockery with the edge of her apron so as not to cut herself. I knew I should go, I knew she wanted me to leave, but her description of Sir William's afternoon of revelry lured me to the door to the main room. I leaned against it, letting it swing open just a crack.

"Here now, what're you doing, mistress?"

I ignored Dame Brewer but realized I could not hang about in the doorway. I would have to choose. In or out. Stay or go.

The kitchen door opened behind and to one side of the bar. The public room was noisy and crowded. I slipped through the door and moved along the wall where benches and stools had been kicked haphazardly out of the way. Master Brewer was at the far end of the bar pouring generous drinks. Keeping my head down, I made my way into a corner near the hearth, unnoticed by the gang of men standing around Sir William.

Master Brewer lowered his pitcher and set it on the bar. He was ruddy-faced and bald, grinning broadly at the bounty this morning's unexpected news had brought him. "Are you certain you must leave us so soon, Sir William?" he inquired.

"Indeed I must," said my husband-to-be from the center of the loud, laughing, drinking crew. "There are purchases I must make, gifts to buy, and sadly, I cannot find them here. No offense to your fair village."

The men guffawed with laughter. The miller slapped him on the back. "None taken, none taken, I assure you, sir. An esteemed personage such as yourself must of course go to Coventry to find what you are looking for."

"Though why he didn't go there for a bride is beyond my understanding," someone said, and they all laughed.

"Now why would you say that?" Sir William said, in good-natured challenge.

"Forgive me for saying…" The miller leaned in close to Sir William. I could imagine the reek of his boozy breath. "But your bride is the most notorious shrew in the country."

Another burst of laughter, and the clink of cups. Sir William laughed along with them. My hands made fists, my nails digging into my palms.

"Go to, gentlemen, I have chosen her for myself. I find my Kate as sweet as honey and fair as a spring morning," Sir William said, and they all laughed again. He continued, his voice firmer. "If she and I be pleased, what's it to you? But never fear," he went on, after taking a quaff from his cup, "never fear. I will show her my will, and she will have no other will than *my* will, and I will be her only will…" He raised his cup in a salute. "And she will be mine."

They all raised their glasses. "To Sir William," they called and drank again. Master Brewer held out his pitcher again, looking as delighted as the day his younger daughter had gotten married.

I stepped forward.

No one saw me.

I climbed over a bench and on top of a stool.

"Just remember, Sir William," I shouted over their raucous voices. They quieted, turning toward me, but it might as well have been only Sir William and me in the inn.

"You would do well to remember, sir, that a woman will have her will."

Someone choked on his beer, another man dared to laugh. Sir William did not.

He walked forward. Standing on the stool, I was as tall as he was, perhaps a bit taller. I had garnered his attention, but I had not thought beyond that. He had punned on his name and made light of my obedience, and I had meant to take back some measure of control. Which I had. Except the common saying I had used to do it had two meanings. *A woman will have her will*— she will have her own way, and she will have her man's....

I felt a hot blush on my cheeks, but what was done, was done. He had arrived at my stool and was looking up at me, amusement bright in his eyes. I glared down at him.

"Though others may have their wishes, you *will* have your Will." He swept another of his broad, graceful bows, and everyone applauded, laughing and cheering. He meant to be charming, I supposed, but I didn't find him so. He was so smug, and determined to have the last word.

My hand flinched with the desire to strike him again. He stayed me by taking hold of both of my hands. With a glance toward the door, he said, "I see my man is ready to depart. Much as it would delight me to stay and enjoy the unexpected pleasure of speaking with you, Kate, I must get to Coventry with all haste. Until Sunday."

He kissed my hands one by one and bowed once more. Then he stepped back and bowed to the rest of the company and swept out the door.

Everyone was staring at me.

I hopped down from the stool—*a stool is movable. Come sit on me,* oh God!—my hands burning from his gallantry, and retreated back through the kitchen.

Ellen, shaking her head, stood in the doorway. "You never will learn to be quiet, will you?"

Just to spite her, I did not answer.

The men made a riot of noise in the front of the inn, seeing Sir William off. I stalked away, too flustered to go home, and found myself on Church Street, in the artisans' part of town. Here, the uneven road was only wide enough for one cart to pass, and the timber-framed, whitewashed buildings leaned close on both sides of the street, barely allowing any light through from above. In fact, if you leaned out from an upper-story window on one side of the street, you could surely touch the sign of a store on the other side.

Head down, shoulders hunched, muttering to myself, I relived the scene in the common room, wishing I had done things differently.

And proceeded to walk straight into someone.

His "oof" of lost breath was followed by an outraged "How dare—" as I bounced off his bony shoulder. I looked up into the ruddy face of our neighbor, Master Carson, a prosperous merchant like my father, but much younger and happily married with a brood of small children like chicks in his yard.

"Oh, Mistress Kathryn." His face went still, careful. He steadied me with a hand on my shoulder. He glanced down, away, anywhere but at me. He stepped away, shaking his hand surreptitiously behind his back. As if he might have been sullied by touching me.

My fists clenched. "Good morrow, Master Carson."

He ducked his head, tugging at his cap. "Good morrow, Mistress Mulleyn," he replied. "My apologies."

"The fault was mine, Master Carson."

"Not at all. Not at all." His words tumbled over each other faster than his feet as he passed me.

I twisted from my waist, watching him go. The devil himself might have dogged his heels for the speed at which he trotted along the street. But at least he had spoken politely to me rather than ignoring me entirely, which his wife always did.

Better, too, than muttering curses under his breath as he passed, as so many of our neighbors did.

Froward wench. Harpy. She-devil. Shrew.

With a sigh, I looked around at the bustle of folk going about their business, in and out of shops, easy smiles on their faces, some arm in arm with friends. How long since I had been so carefree, so easy with someone?

Blanche and I had been that way once, long ago, so long I could barely remember. Most days, I didn't even try.

A painted sign indicated Dame Hutton's dress shop a few doors ahead. I hesitated, then headed that way.

A small bell jingled as I shut the shop door behind me.

Every eye in the place slammed into me, an arrow to the bull's-eye.

I met their stares, one by one.

Girls my own age watched with wide eyes and smirking lips. Matrons, their mothers and aunts and married older sisters, tipped their heads together and murmured. An Alice, one of Blanche's herd of swine, peered around a bolt of pink linen, eagerly gathering gossip to share with the rest of them later.

How well I could read their expressions. How easily I could hear the whispers they tried to conceal. Kathryn Mulleyn a bride, they said. How preposterous. No one here in Whitelock would have her, so her father had to pay a stranger to take her away. Twenty thousand crowns— practically a king's ransom! But he doesn't know yet that he's got the worse end of the bargain. He'll learn. Soon enough, he'll learn....

Dame Hutton glided over to me, her movements smooth and unhurried. "Mistress Kathryn, how lovely to see you." Her light, friendly tone even sounded like she meant it.

"I see you are...quite busy today, Dame Hutton," I said, feeling behind me for the latch on the door. "I can come back, or perhaps you can come by my house later? To discuss the... ah...."

"Yes," she said brightly, "yes, of course. Come right in and I can help you at once."

I could not tear my eyes off the other women. "It seems my situation is fascinating to you all." My voice rose. "Is there something you'd like to say to me? Congratulations, perhaps?"

They all made a show of turning back to their perusal of fabrics and ribbons and lace, whispering. A hard, cold knot formed in my stomach.

Dame Hutton placed a hand on my arm. Startled, I looked down at her strong, capable fingers, at her firm, comforting grip, then up at her face. She was smiling.

I drew in a shaky breath. "I came to see you. I'm not even sure.... There is so little time."

She nodded.

The words kept flowing; I could not understand why. "I probably should have stayed at home. The Moun— My father's—my mother—she was out of bed and in the kitchen. She never goes in there. Poor Cook! But there is so little time," I finished lamely.

"Come, Kathryn," Dame Hutton said quietly. "Let's have a look around."

That tapping sound again.

This time, I was awake, unable to sleep after the unexpected events of the day. And this time, I knew full well the cause of the sound.

I sprang from the bed and crept to the shutters, groping in the dark for the handles. Standing directly in front of the window, I yanked both shutters open in one swift motion and leaned forward, insults ready on my tongue to hurl at the fool below.

But the fool was in my window.

I nearly collided with him, face to face.

I gasped. His eyes went wide as he lost his grip on the windowsill and began to fall backward.

Without thinking, I reached out for him. His hands caught my forearms in an iron grip, pulling me forward. My gut slammed into the sill, knocking the breath out of me. Bracing my legs against the wall, I hauled back against him. He teetered and wobbled and pitched forward.

With a grunt, he fell face-first into my breasts.

I pushed him off.

Laughing, he clung to my arms and held himself steady.

"What," I said through my teeth, "are you doing here?"

He couldn't stop laughing. He bowed his head down against his forearm. His hair was dark in the moonlight, silver-limned. I could see every short-clipped hair on the back of his neck. I could smell his harsh, unscented soap.

"Sir William," I said sharply. "You will rattle the nails out of your ladder and then where will you be?"

He collected himself and looked down at the ground between his feet before turning his face toward me. I had not even a candle to illuminate the night. His face was almost entirely in shadow. "I will fall to my death beneath your window."

"Surely you did not come here tonight intending to die at my feet."

"To die in your arms, perhaps."

A bolt shot through me, settling to a thrum deep within. Thankful for the absence of light, I pulled back, trying to escape his touch which was suddenly heated. "How dare you?"

"We are betrothed," he said. "Sunday is only days away."

My heart stopped, then lurched into its course again. Days. What he was suggesting, people did it all the time. Out in the countryside, men and women who didn't want to wait for a priest lived together, had children, grew old and died, often never receiving the church's blessing. We wouldn't be so bold, just take our marriage rights a little early....

And then maybe he'd never come back.

"I thank you for the offer, but I will wait till the bed has been properly blessed."

He chuckled. "Wise woman. I knew it, but I had to ask." And he winked.

Too late I noticed that I was illuminated by a pool of moonlight that poured over my thin linen nightgown like water.

"My Kate is slender as the hazel branch, brown as hazel nuts, and sweeter than the kernels," he murmured, his gaze roving over my body, my hair, my face.

My will faltered. Would it be so terribly wrong, after all? If his gaze set me alight, what else might he do if I let him in?

But I would not—I could not—yield so easily, not any part of me.

I rushed to the bed for a blanket to pull tight around me, hunching my shoulders. "What are you doing here? You should be halfway to Coventry by now."

Perching his elbows on the sill, he looked up at me, still smiling, still shrouded in shadow.

"I found it much harder to leave than I expected, when it came to it."

I returned his smile. It was so easy.

"Oh, and I brought you something," he said, reaching down toward his belt. Curious, I took a step closer, then another as he fumbled one-handed with his belt-purse.

"Here!" He held out a fistful of tiny, crumpled flowers yanked up by their roots, dirt still clinging to them. I reached out hesitantly to take them from him.

"Thank you," I said, half a question. "Where did you—?"

"A field on the way out of town, miles from here. When I saw them, I knew I had to come back."

I looked from the flowers to him. "Because—?"

"Because the flowers are Sweet William. William. Me. You see?"

I took the little water cup from my bedside table and dropped the flowers in. "They are lovely."

In a way, they were. I could imagine him pulling that immense horse to a stop, sliding off, curling his fist around them, and pulling them up out of the ground, turning around, and riding back to give them to me....

The ladder. Where on earth...?

"I am glad you're pleased." His voice cut into my thoughts. "What else can I bring you?"

"What?"

"From Coventry. What shall I bring back to my fair bride from Coventry, Kate?"

Oh aye, his fair bride. Just like that, the afternoon fell upon me again. Sir William's proposal, the words we exchanged like blows...and the blows that had been struck as well. Being sold like a pig at the market with nothing to say about it. The way he presumed I would say yes to his proposal, the same way he presumed I'd let him in here tonight....

"I want no gifts from you."

"There must be something you lack, something your heart desires...."

He was leaning forward in the window, trying to see me better. I remained in the shadows. I would not reveal my desires to him.

"Nothing, sir. Pray do not trouble yourself."

"Alas, then, I shall content myself." He shook a finger at me. "But then you may not berate me for choosing ill."

"I think you may be certain I shall find many other reasons to berate you once we are married."

"Oh!" His hand flew to his heart so violently he almost overset himself. "How you wound me."

"Indeed? I am not sorry. And now, good night." I moved forward and took hold of one shutter, pressing it closed on him and reaching for the other.

"Wait!" He slapped a hand on the wood. Without seeming to exert himself, he prevented me from closing it. I pressed harder. He pushed back.

"Wait, I beg you."

One more effort and I gave up with a groan. "What?"

"Gifts. What shall I bring for your family?"

"I care not."

He shook his head. "Nay, you must." He shifted his hand on the shutter so it touched mine; I did not like the way my heart leaped in response. "They will be my family, too, come Sunday."

I moved my hand. "I pity you that. A wiser man would go to Coventry and not return."

"Nevertheless. Gifts."

I put my hands on my hips. "Sweets, for Blanche's mother. A pretty bauble to feed Blanche's vanity. And for my father...." I paused. What for my father?

Oh yes.

"For my father, a hawk."

"A hawk?"

"Yes. He speaks of little else when he returns from the larger towns. He sees wealthy men with a falcon on their fists and he chokes on his envy."

Sir William was silent a moment. "Does your father have the smallest idea of how to keep one?"

"I think not. Is it difficult?"

He gave a short laugh. "The cost in raw meat alone, to a man like your father who does not hunt.... Does he have a proper mews? Does he have a trained falconer on his staff?" He leaned against the window frame, looking at me closely. "The birds are trapped wild, my lady, and they remain wild all their lives. They have sharp talons, and beaks like a mason's chisel. A man like your father could not begin—"

He cut his words off sharply and pulled away. "A hawk. Indeed," he said, backing down the ladder.

I stuck my head out the window, confused. Why this abrupt departure?

"Sir William?"

He waved a hand at me, not looking up, not pausing in his descent.

"Until Sunday," he called.

I refused to watch him go. I slammed the shutter closed and stalked back to bed. But with my heart pounding so, I had a hard time finding my way into sleep.

Chapter Seven

Friday

Dame Hutton arrived early on Friday morning to fit me for my wedding clothes. My eyes burned with lack of sleep, and my mind struggled to believe that this was truly happening. I was being pinned into the garments I would wear to marry Sir William. Dame Hutton moved around me with quick efficiency, her mouth full of pins, her hands pinching and tucking the fabric of a pink silk chemise that, until this morning, had belonged to Blanche.

In her bedroom across the landing, Blanche complained to her mother. "I'll never get it back," she said. "Why can she not wear one of her own?"

The Mountain made a noncommittal sound. "You know that none of her things are fine enough for a wedding," she said, her voice like two boulders grinding. "Besides, your father will buy you a dozen more like it, and better, once she is gone." She said "gone" like a child would say "Yuletide" or "sweetmeats."

Dame Hutton glanced at me as she gathered the loose fabric at my right shoulder, but I kept my eyes focused on a dark spot on the plastered wall opposite me. Margaret stood patiently nearby, watching Dame Hutton work, my green satin kirtle held carefully in her arms.

"When she is gone," Blanche repeated breezily. "Why, then Father will have to buy me clothes for my own wedding!" The two of them cackled like a pair of geese.

Dame Hutton's lips tightened around the pins and spots of red flared on her cheeks. Her hands flew around my body, pulling the chemise snug. Blanche was both taller and more voluptuous than I, so this borrowed undergown needed quite a bit of tailoring to fit me.

I am getting married. On Sunday, I will be a bride.

But after so many years of thinking it would never happen—indeed, of being told by everyone around me that I would live and die a maid, and for good reason—the thought was feeble as a shout in the face of a storm's gale. I could not make myself believe it.

"Now, Mistress Kathryn," Dame Hutton said, pulling me out of my reverie. Blinking, I forced my eyes to focus on the shimmer of green fabric before me. Margaret gave me a wink as she draped the kirtle in front of her body with a saucy swoosh. "Let us talk about this dress."

The seamstress's words acted as a summons, for Blanche floated into the room, a vision in sky blue. Her cornflower eyes swept over me as she draped herself across the bed, tucking her feet under her skirts. Absently, with a half-smile on her face as she looked at me, she smoothed the gossamer veil covering hair that tumbled over her shoulders and down to her waist like Rumpelstiltskin's bounty.

The Mountain heaved her enormous body through the door one step at a time, panting with effort. She eyed the bed longingly, but when Blanche showed no inclination to rise, she forced her legs to carry her to my room's one chair. It gave a wretched groan when she dumped her body on it.

"Well," she puffed. "I can't think that I've been out of my bed so much in ten years as I've been this week. All this fuss over Kathryn's wedding."

"Yes, who'd have thought?" Blanche said. "All this fuss for Kathryn." She smiled at Dame Hutton. "So. The dress?"

We all turned critical eyes upon it. The bodice was a pale green, the color of new spring leaves, while the skirt and sleeves were a darker green, reflecting summer's richness. My first thought was that the sleeves could be removed and changed, and of course Blanche's blush-pink chemise would provide interesting contrast.

I could see the Mountain contemplating the same thing. "New sleeves," she muttered, breathing heavily through her nose. "In the latest style. I'll not let it be said that we shirked you, Kathryn. And a hem for decoration, and a train of the same color as the sleeves...." Her hand wove in the air. "What say you to yellow?"

"More of a gold," I said, then remembered to give her the respect she was entitled to as my father's wife. "Mother."

"What, would you bankrupt us? Think of your sister, still to be married."

I gritted my teeth. "I did not say cloth of gold, Mother. I meant a golden *hue*, like a goldenrod flower."

Dame Hutton jumped in. "I have just the thing in my shop, Mistress Kathryn. And, Dame Mulleyn, I can make angel sleeves for the kirtle; I have heard they are the very latest fashion from the royal court."

"Angel sleeves?"

She gestured with her hands. "Very long, and very wide at the wrist, so that they almost touch the floor even when you hold your hands straight out in front of you. Like the gown of an angel."

Blanche cooed, and I could tell she was already imagining angel sleeves on a dress of her own.

"Also," Dame Hutton went on, "I have some very pretty brocade borders in my shop shot through with gold thread." At the Mountain's frown, she hurried on. "Not too expensive, but very impressive. We could decorate the cuffs of the sleeves, and the neckline, and perhaps accent the waist? Perhaps also the hemline and the train, if you will permit? It will make the dress look entirely new."

The Mountain was still frowning, her heavy brows pulled down over her dark eyes. "I will not be bankrupted by this wedding. Still, we must make her presentable. A worthy bride for a knight." There was the tiniest of tremors in her voice, but I couldn't place it. It might have been true emotion, but it might just as easily have been annoyance at the expense, or concern over how Sir William would view me, as the family's offering.

"And..." My voice was rough, so I cleared my throat and tried again. "And beads. For the bodice."

"Oh yes." Dame Hutton tipped her head to the side and pulled a stick of charcoal from some hidden recess in her apron. "A few lines of sparkle, here..." Pressing the dress flat against Margaret, she drew a line down the bodice. "And here..." She sketched the places where the beads would go and nodded. "A lovely accent. Excellent idea. And inexpensive," she added, with a glance at my father's wife, who grunted. "If you will do the needlework, Mistress Kathryn, it will not add any time to altering the dress." She put away her charcoal and reached for the laces on the kirtle's sleeves. "If you come to the shop again this afternoon, you can pick out a border then."

Her shop again. All the eyes of the village on me. I shook my head. "That's all right, Dame Hutton. I trust your judgment."

We were talking about my wedding. Making a wedding dress. For Sunday.

On my little dressing table, a plain, clay cup held a posy of pale blue and lavender star-shaped flowers. They were half-crushed and none too fresh from their rough journey the night before, but they still had the power to smile at me. To taunt me from across the room.

Sweet William.

If nothing else, the man had a sense of humor.

Together, Dame Hutton and Margaret reached for me to extricate me from the chemise full of pins, carefully lifting it off my body and over my head. I slipped back into a chemise of my own. Plain undyed linen, only marginally finer than what Margaret herself wore and a far cry from the whisper of silk. Dame Hutton settled on the edge of the bed with the green kirtle in her lap, pointedly sitting close to Blanche to make her move aside. With a little sniff, Blanche slid to the other side of the bed and then off, exiting the room with a rustle of disapproving skirts. Dame Hutton paid her no heed but got to work ripping the seam holding the bodice and skirt of my dress together. Margaret helped the Mountain return to the comfort of her room. The stairs complained nearly as much as Blanche's mother all the way down.

The seamstress left the bodice on the bed and carefully folded the skirt and sleeves into a bag to carry back to her shop where she could work on them in peace. Just as carefully, she avoided looking at me.

Margaret returned, shaking out her arms from the strain of supporting the Mountain. She glanced from me to Dame Hutton and back, then went to help with packing up.

Dame Hutton straightened, lifting her basket. "I will choose some beads and send them over this morning, Mistress Kathryn, so you can get to work today."

"Thank you," I said, my voice squeaking out like a rusty hinge.

"And I'll make my choices based on what we've discussed here today, and what you and I looked at yesterday in my shop. Bearing in mind the restrictions your mother has put on price, and of course the limited time we have to work with."

I nodded, no longer trusting myself to speak.

Margaret handed Dame Hutton the bag holding the pieces of my wedding clothes and came to help me into my kirtle. My head was hidden inside the blue damask when I heard the seamstress address me again. "So that's how it is?"

Popping my head and arms out through the waist of the kirtle, I gestured Margaret to wait. Dame Hutton had paused in the doorway and was looking back at me, a curious mixture of anger and pity on her face. "I don't know what you mean," I said.

"Your sister. Her mother. This is what it's like for you?"

Margaret looked down, away, a sleeve dangling limply in her grasp. I shot Dame Hutton a tight smile. "How else should it be, Dame Hutton? Everyone knows I am the shrew."

A few hours later, the bodice of the green kirtle lay on my lap. Morning sunlight streaming through the solar window illuminated it, catching in the weave so it gleamed softly as I moved it, looking over Dame Hutton's pattern for the beadwork. I reached over to the little table beside my chair and opened the bags of beads Dame Hutton had sent over—tiny bits of glass in round and tube shapes, clear and gold and dark green—and ran my finger through them, rolling them like seeds over my skin. I thought about where each shape and color should go, and tried very hard not to think about Sunday.

When I could avoid it no longer, I threaded a fine needle with delicate thread and reached for the bag of dark green beads.

Blanche burst into the solar. "So."

I kept my eyes on the beads, counting four of them onto the thread. I would have liked to set each bead individually, but there was simply no time. Two more days. What the Mountain had said was right. It *was* outrageous.

Standing over me, fists on her lovely, ample hips, Blanche said, "I suppose you're very proud of yourself."

I said nothing. With studied concentration, I stitched the first beads down onto the fabric. I could feel the expectation pouring off my sister. Why didn't I speak? "I told Father I wouldn't have him. You must know that. I wouldn't have him, even if he was a knight."

I glanced up, catching myself before I met her eyes or responded to what she was saying. Of course she had to save face in this way. He had not rejected her and chosen me. No, she had not wanted him.

She strolled to the bed, picked up a pillow and plumped it needlessly into shape.

"He has a castle, you know—of course you must know that. A small keep with a tower and moat, with several hundred tenants beholden to him."

These were details I had not known—I was to marry him, and no one had thought to tell me aught of the place I was to live in besides its name—but I wasn't going to let *her* know that. I picked a few more beads onto the thread.

"But did you know he has no money?"

My skin bristled, crawling all over the way a dog's must when it senses a threat. *Of course*, I thought. As I stitched down the next set of beads, I tried to ignore the squeezing around my heart.

Blanche tossed the pillow back onto the bed. "How does that feel, Kathryn?" She leaned in close, looking down at my needlework, then tipping her face up into mine. "The only reason he wants your stick-skinny body is for your big, fat dowry."

"Blanche." I stilled my hands, stilled the blood rushing through my veins. "Is there something I can do for you?"

Blanche stamped her foot. "Ooooh! You can't even see what's right before you!"

"Well, no," I said mildly. "You're standing in my light."

"That's not what I—oh, fine." She stomped away and flounced down on the bed, her skirts belling around her. Even annoyed, she was beautiful, and I couldn't bear to look at her for long.

"Do you want to hear me say it?"

"Say what?"

She flipped her hands in the air. "It seems you do. Fine. I'll say it. You won. All right? You won. He chose you over me."

A little thrill danced up and down my spine. "Yes. Yes, he did."

"Now can you stop lording it over me?"

I looked up from the beads to gape at her. "Lording—? Blanche, what are you talking about?"

She got up from the bed and began to pace. "You always act like you're better than me, than all of us, with your books and your Latin and doing Father's sums. That's why no one likes you."

"I'm well aware of why no one likes me," I said, looking down at the needle in my hand, fighting to keep it from trembling.

"But *he* likes it!" she protested. "He chose you *for* your learning, not in spite of it." She quit her pacing and stood over me. "It was the one thing I had always counted on, that no one would want you the way you are."

"Blanche," I said, pinching the bridge of my nose. "Is there a lesson to your sermon, or are you just trying to hurt me?"

"I thought you'd never get a husband if you weren't more like me. I thought that one day, you'd be forced to humble yourself and ask for my help, and then I would be gracious and magnamonious—"

I barely restrained my titter of laughter.

"You were supposed to need me. All these years, you've ignored me and scorned me, and I've—" She stopped. "You don't know what it's been like."

I jumped out of my seat, the bodice tumbling to the floor. "I don't know what it's been like? *You* don't know what it's been like! You are Father's favorite, you get everything you desire—"

"But he *needs* you!"

We stood staring at each other, fists clenched, mouths agape. It was as though I had never seen her before.

Blanche, jealous of me?

Impossible.

Some opaque wall crashed down behind her eyes and she looked away. I retrieved the bodice and found the dangling needle. The moment had passed, scarcely to be credited.

Father's voice drifted up through my casement. I was determined to disregard him. Count beads, place stitch.

Blanche, recovering herself, did not flee the room as I expected, but went to the window to eavesdrop on Father's conversation.

Somehow, watching her listening forced me to listen as well.

"One hundred milk cows and one hundred twenty head of oxen...."

Blanche rolled her eyes and fell back against the window frame. "Ugh. It's old Master Greenwood again. Will he never give up?"

Another voice rose from the courtyard. "...my father's only son and heir. The house Master Greenwood keeps here in Whitelock may be very fine, but my father has three such houses, the finest of them in Leicester itself."

Blanche gasped, peeking out the window as best she could without revealing herself. "Why, it's Master Lawry!"

I repeated, "Master Lawry?" before I could stop myself.

In light of Ellen's words, I set down my stitching and tilted my chair back against the window. By angling my head just so, I could see Master Lawry where he stood near the fountain. For certes, his clothes did not fit properly, but that did not make him an imposter. He spoke well once he was at ease in company and seemed wise and clever.... Ellen could not possibly be correct.

Blanche crouched beside the window and whispered, loud enough to be heard in the next house, "They must have heard of your betrothal and now they come to court me!"

I continued to string beads onto my needle and pin them fiercely onto the bodice of my wedding dress.

The discussion below moved on to the gentlemen's prospects in trade: wagons, shops, market stalls, trade routes, ships. Blanche was entranced.

I worked steadily, listening with half an ear. Master Greenwood appeared to be coming up short in every measure.

"What of her jointure?" Father asked. "What if she is made a widow?"

Master Greenwood answered quickly, "I am advanced in years, Master Mulleyn, and have no other heirs. If I were to die before your daughter—if she were my wife—all that I have would be hers."

"Ha!" I laughed. "Master Greenwood sees it as an advantage that he is old and soon to die!"

Blanche made a face. "Well, if I must marry him that *would* be an advantage."

I shook my head, leaning closer over my beadwork. The light was fading; the sun had passed behind some clouds. It seemed likely to rain.

"You see, Master Lawry," Father said, and I imagined him turning toward the younger man with an expansive gesture, "I am here on the horns of a dilemma. Master Greenwood offers less, but he offers all. You make the better offer, but all that you offer yet belongs to your father while he lives. You must pardon me, but if you were to die before him, where is her portion? What is to become of my poor daughter?"

Master Lawry's tone was cavalier. "It is nothing to worry about. My father is old; I am young."

Master Greenwood laughed harshly. "And may not young men die as well as old?"

They began to quarrel like a couple of squawking chickens, but Father interrupted them. "Gentlemen," he said, "here is my resolve. On Sunday, my daughter Kathryn will be married. Then, Master Lawry, if your father will give assurances of her protection, on the following Sunday, you may post the banns for your marriage to my daughter Blanche. Otherwise, Master Greenwood shall do so. Now, farewell, gentlemen."

Father went inside. Even from so far above, I could feel his triumph. What a week he was having!

The other men lingered to continue their argument, their voices fading as they moved away from the window. "Ha!" Master Greenwood rumbled. "Your father is a fool if he gives over everything to you while he still lives, just so you can marry a pretty girl. It's nonsense. Never happen. We'll see what will come on the Sunday after Kathryn is finally gone."

"Think what you will, old man," Master Lawry retorted. "We shall indeed see what will come."

I kept my head down. I did not want Blanche to see my face. How did *she* like being bargained for like a suckling pig at the market?

She turned from the window, her eyes wide. "Did you hear?"

"What did you expect? Declarations of undying love and devotion?"

She seemed not to have heard me. "Three houses, he has. Land that produces over 3,000 crowns a year! He is rich!"

"His *father* is rich."

Blanche waved a hand at me. She had no use for such trifles as facts. "I will be rich!" She looked at me with shining eyes. "You may become a lady, but I will be rich!"

As Blanche said, I was a great lady now. Betrothed to a man of, if not wealth, at least of status and prospects, in favor at King Richard's court. I was moving up in the world.

I did not have to sit for pointless lessons any longer.

The graying skies of morning had opened up with a gentle rain, keeping Blanche and her tutors indoors. I had hoped they would stay downstairs in the hall, but they, or rather Blanche, decided that the solar, where I sat trying to distract myself with a book of my own, would be more comfortable. The music master and the language master immediately fell to bickering over which of their lessons should commence first. Pretty, young Cameron insisted that music should follow more strenuous work as a respite. Master Horton claimed music took precedence over all else as the promoter of heavenly harmony on earth.

"Gentlemen," Blanche said, interrupting them gently. "You do me wrong by striving over what is, in fact, my choice. I am no schoolboy in breeches." She swished her hips, allowing them to soak in that image for a moment. "I am not tied to hours or appointed times, but learn my lessons to please myself."

Both men stared at her—I could tell Master Horton was struggling to get "Blanche in breeches" out of his mind—and then Master Cameron bowed his acquiescence. Master Horton hastened to follow.

Smiling her satisfaction, Blanche perched herself on the settle with room for one of them next to her. I sighed into my book. As if there was any doubt which lesson she would choose.

"Good Master Cameron, come sit you by me. Master Lucas, take your instrument and play meanwhile. His lecture will be done even before you have tuned."

The fake music master had brought his harp today. He carried it to a plush chair, which he hooked with his foot and slid as close to them as he could without being noticed. Sitting upon it, he inched it closer still, until a screech of wood betrayed him. Both Blanche's blue eyes and Cameron's hazel fell sharply upon him. Nodding an apology, he set about tuning his instrument. With all those strings, it would take a long while to perfect the sound, as was surely Blanche's intent. He glanced at the couple, clearly worried about his chances of gaining a place on the settle. "You will leave your lesson when I am in tune?"

"That will be never," Master Cameron said. Blanche hid a smirk by turning her face into her shoulder.

Sparks shot between the men and yet no further words were spoken. Blanche let them bristle for a moment more, then drew Master Cameron's attention back to her with a light touch on his sleeve. "Pray, where did we last leave off?"

Master Cameron opened a book and cleared his throat, flipping through the pages. Blanche leaned in closer. His hands trembled a little. "Ovid, mistress. We have been... reading Ovid."

"Yes," she said, hissing the word softly in his ear. "Ovid."

The drone of Latin, the pluck-whine of the harp strings, the soft drip of the rain on the casements and hurrying in the gutters.... My eyes drifted closed. After Sir William's late night visit, I had spent the night alternately pacing my room and tossing uncomfortably in my bed. Then there was all that close beadwork this morning. These quiet sounds soothed me, urging me toward sleep.

"Please, lady, listen carefully to what I say."

Jolting awake, I had to grab at my book to keep it from falling out of my lap. Blinking, I looked around to see if the others had noticed.

Master Cameron was reading the Ovid aloud in a strong, pleasant voice, and Blanche was intent on every word, leaning forward slightly, her hands gripping the edge of the settle. Her interest could only be in him. This translation was nothing we had not done years before.

"*Hic ibat Simois...*," Cameron intoned, then leaned closer to Blanche and, with a glance at Horton, who was furiously twiddling the keys of his harp, he lowered his voice and murmured, "I have something that I must tell you. Something very important, and very secret."

Blanche, to her credit, did not flinch. She simply nodded and glanced down at the book in his hands as though he had drawn her attention to the words there. Following her lead, he pointed to the page.

"*Hic est...*," Cameron went on, declaiming the Latin. "I am the true Matthew Lawry," he said softly, his mouth next to her ear, so that I almost didn't hear it.

I did hear her tiny gasp.

"*Sigeia tellus...*," he said quickly to cover the sound.

"How?" she breathed. "Why?"

"The other is my servant, dressed as the master... *Hic steterat....*" When he spoke the Latin, it was loud, louder than Master Horton's half-tuned harp, while the English was whispered urgently in her ear. "When I saw you, when I first arrived, I had to get close to you, and when I heard that your father would not permit anyone to court you, I devised this scheme...*Priami....*" He glanced at the music master and continued in a rush. "My servant has won your father's approval for us to wed...*regia!*" The Latin word burst from his lips with such force even Master Horton shot him a look.

Trying not to stare, I forced myself to look out at the rain. Ellen had been correct after all! And then I had to acknowledge the clues that had been there all along, if only I had allowed myself to see them, if I had not been so determined to explain them away. The ill-fitting clothes on both of them. The awkwardness of "Master Lawry" at my father's hearth that first day. He was a servant among his master's equals, playing a part. And this "Master Cameron's" sharp glances and aggressive ways toward Master Horton, whom he presumed to be a mere servant and therefore beneath him. Anger flared in me against this foolish, arrogant young man. If the servant were caught impersonating his master, he would be considered no better than a common thief and branded or worse, and all because this boy was in love with my sister! I wanted to speak out now, but for the false Master Lawry's sake, I knew I should not.

Master Horton, having seen enough, leaped from his chair. "I am ready now."

"Play," Blanche said, too surprised by Master Cameron's revelation to toy with the fat musician.

He drew his fingers along the harp strings, playing a pretty melody. Blanche shook her head. "Nay, master, the treble jars my ears."

Grinding his teeth, Horton sent a killing look at Cameron, who, his face turned away from Blanche, gave him a smug grin. With a slight bow, Horton replied, "I would fain disturb your delicate ears, mistress. I will try again."

Blanche took the book from the hands of her tutor, or rather, her true suitor. She glanced at me, and I quickly ducked my head down into my own book again. Waiting until Horton had settled back into his seat and was plucking away at the harp's strings again, she said in a loud voice, "Now let me see if I have learned it well. Tell me how I do, if you please. *Hic ibat Simois...*" Then, as her tutor had done, she leaned toward him and murmured in his ear, "You shock me, Master Cameron, or is it Lawry? I know you not and cannot tell if I should trust you."

Cameron's—nay, Lawry's—face fell. Blanche traced the words on the page with a delicate finger, and he shuddered as if she touched his own skin.

"*Hic est Sigeia tellus....*" She glanced at me again, and I turned a page, having no idea what I had just read. "We are not alone here and your speech is ill-advised," she murmured in a tone that said just the opposite. "*Hic steterat Priami....* Your servant may have spoken to my father, but you have not spoken properly to me... *regia.*" She paused, and his head drooped, defeated. "Yet," she whispered, leaning close to him once again, "do not despair." She snapped the book shut with a smile and handed it back to him. "How did I do?"

Lawry gaped, the book hanging in his hand like an overripe fruit on the branch.

"Mistress!" Master Horton called, and we all jumped in our seats. "My harp is in tune." He strummed once to prove it.

It sounded fine to me, but Master Lawry, now proven as false as the other, growled, "Nay, the bass is off."

"The bass is right, it is the base knave that jars," Master Horton shot back.

"Gentlemen, please." Blanche patted the language master on the knee. "Good Master Cameron," she said, the tiny emphasis she placed on his false name making her power over him clear, "it is time for my music lesson."

Master Horton rose and carried his harp over to the settle. As he passed Master Lawry, he bumped him with his shoulder. "You may go walk. I make no music in three parts."

"I shall not walk out in the rain," Master Lawry said, but he did withdraw to the chair where Master Horton had been. He opened the book in his lap but watched the two upon the settle carefully. Whether he knew that Master Horton was as much an imposter as himself, or whether he simply had the natural mistrust of a liar—"he that is giddy thinks the world turns round," as the saying goes—he would see what transpired.

So would I.

Blanche reached for the harp, but Master Horton stayed her hands. She pouted prettily.

"Nay, mistress, before we begin with the harp, I wish to acquaint you today with the rudiments of the art of music: the gamut."

"The gamut?" Blanche repeated.

Taking her response for ignorance, Master Horton said, "The notes, the scales, the means by which we learn music."

"But Master Lucas, I learned my gamut long ago."

Master Horton was sweating under his hat, worn even indoors as part of his disguise, his hands quivering on the harp. "Yet, this is a most excellent gamut, more intriguing and delightful than any ever taught by any of my trade." He pulled a tightly folded square of parchment out of his belt-purse. "Learn you now the gamut of"—he dropped his voice to a dramatic whisper—"Master Robert Horton."

Blanche gave him a quizzical look, Master Lawry a piercing one. Had it been his plan all along to reveal himself so soon, or had Master Lawry's sudden revelation, which Horton could not have missed, pushed him to expose himself now? Surely this was not the way Horton had imagined declaring himself to Blanche, with Lawry scowling at him, and with me a few feet away.

Blanche unfolded the parchment and hummed a few measures. Just to prove to him that she did not need any teaching, I suppose.

"This was written to plead all Master Horton's passion," she sang softly. Horton nodded with enthusiasm, urging her on.

"Blanche, take him for your husband;

"He loves you with all affection;

"One clef, two notes have I;

"Show pity or I die…."

It was all I could do to stifle a laugh and turn it into a cough. Would Blanche take a hint from me and smash the harp over his deceitful head?

Blanche dropped the parchment into her lap and pivoted her body toward him. Her face was as clouded with anger as I had ever seen her show to anyone other than me. "Call you *this* the gamut? I like it not. I prefer the traditional one. Do you understand me, Master *Lucas*?"

Trembling, he adjusted his hat and grabbed the parchment back, crumpling it in his thick fist. "Full well, Mistress Blanche. Perhaps…" He stood. "Perhaps you would prefer not to have a music lesson today."

She sat looking up at him for a long moment. Then she placed the harp in his hands and said, "Yes, Master Lucas, I believe you are right. I would prefer not to have any more music lessons. Today."

But there was something in the way she said "today," and something in the way he received it, that made it clear that "Master Lucas" would not be returning to our house again.

As he left the room, Master Cameron dared to return to Blanche on the settle. He had no book in his hand.

I did not want to discover what was going to pass between the two of them, so I followed Master Horton out.

Chapter Eight

Saturday

Dame Hutton returned to the house on Saturday afternoon to put the wedding dress back together, and it was much prettier than I had hoped for. She had given the cuffs of the sleeves and the hem of the skirt a wide brocade border, a pattern of leaves and flowers that accentuated the greens of the kirtle. The train, which tied on with large bows, consisted of enough fabric to be reused later for something else. Perhaps a new bodice, or new sleeves, or a headdress and matching slippers. With the new beadwork on the bodice—which, I had to admit, was quite fine—I had an entirely new dress for my wedding.

There was no looking glass in the house large enough for me to see the final result of Dame Hutton's efforts. Blanche had a looking glass that fit in her palm, but that was too small to be of any help to me even if she had allowed me to use it. But Blanche was more than happy to sit in judgment as Dame Hutton made the final stitches and Margaret tied the bows on the train.

My hands trembled inside the long angel sleeves. Would I be pleasing to him? Would he care what I looked like, or would he care only for the sack of gold that came along with me?

Blanche sighed faintly. "I suppose it's the best you can hope for."

I gritted my teeth and growled back at her, "Gloat now while you may, but we both know your own wedding will be the highlight of your sad little life, and Master Greenwood is fast approaching."

"I'll never marry him, no matter what Father says," she spat back.

"If I must do as he says, so must you." I could see I had touched the heart of her fears, so I kept pressing the sore spot.

"I will get my own way," she insisted. "You'll see. I will." She wrapped her arms around herself, shrinking smaller despite her confident tone.

From across the hall came the Mountain's booming voice. "Bring her here. I want to see."

Margaret took hold of the train, lifting it high off the floorboards so it would not catch a stray splinter, and Dame Hutton helped me step down off the stool. We paraded across the landing into my parents' room, Blanche trailing after.

In the shadows of the wide, curtained bed, the Mountain reclined under a light blanket, propped on goose-feather pillows the size of hay bales. I stopped at the foot of the bed for her inspection.

She squinted and puckered, not just her eyes but her whole face. "Yes, good," she mumbled. "Presentable. Suitable."

Dame Hutton smoothed the train, adjusting the bows. "Green was the right choice, don't you agree, Dame Mulleyn?"

The Mountain grunted, picking over the plate of sweets and savories on the bedside table.

"Oh yes," Blanche replied for her. "It saves her complexion from being entirely sallow." She selected a little tart from her mother's tray and nibbled at the crust. "Too bad nothing can be done about her eyes." She held the tart up in front of her own eye, demonstrating. "Like a cow's, big and round and brown." She giggled a little and said, "Oh, I know! I will allow you to use some of my creams tomorrow for the wedding." She gestured vaguely toward my face as though she were painting it. "Would you like that, Kathryn?"

"Mistress Blanche," Dame Hutton began.

"Can you not add more padding, Dame Hutton?" Blanche continued, her tone a little sad. "Poor Kathryn is so skinny, Sir William will think we don't feed her." And she smiled to show that her words were not to be taken as a criticism of me.

"Now, Mistress Blanche," Dame Hutton said, more sternly this time, "there is nothing—"

"No, Dame Hutton," I said, "it's quite all right." I looked at my sister. A body like Blanche's spoke of prosperity, richness, wealth. It promised ease in birthing children, and delight in getting them. What did I offer?

What *did* I offer?

I could not breathe. "Margaret, get me out of this dress." I charged out of the room, yanking Margaret behind me on my train.

There was no good reason for the language tutor to come to our house any longer, now that the fiction of the tutors had accomplished its goal. I was betrothed, and Blanche's hand would be decided once word was received from Master Lawry's father. Yet, Master Cameron came uninvited, and my sister did not send him away. Had my father given it any thought at all, he would have been suspicious, or at least wary, but my father, like my sister, never exercised his brain if it were not required of him.

After Friday's rain, the courtyard was fresh and sparkling, and they sat together on a bench while the gardeners worked around them frantically preparing for the wedding on the morrow. I watched them from the doorway of the hall, hip to hip and shoulder to shoulder on the bench, having all but abandoned the pretense of studying. I saw the way he looked at her, the way she half looked at him from under her lashes. The way he spoke and she laughed, so softly. The way he leaned in and she leaned in, then away. It was a dance, a dance I had never learned, a dance I had never had the chance to learn.

I leaned my forehead on the doorframe. If I had a different sister—if things between us were different—I could ask her, How does that happen? How do you make him attend to you like there is no one and nothing else in the world? I could ask, How do you curb your tongue and speak only sweet words? Why was this so easy for her and so impossible for me?

She had nearly offered her help yesterday. She'd expected me to ask, but after that argument, there was no way I could.

Why did I care? What did it matter? My wedding was a business transaction, my husband a fortune seeker.

Still....

It would have been nice to have some idea of how to act, of how to be different from who I was.

I slapped my palm against the doorframe and went away.

Nightfall. At last, or already, depending on how one looked at it.

The dress hung on hooks in my bedchamber, stuffed with clean rags to keep its shape.

The whole house smelled like heaven, for Cook and her staff had been making ready since Friday morning. An array of breads had been ordered from the bakery and nestled, covered in cloths, in baskets around the kitchen. Before dawn, a side of beef would be set over the massive kitchen fire. There was blancmanger—a thick, pasty stew of chicken and rice, sweet with spices and almonds—platters of roasted pork, bowls of peas with onions, vats of salted herring, a giant crock of beans in a sweet-spicy sauce that was Cook's specialty, huge wheels of cheese, cinnamon-stewed apples, fresh fruits, and, of course, a cake.

The courtyard had been raked and weeded, the gravel of the path washed and relaid, the bushes trimmed, new flowers planted. Trestle tables had been set up for all the guests. Father had invited everyone of note in town to this event he had imagined would never take place. In the morning, the tables would be covered with white cloths, decked with flowers, and laid with trenchers and goblets of silver-chased pewter. Garlands of ribbons and flowers would be hung from window to window across the courtyard and over the door at the front of the house. It would announce to the world that here, here we were having a wedding.

As I drifted from room to room, cataloguing the preparations, I still couldn't decide how I felt about that.

The Mountain sent Margaret to find me, ordering me to my chamber shortly after the sun went down. When I gave her a look, she said I'd want to look well in the morning and added, blushing pink, "You'll probably not have much time for sleep tomorrow night, mistress."

That was not a conversation I wanted to continue, so off to my bedchamber I went.

Although sleep was no closer for all that I was lying in bed in my nightgown. Flashes, snippets, ribbons of memory wove through my mind. Memories. Images. Words. Feelings.

Tomorrow, I would be married.

Tomorrow, I would escape.

True, I would have liked knowing better what I was escaping *to* besides a keep with a moat, but at the least I would not be here any longer. No Father, no Mountain, and, ah! No Blanche. Mistress of my own home, free to do as I pleased. Well, as long as it pleased my husband too.

But he chose me. He could have had Blanche, but he wanted me.

A memory flashed, like lightning. The crack of sound, the sting of flesh. I had slapped him.

Another flash. He held me tight against him, his palm pressed low on my back, every inch of our bodies touching.

A sleepless night tomorrow. My skin flushed, and something fluttered, low in my belly.

Tomorrow.

I wondered, that Saturday night, lying awake and watching the moon trace patterns on my walls, whether I ought to have let him in.

Chapter Nine

Sunday

I woke at dawn with the cock's crowing, the birds singing, and the church bells ringing. We were to be married at *terce*, several hours hence, plenty of time to get ready. Since it was Sunday, after the wedding we would attend Mass together and then return home for the wedding dinner. And since we were going to attend Mass, we could not break our fast before receiving the holy Eucharist. That was all right. I was too nervous to eat.

The house was waking up around me. Servants, already up for hours, began moving about the family rooms.

There was a knock on my door, and Margaret pushed it open a crack, not waiting for my call. "I've come to help you first today, mistress. Mistress Blanche can wait."

"Thank you, Margaret."

"What'll you have first, mistress?"

"Some water to wash, I think."

It took a surprisingly short time to make a bride out of me. Margaret had brought Blanche's cosmetics, as promised, although I could not see the results. Blanche's generosity did not extend to sharing her mirror. The last step, and the most tedious, was plaiting my long, dark hair as befit a bride.

Blanche flounced into my bedchamber without knocking, still in her nightgown.

"Margaret," she demanded, "are you nearly done?"

"Very nearly, mistress."

"Good. I'm tired of waiting." She paused, looking me over.

"Well, you look rather nice."

"Thank you, Blanche." I closed my eyes. I had vowed I would not fight with her on my wedding day no matter how she provoked me.

"Here," she said, holding something out toward me. With my head held still for Margaret, I couldn't see it.

"Blanche, I can't—" I heard my voice rising and pulled it back down. "What is it?"

She dropped something in my lap. I could just see it if I strained my eyes.

"It's a garland for your hair," she said. "I made it for you."

For perhaps the first time in my life, I had nothing to say to her.

"Good luck on your wedding day," she said, "and good luck to *him* every day thereafter."

I breathed in, a long, slow breath through my nose, remembering my vow. "Thank you, Blanche, for the flowers."

She paused at the door, made a dismissive noise. "It'll be my turn to wed soon enough. Margaret, do hurry."

On my way out of the house's double doors, flung wide and ribbon-decked, I had a brief moment of panic. *When I come back, I will be Lady Kathryn. I will be married.* I had to fight the instinct to turn around and flee back up the stairs. As though any safety, any comfort, lay there.

Still....

"Margaret," I said. "Come with me."

As we charged upstairs, Margaret holding my train high, Blanche called after me, "What is it now? You can't get out of this, you know."

The clump of wilting flowers still sat in their cup by my bed. I scooped them up, dripping muddy water on the floor.

"Mistress!" Margaret gasped, grabbing them from my hand. "What are you doing?"

"These. I'm bringing them with me."

She stared at me as though I'd gone mad, then shook her head. "Well, you can't take them like this." She hurried from the room and returned with her sewing basket. Taking the flowers from me, she knelt on the floor and worked with terrible efficiency, snipping off the ragged roots and dead flowers with her scissors, then wrapping the little bundle in a plain, white ribbon.

"There," she said, handing it over. "If you must."

"Sweet William," I murmured, turning the fragile blooms over in my hands. "Yes, I think I must."

A squat building of old, dull stone, St. Bernard's had been built in Norman times—some three hundred years ago, when this part of the country was a bulwark against the heathen Welsh—and was typically Norman: a simple rectangle with one fat, square bell tower. Two windows of precious glass adorned each side of the church, and the top of the bell tower was cut through with apertures for sound that could double as hideouts for archers in the event the village ever needed to defend itself.

We arrived at the church well before the bells were to toll the third hour. It was the Mountain's first day out of the house in years, a special occasion if only for that. She squinted and blinked, puffed and sweated, and by the time we reached the church, her face was red as a cherry and she needed to sit down inside. Father, Blanche, and I waited just inside the doors, for the sun was strong and the morning was growing hot.

A trickle of people followed us as we walked from our house to the church, and then a crowd began to gather in front of the church, all come to witness this unthinkable event: Kathryn Mulleyn getting married. I stayed within the church, avoiding all eyes. My stomach was knotted with fear.

Master Greenwood and Master Lawry—the false Master Lawry, as I now knew, the servant in his master's clothes—arrived together or at least at the same time. It seemed that both wanted to be sure that this wedding went forward so that one of them could claim Blanche as his prize one week hence, even though which one of them was still uncertain. They came into the shade with us. Father greeted them warmly. Blanche smiled and flashed her eyelashes at them.

"How now, Master Lawry?" Father said. "Any word from your father?"

"Not yet," said the servant in disguise, "but it is a long road over rough country."

"And a harsh message," Master Greenwood said. "I think you will not like your father's answer when it comes."

The other remained unruffled. "And where is Master Horton?" Father asked. "Is he not coming to wish us well?"

Master Greenwood laughed, turning it into a cough. "Ah, it appears Master Horton has gone into the country to a cousin's house for a visit. I hear there is a widow in that household of some charm and a pleasant demeanor. I do not expect to see him hereabouts for some time."

"So quickly do men change their minds," Blanche said, then added sweetly, "Pray, has anyone seen the groom?"

The men fell silent and all eyes went to me.

"Where did Sir William stay when last he came?" Father asked. "Was it at the inn?"

Master Greenwood and the false Master Lawry exchanged a look. "Yes," the latter said, "but he was not there last night."

"I will send my man," Master Greenwood said. The fellow went off at a trot in that direction.

I turned my back on the others. *What if he does not come? What if, for all his fine words, he never meant to marry me?* Perhaps I had thought him foolish, perhaps mad to seek my hand so swiftly, but I had not imagined he could be so cruel as this. The knots in my stomach cooled, froze, turned into solid stone. I struggled to breathe. Nay. I would not believe it. He would come.

The sexton rang the bell for *terce*, the appointed hour for the wedding—one, two, three. Master Greenwood's man returned, whispered in his master's ear. Master Greenwood slowly shook his head. He turned to me. "Mistress Kathryn," he said, with more kindness than he had ever shown before, "there is no sign of Sir William at the inn. But perhaps he meant to come straight here to the church and he is but delayed."

Father nodded, wringing his hands. "Indeed, Master Greenwood, you have it there. Perhaps he has been delayed on the road. You,

Andrew, and you there, what's your name? You fellows go to the west end of High Street and see when he comes. Make sure he is in good state and unharmed." As the men hurried off down the road, Father turned back to the other gentlemen. "Do you think he could have run afoul of brigands? Might he be in need of help?"

False Master Lawry clapped a hand on Father's shoulder. "My dear Master Mulleyn, the man is trained in the knightly arts, and surely he would not come unescorted. Never fear, there is just some delay. His horse threw a shoe, perhaps. Come, let us wait within."

We waited within.

An hour passed, and the men who had been watching on High Street came back complaining of the heat. The sexton gave them ale and some bread and sent them back.

Another hour passed, and the priest brought out wine for all of us waiting in the church. The servant posing as Master Lawry was making Blanche laugh. I wished there was someone to make me laugh, someone who cared enough to try to put me at ease.

Another hour, and the priest slipped out of the vestry to talk quietly with Father. I knew what they were saying. What else could they be saying? The groom was not here. He was not coming.

I fought against the tears that burned at my eyes. Should I be surprised that he had changed his mind and decided not to marry Kathryn the shrew after all? Or perhaps he had never meant to come back. I remembered his proposal, how swept up I had been in the sensation of him, how I had nearly said "yes" before my father walked in. Had it all been a jest he indulged in at my expense? A sound—half howl, half sob—rose up in my throat, and I choked it down, pounding with my fist on my breastbone until the sensation of strangling went away. No. No tears, no anger, nothing. *This is what happens when you allow yourself to hope, Kathryn.*

I looked at the people waiting in the church, their faces a mixture of pity and amusement. I watched my father twisting his cap, nodding at the priest's words, both of them looking at me as one would keep a wary eye on a coiled and venomous snake, waiting for it to strike, hoping someone else will come along and dispatch it. Blanche laughed, too loudly, and it echoed in the rafters.

I pushed myself up from my seat and made my way to Father. "Is this what you hoped for, with your grand plans? You hoped to buy me a husband, but perhaps now he is showing you what he thinks of the bargain, Master Merchant. You refused him first, and now he pays you back in kind. I must thank you for my public disgrace."

Even for me, even for the shrew, such insult to my father in front of others was unthinkable. As he raised his hands, I flinched, but for once, he did not shake or strike me for my sharp tongue. Instead, he reached for me.

His voice was gentle. "Kathryn...."

I jerked away, my pain somehow worsened by his attempt at compassion. "Look at me, Father. Look at me!" I swept my hands the length of my body, taking in the dress, the hair, the paint on my face. "Here I am, and *where is he?* Everyone has seen me here today, ready to marry, and where is he?" I swept my arm out toward the open door of the church, to where the whole village had gathered earlier to witness my wedding and now had enjoyed my utter humiliation.

"For the rest of my days, Father, do you know what I will hear? 'Look, there goes Sir William's wife, if he would just trouble himself to come and marry her.'"

I wheeled about, lurching like a drunk. Father's hands went out again, but I swept away from him, racing up the aisle. Blanche was staring at me, her eyes wide. I paused long enough to pull her garland of flowers off my head. The pins holding it in place ripped at my scalp, tearing at Margaret's careful arrangement of braids, and long, dark hairs yanked free, but I spared not a thought for how I looked. I was beyond feeling mere pain. I threw the garland at her, hard. She caught it with a puzzled look.

"There. I am betrothed, if not truly wed. That ought to be enough for you and whatever grasping man wins you. I wish you joy."

I walked out of the church. As I suspected, so many hours later, none of the villagers remained out front. The area in front of the church was empty. The village was quiet, dozing under the beaming sun. It was Sunday, after all. A day of rest and quiet contemplation.

I dropped my hopeful little bundle of blooms on the stoop of the church and crushed them under my heel. Sweet William indeed.

I went home.

It felt like hours later when Father and the others arrived, but it could not have been. The sun was still high in the sky, the air still oppressive, the shadows on my bedchamber floor barely shifted from where they lay. I stared down at my hands, clasped in my lap, and past that at the green skirt with its elaborate brocade trim. The beads winked and sparkled at the edge of my vision, taunting me. *Almost married*, they said. *Almost. No one could want you, in the end.*

But I wasn't angry anymore. I couldn't summon the strength. I was just... numb.

The Mountain, grumbling, heaved her way up the stairs and was put to bed. I could hear the voices of Margaret and the other housemaids in her bedchamber one floor below mine. After all this activity, it was unlikely she would arise again for weeks.

Father and Blanche stopped in the street in front of the house, saying farewell to some of the guests who had lingered until the very end. These included Blanche's suitors, of course. I stood up to close my shutters so I wouldn't have to listen.

"But Father!" Blanche's voice was so clear, she could only have intended for me to hear it. "Father, there's all that food in there, and it has all been made ready, and if we don't eat it we shall have to throw it away. Think of the expense!" Her voice, if possible, came closer. Perhaps they had come nearer to the house or onto the steps before the door. "Think, Father. Kathryn was right. She *is* betrothed, even if he didn't come to claim her, so you have done all you can for her. There is nothing now standing in my way. Allow me to celebrate my own freedom. *She* cannot enjoy it, but that doesn't mean we must all suffer."

There was silence and I waited for Father to refuse her. What she asked was wrong, it was unthinkable, it was—

"You are right, Blanche. Surely it would be a sin to discard all of this marvelous food. And after all, it will be your wedding next. Master Lawry." He raised his voice to say the name. "Will you not join us for dinner? Though we cannot celebrate a wedding today, surely we can celebrate your betrothal?"

I fell to my knees.

If I had any food in my gut, I am sure I would have lost it.

As the sun dropped lower and lower, the front door opened and slammed with a steady stream of neighbors as word began to spread. Laughter and conversation drifted up from the courtyard at the back of the house, seeping in through windows and doors, crawling up the stairs.

Even with my head under the pillow, I could hear them. There was, after all, a great deal of very fine wine.

I don't know what sound, what motion of air, alerted me, but suddenly I was wide awake. Sitting up in my narrow bed, I breathed in, trying to still my pounding heart.

Though it was past *matins*, past moon-set, deep in the watch of the night, though it was so dark I could not see the beads on my kirtle, though the stars outside were so faint they illumined only the faintest outline of an open window, I knew.

I was not alone.

I could taste his sweat in the air I breathed. I could feel his presence as an alteration in the weight of it.

I knew I had not left the window open.

"Are you ready to go now?"

Fury surged. I took up my pillow and flung it in his direction. From the soft plop, I could not be sure what or where it hit, but I didn't wait to find out. I followed it, flying out of bed in the direction of his voice. The embarrassment of having struck him the other day was gone. He had acted abominably, unforgivably, and he deserved any punishment I could wreak upon him.

I stumbled on a pile of bedclothes and reached empty air where his voice had been. Powerful hands grabbed my wrists and twisted, pinning both arms behind my back.

"Now, Kate," he murmured, his breath pressing my hair against my ear. "Is that any way to greet your husband?"

"What husband?" I shrieked, but it came out only as a harsh, broken whisper. "I have no husband. There was a man who lied and abandoned me, humiliating me in front of my family, my entire town. Is this the one you mean?"

"What?" I could almost hear him smiling and struggled uselessly against his strength. "I thought you didn't want to marry me."

"I didn't! I don't!" I stomped down on his booted foot and he let me go, but I sensed it was only his choice and none of my doing. I spun away from him, rubbing my wrists. "What do you know of what I want and what I don't want?"

He was silent for a moment, and then I sensed him moving about the room, reaching, touching things.

"What are you doing?"

"You must have a bag or a trunk here somewhere. It is time to go."

I drew in my breath sharply. "Go where?"

He straightened. I could tell, because he was framed, just barely, in the window again. "Go. To my keep. You are my wife. It is time to go."

I folded my arms. "We are not married."

"A mere formality. Your father and I have an agreement, and your whole village saw you ready to marry me. You just told me that yourself." He paused. "Or would you prefer to stay?"

Would my father complain if I was taken from this house without a church ceremony? Would he object to the idea of Sir William's invasion of his home and abduction of his daughter? I heard in my mind the echo of laughter in the courtyard this very night, their reveling after my humiliation. I knew the answer. They would care nothing for the formalities, so long as Blanche was free.

I took my cloak from the hook beside the door. "You can send a servant for my things in the morning. Husband."

The same ladder from his last visit stood propped under my window. The distance to the cobbled streets below, lost in darkness, had never appeared so long. Before I could think any more about it, I tucked my skirts and bulky train up over one arm and clambered up onto the windowsill. There, with my feet hanging over empty space, I froze. Once I set off down the ladder, my choice was irrevocable. If I came back—and I did not ever want to—but if I did, it would not be as a daughter of this house but as Lady Kathryn Pendaran. I shot a glance back over my shoulder. Sir William waited, hands on hips, not quite ready to toss me out the window but nearly.

I set one foot in its delicate wedding slipper on the ladder, setting the wood quivering all along its length. I gripped the windowsill, digging in my nails. My teeth began to chatter, even though the night air was not cold at all. I was sleepy, and hungry, and still angry with him for... well, for all of this. Not a good state for climbing down unstable ladders.

His hands suddenly on my waist made me start, and I nearly pitched out the window with a gasp. "Kate," he said in my ear. "Climb down. You will come to no harm."

Making a dubious noise, I forced myself to move. I put all of my weight onto the ladder and turned carefully to face the house. Sir William released my waist as I went, but his hands hovered near, and despite my wish to ignore him, it was comforting to know that his strength was there in the event I faltered. The ladder shuddered and shook with each step as I descended, and I wondered why there was no man at the bottom to hold it steady. Why had he, a knight with servants, come alone? Then, too, should he not have come to the church and married me this morning? None of this made any sense.

Only for tonight, I would do as he asked. Let him get me away from this horrible place, and then all would be different between us.

Once I was safe on the ground, he climbed down nimble as a thief and hoisted the ladder onto his shoulder. The sight of it, so long in front of him and behind, made me realize at last how improbable it was that he had such a ladder at all, one high enough to reach my window on the third story of the house. I looked around for a horse or wagon, any hint of his plans from here.

"What—?"

"Hush!" he commanded, and led the way along High Street in the faint moonlight.

I watched him go, staggering a little under the burden of the ladder, then followed. What else was there to do?

Just off the village square, he turned aside toward the stable at the back of the inn. I watched as he deposited the ladder back where it belonged, leaning against the stable with its top end just under the little door to the hay loft. Of course. I should have known. Where else would he have come by such a ladder? As he came back to me in the street, I said, "A woman less angry might admire your audacity, sir."

He bowed slightly and took my arm. "This way, my lady," he said and escorted me west along High Street. The buildings of the town ended. The grass of the market green yielded to the pounded earth of the outskirts which dwindled to two wagon ruts with a trail of hooves between them beaten into the earth, and we continued to walk in silence.

"Exactly how far is it to your home, sir?" I asked, feeling every pebble through the thin leather bottom of my silk slippers. "If I had known we were going to walk halfway to Wales, I would have worn my boots."

"Not long now, not long," he said, and just at that moment, a man emerged from a thick stand of hazel bushes, making me gasp and start with fear.

"Good evening, sir, milady," the man said, bowing low. "I've the horses ready. Right this way, milady."

We stepped off the road, and now the prickles of thorny weeds pierced my feet and snatched at my dress. I muttered wordless complaints, but we did not have far to go. Behind the holly, three mismatched horses waited: a ragged little hill-pony as silver-white as the moonlight itself; a pretty bay saddle horse, mahogany under the moon, with a black mane and tail, four white stockings, and a long blaze streaming down his face; and behind them, like a giant guardian, the knight's destrier, red as wine, red as blood, each hoof larger than my head and heavy enough to crush it without noticing. I froze when he swung his huge face around to look at me, to snort at my arrival. Big as he had seemed at a distance in the stable yard, he was a nightmare up close.

As I shrank back from the beast, Sir William came up behind me and put his hands on my waist. Before I could protest, he had lifted me and deposited me in the saddle of the pretty bay, who danced a little as I grabbed his mane and tried to settle my seat.

For once in my life, words failed me.

"Your wedding gift," he said before walking away to swing easily into the saddle of his own horse.

"What shall I call him?" I asked.

He paused, considering. "For the moment, call him Conveyance, a means to get you home," Sir William said. "After that, we shall see." He turned his head away. "Gregory."

His servant, holding the reins of the pony, looked like a child beside that immense destrier. "Yes, sir?"

"See to the lead, will you?"

"Yes, sir."

Gregory looped his pony's reins around his wrist and came over to my horse's head. The bay snuffled eagerly at his hands, searching for a treat, and Gregory gave him something while taking hold of his headstall and clipping a rope onto it.

"What is that?" I asked.

He glanced up at me. "It's a leading rope, milady."

"I know very well what it is. I want to know what it is doing on my horse."

"Well, one end of it is going to stay there, milady, and the other end of it is going to be attached to me and my little mount here."

"Why?"

"Because," cut in Sir William, who had wheeled his mount in a circle and was now right next to us, "I have seen your behavior and I do not trust you to do as you are told."

I scolded both of them, master and man, as we set out. Receiving no response from either of them, I gave it up. It was to be a long ride, after all.

By my best reckoning, we had been riding for more than two hours with the waxing crescent moon setting in front of us. Sir William led the way, his destrier's long strides putting the familiar country surrounding my town far behind us. During this time,

Gregory's pony had two problems. First, it had to keep up with the strong, steady pace of the warhorse, which required frequent outbreaks of a bouncy trot, clearly jarring to its rider. Second, and more vexing, it had to contend with leading my "Conveyance," whose longer legs meant that he was always covering more ground than the pony. Creeping close, he would brush his nose or shoulder against the pony's rump, causing the pony to flick his tail in annoyance, or stamp a hoof in warning, or—again—trot away. Conveyance and I found this all rather amusing. The pony did not.

"Milady, please," Gregory said, "I don't want my pony to kick."

"I'm very sorry, Gregory," I replied. "I don't want your pony to kick either. But as you are aware, I really have no control."

"Now, milady," Gregory said, but that was all I heard.

The pony took that moment, that very moment, to make it clear that the encroachment on his rear end was no longer acceptable. He tucked both of his hind legs under him and lashed out with his sharp little heels. Conveyance, startled and offended by this sudden change in the pony's demeanor, jerked up and back, but the lead rope prevented him from moving as far as he would have liked. I grabbed his mane, having been denied reins, and slammed my heels down in the stirrups. Conveyance tossed his head against the lead rope and pulled back again, rearing up a little on his hind legs, then a little more.

I wanted to cry out for help, but my throat was frozen, airless.

The pony kicked out again, whinnying at the ruckus.

Conveyance bucked, and I went off.

The world went upside down, slowly, silently, and then I was slammed on my back in the middle of the road in the one place—the *one* place—that still held any moisture from Friday's rain. I lay still for a long moment, taking stock, judging whether anything was broken, realizing that some of the soft dampness was horse manure—horse manure on my wedding dress!—until I heard raised voices and forced myself to sit up.

Sir William and Gregory were standing in the road, facing each other. The knight's rapid, staccato phrases were punctuated by a finger pointed at Gregory's breastbone. "My lady was in your charge," he was saying as I approached. "A less tolerant master would beat the stuffing out of you!"

For his part, Gregory looked just as angry, but, as a good servant, he could not articulate it. Fists clenched, body tense, he sputtered and blurted a few words in his defense. "I didn't—I tried—" I could tell he longed to smack Sir William's finger away and yell right back at him.

Something about this seemed so familiar....

I struggled to my feet, the back of my kirtle heavy with the damp. "Sir William," I said, making my unsteady way toward them.

He turned on me. "What?"

His eyes snapped with dark fire. I recoiled but spoke up for Gregory. "Why do you chastise your servant for your own mistake? You put a leading rope on my horse when I am perfectly able to direct the creature myself, and you put the slower horse to leading the faster. You should have known this would happen, and yet when it did, here you are passing off the blame! Shame on you, and shame on you for punishing your servant for your own failure."

His hand twitched and my eyes darted to it. I did not flinch, but I threw his own words back at him: "I swear I will cuff you if you strike me."

He blinked and the ghost of a smile touched his lips. I released my breath slowly.

"You have a good memory," he said.

"Oh yes," I replied. "I remember everything."

He nodded and said, "Good." He glanced at Gregory, who had gone to attend the horses, all now grazing in the thick grasses and weeds at the side of the road. With a graceful hand, he gestured toward Conveyance. "Please."

I was not going to argue.

I should have untied my filthy, mud-soaked, manure-stained train and left it there, instead of sitting on it all the way to Bitterbrook Keep. I would have plenty to regret later, but that night, a wet, cold seat was all I had to complain about.

PART TWO

Bitterbrook Keep

Chapter Ten

Monday

I must have fallen asleep on the horse's back, his leading rope now tethered to Sir William's saddle instead of poor Gregory's. The journey seemed interminable, though of course in the uninterrupted dark once the moon had set, it was hard to tell which direction our path took and impossible to know how long we had been riding. We splashed across several streams, waded a river up to the horses' knees, climbed steadily up a long rise of land, drifted in and out of woods…. I was in utterly unfamiliar surroundings I could not even see properly. Yet Sir William rode on, never hesitating, never turning around to check on me, never stopping for a rest.

It was the sound of birds that stirred me, and coming awake on horseback was so disorienting, I nearly toppled off. I caught myself with fistfuls of mane, with knees clamped tight, and shook myself fully awake. The first pale light of day was washing over the world, turning it from black to colorless. Instead of black columns reaching from a black ground into a blue-black sky, now I could see trees, grass, clouds, all doused in lye, stripped of color.

Sir William said, "Halt," and pulled up his destrier.

My Conveyance sighed and stumbled to a stop behind him.

Blinking, I looked up, past Sir William. I could hear Blanche's voice in my mind: *"A small keep with a tower and a moat…"*

On a flat-topped hill before us was a stone castle with a crenellated tower and a massive curtain wall. A stream had been diverted to flow around the base of the hill, which had been stripped clean of all vegetation but grass. Where our horses stood and for as far as I could see, there was not a tree I could have wrapped two hands around.

Gregory pulled his little pony up alongside me. "Ah," he said. "Home."

"Gregory," Sir William said, "go on ahead. Make ready for your lady's arrival."

"Yes, sir." With a slap of his heels to his weary pony's sides, he sent it jogging off toward the keep. Perhaps the thought of its own stall and some oats encouraged it, for it made a good pace.

I stared ahead. What to do now? Ought I to say something? If so, what? *It's a very old keep, isn't it?* Or, *That's a lovely keep you have?*

"Bitterbrook Keep," Sir William said at last. "You shall be lady and mistress there."

"Aye, I *will* be," I corrected him. He turned his face toward me, surprised by my vehement tone. "And judging by what I have seen of you so far, a better lord I will be, for all that I wear these skirts. Your servants must live in terror of a master who cannot be trusted."

"What a rogue and arrant knave am I!" he exclaimed.

"Indeed you are!"

With his lopsided grin, he was clearly more amused than offended. "So you say from such a short acquaintance?"

"It is no hardship to see to the bottom of a shallow pond," I said coldly. "I do not need the eyes of an eagle to see into the next room."

"Ah," he said, still half smiling. "But, my lady, you of all people must know that you will only see what you are looking for. *Quaerite et invenietis.*"

"Again you quote scripture at me? To what end, sir?"

He continued to smile. "I depend upon your knowing exactly what I mean. At some point, you will admit it to me."

"It is interesting that you have such intimate knowledge of the Bible, a man who would not show his face in church to get married and instead sneaks about in the middle of night abducting helpless women."

He laughed, only increasing my frustration with him. If I had had control of my horse, I would have ridden off in disdain. As it was, I could only dig my heels down in the stirrups, making my Conveyance dance and fidget under me.

Sir William looked away and clicked his tongue at his monstrous beast. My horse and I had no choice but to follow.

"Seek and thou shalt find," I muttered the scripture under my breath, burning holes in his back with my eyes, hoping he would feel it. But somewhere in the deep recesses of my mind, his words teased. *"I depend upon your knowing exactly what I mean."* Well, I did. What did it matter to him that I did? And why was he depending on it? What was I supposed to seek, and what did he intend that I find?

I glared some more, and yet his back was impervious. Holding tight to my anger, I tried to shake loose his words and instead raised my eyes to the view ahead.

Despite its dreary name, Bitterbrook Keep appeared to very good effect as we approached. The dawn sun struck it from behind us, painting the gray granite a rosy-gold. I could see nothing but the tower behind the curtain wall, and of course the closer we rode, the less I could see. As we approached the entry, all that was visible was the massive, hulking wall comprised of enormous stones stacked one upon the other higher than several men. The sheer size of it took my breath away, a town girl with no first-hand experience of castles or war or knights.

Except now I was married to one.

Almost.

With a shiver in my belly, I pushed away the thought of what it would require to make this a true marriage.

The entrance to the keep was a broad archway through the wall, wide enough for two horses side by side. Thick wooden doors on both ends of the archway stood open, and as we entered, we rode under the portcullis, a wooden, lattice-like gate, its bottom edges sharpened like spear points. Arrow slits and other holes were punched at intervals into the walls and ceiling. I trembled a little in that dark space within the wall. If the doors were slammed shut, the keep's defenders would have no difficulty killing anyone trapped there.

We emerged from the darkness into a wide courtyard, its grass mostly trampled into dust. Directly ahead was the tower, three tall stories watching over the countryside, and attached to its south side was a long, low stone hall. Pressed up against the hall and the outer wall were various wooden structures whose purposes I could only guess at. Stables? Storage? Servant quarters?

The ears of both horses perked up as they walked into the yard, recognizing the end of their journey. My spirits lifted as well, for though what lay ahead was uncertain, I was the lady of this place. I was here.

And my family was not.

A line of servants awaited us on the lowest step leading up to the hall, tugging at their clothes to set them right. Sir William drew his charger to a halt at the mounting block beside the steps, and one of the men hurried down to hold the bridle. Another quickly followed to assist his lord in dismounting. He barely glanced at them, saying neither a word of greeting nor of thanks.

He stalked back to my horse. Conveyance snorted and stamped nervously. Sir William reached up toward me with an impatient gesture.

"Come," he said.

I was so stiff and sore from the long ride, I could hardly make my legs respond. Before I knew what was happening, he grabbed me around the waist and hauled me off like so much baggage. When my feet hit the ground, my legs buckled and I found myself on my hands and knees under Conveyance. Too startled to cry out, I gasped and scrambled backward, out of range of his hooves.

A rough hand grabbed hold of the lacings up the back of my kirtle. The breath whooshed out of me as Sir William hauled me to my feet.

I whirled around, spitting like a cat. "How dare you treat me so?"

But he was already halfway up the stairs to the keep.

"Where are my servants?" he bellowed as he entered the hall. I was only a few steps behind him, stumbling on numb legs in my filthy wedding dress. I wanted nothing more than to take a look around, have a bath, and get to sleep.

This hall, the kind of great room on which the hall in my father's townhome had been modeled, was a cavernous chamber with a dais at the far end, big enough to demand four hearths, large enough to host a feast of five hundred people, just like in stories I had heard about the courts of great lords and kings. But it lacked the grace of those halls I had heard described. The walls were bare of tapestries and marked with soot above the torch sconces. The windows were mere slits set high overhead, letting in only thin bars of light; no furniture or objects of any value served to impose a sense of majesty or grandeur on the place. My father's hall, though smaller, was far more richly appointed. Blanche's words chimed in my mind. *"The only reason he wants your stick-skinny body is for your big, fat dowry."*

I shook my head. I had escaped her. I could not allow her here.

"Where are those knaves hiding?" Sir William's voice echoed among the rafters.

"The servants are coming behind us, sir," I chided him, "having met us outside as is proper."

"Here, sir," Gregory said, hurrying in to stand before his master. The others followed in a flurry of movement. "We are all here."

"Here, sir," Sir William repeated, mocking him. "Gregory, did I not give you instruction on what you were to do?"

Gregory looked confused. "Well, yes, sir, you told me to make all ready for my lady, and so—"

"Silence, fool! I cannot abide being kept waiting. Do not let it happen again. Where is my food?"

I was as stunned as Gregory appeared to be. In my father's house, this knight had been courteous and charming. Infuriating and arrogant, to be sure, but never uncivil. But since we had left Whitelock last night, his behavior was… well, it was awful.

Was this what my life was to be?

No. It had been a long night and we were all tired. Surely when he had had time to reflect upon his actions, he would regret his behavior toward his servants. I had to take some control of the situation.

First things first. While it had been a long time—a very long time, in fact—since I had eaten, I was filthy from my fall on the road and again in the courtyard. I placed a light hand on Sir William's sleeve and said, "I would prefer to wash and rest first."

He shook my hand off. It might have been a stinging wasp on his arm. "Nonsense. You will sit with me and eat."

He grabbed my hand and started toward the dais where his servants had placed two tall-backed wooden chairs in front of a long table draped with a white cloth and set with pewter dishes and goblets.

Frowning, I pulled back against him. "No," I said. "I do not want to eat now. I want to wash and rest first."

He ignored my words and pulled harder. Like a reluctant mule, I was dragged to the dais. He charged up the steps, making me stumble.

"Sit, Kate," he said, spinning me into a chair. "Sit and eat." He picked up a knife from the table and held it out to me. When I reached for it, he snatched it away. "Best not, with your temper," he said. "I'll cut your meat for you."

I gasped and spluttered. I could hardly frame words to express my outrage. "My temper? *My* temper?" But he did not seem to hear me.

"In God's name, where is the food?" he yelled, and several harried servants rushed to a side door, heading, I supposed, to the kitchen. Their faces spoke volumes of resentment at being treated so.

Sir William smiled at me. "Be merry, Kate," he said.

His mood changed like lightning flashes. I was unsettled enough from the night's long ride and the humiliation of the day before. I had no desire to puzzle through his behavior. Through gritted teeth, I said, "I would like to wash before I eat."

"Well, you went and fell in the mud. That's not my fault. Wine, here!"

"Actually, as I told you before, it very much was," I retorted loudly, as if increased strength would convince him. "You put my horse on a short rope and forced him to follow that pony."

"Oh, enough." He waved a hand at me. "Your father was right, you know. A veritable shrew."

Oh no. Not that word. I leaped out of my chair. He reached out and with one firm hand, pushed me back into my seat.

That easily.

While I contemplated that fact, he raised his voice to call to another servant. "Come, we'll have water to wash."

At last, I thought.

The man approached slowly, carrying a large basin of water and a towel. Sir William gestured him toward me. "Allow my lady to wash first," he said. A glow of righteous satisfaction warmed me. At last I was being accorded the proper courtesy and honor due to me as his wife and lady.

But a moment later, that was snatched away when he muttered under his breath, "Right slovenly she is."

Clean water and a towel, only a few feet away. I didn't want to jeopardize it by sniping. I fumed in silence, glaring at Sir William as the servant skirted the table.

I leaned forward, longing to wash the dirt and grit off my hands and face at least.

Perhaps the basin was too full. Perhaps the fellow was clumsy, or his foot caught on the tablecloth that draped all the way to the floor.

Or perhaps—oh, surely not, surely I did not see it—the master of the house slid his foot into the servant's path.

It seemed so slow, it seemed to take such a long time to fall, the water curving in a long, graceful arc directly into my lap.

I shrieked and jumped out of my chair, knocking it backward. My heel caught on the long train of my kirtle and I heard, and felt, the bows anchoring it at my waist rip.

I twisted to look at the damage to my dress before sinking back down into my seat. Sir William did not stir. He was trimming his fingernails with the knife.

Before I could give voice to my rage, he looked up, eyes bright, as though he had just remembered something. "Where are my dogs?" he called. "Bring in Ajax and Acteon, Theseus and Telamon, Zeus and Nemo."

My jaw dropped as yet another of the servants opened a door and ushered in six enormous, slobbering hunting hounds with heads the size and shape of anvils and tails like whips. They galloped into the hall, overjoyed at the sight of their master, baying their excitement.

At the same moment, the door at the other side of the hall opened, admitting the men who had gone to get food.

My stomach let out a growl at the sight of the covered platters they carried.

The dogs, scenting a meal, shifted the course of their headlong rush for Sir William.

"No!" I cried, jumping out of my chair again.

At top speed, the first of the dogs slammed into one of the men carrying the food, knocking him off his feet and into the man behind him. Their dishes flew up in the air, fluffy eggs and rashers of bacon soaring, rising, falling, hitting the ground with a wet splat. The rest of the dogs altered their course from their master to the spilled food, knocking over the next two men in the process. The men shouted, the dishes clattered—bread and cheese and stewed prunes and onions hit the floor—the dogs snuffled and growled and consumed my breakfast.

Sir William laughed.

I stared at him. "Your behavior is unaccountable, sir!" I exclaimed.

"Nay, you do not know these louts. They are the most lazy, disreputable, impossible servants in the country."

I could not miss the look Gregory cast at his master, an odd combination of confusion, anger and disapproval I had no name for.

I could have defended them. I could have set forth for Sir William in great detail exactly how this was all his very own fault and no fault of the servants. But I was starting to shiver from the water on my kirtle; even in June, the warmth of outdoors did not penetrate such thick stone walls. Dare I ask where I might dry off and change my kirtle? But no. I stifled a groan. We had left my father's house empty-handed. I had nothing to change into.

Sir William frowned at the food on the floor. Rising from his chair, he nudged one of the dogs away from a half-chewed lump of meat with his foot. "What's this? Mutton?"

The nearest servant nodded, bowing. His demeanor was hesitant, cautious. "Yes, sir, it is."

"It is burnt," Sir William said.

The man looked puzzled. "But, sir—" the man protested.

"Oh, for heaven's sake!" I burst out. "As if it matters when it is food for the dogs!"

He heeded neither of us. "Fools!" he said, swinging an arm wide, encompassing all of them. "How dare you serve this to me? How can you offer this to your new lady?"

The servants fled.

I stared at him. He stared at me, challenging. I wanted to scream.

I forced myself to speak calmly. "Why do you act thus? The meat was fine, as it seemed to me, if it were not devoured by dogs."

He sat at the table and leaned back in his chair, crossing his legs at the ankles, a man with no cares in the world. He was making my head to spin! "Surely you know, Kate," he said, shaking his head, "that burnt meat engenders anger in the blood. Thus it were better that both of us did not eat it, since we both are choleric by nature."

Other than this morning, I would not have described him as a particularly angry man. Yet I could not disagree with the truth of his words. "What you say is well known, but—"

"Be patient, Kate," he said, patting my hand. "Tonight it will be mended. This morning we'll fast together. Come, I'll show you to your bedchamber where you may rest."

He rose and offered me his hand. I stared at it as if I had never seen its like before. He waited, and waited, and waited some more. I could not help comparing this to the man who had dragged me off the horse. A giggle bubbled up in my nose and I fought it down.

What was I to make of this? Would nothing ever make sense again?

With a sigh, I placed my hand in his. What choice did I have? I was shivering and the dogs were eating my breakfast.

We left the hall by one of the many arched openings and entered the stairwell at the base of the tower. The steps were wide slabs of cold stone worn smooth by the passage of hundreds of feet over hundreds of years, and as we started up, I felt the chill of that history cutting through the slight leather soles of my slippers. I imagined a warm room and a cheery fire, a hot bath and, God willing, some time away from Sir William.

On the second landing we stopped and he opened one of the two doors. "Here is your chamber," he said.

I went inside and stopped. I turned back to look at him. He was waiting for my reaction. "This... this is for me?" I stammered. Even after all that the long night and morning had brought, I was yet unable to credit what I was seeing.

This was no bridal chamber. This was not even the accommodation a wealthy man would provide for a guest. This was, in essence, a servant's room—no, worse. A peasant's hovel. A narrow bed with a straw mattress, a wool blanket that even from the doorway looked moth-eaten, a pillow that might have once belonged to one of his hideous hounds, a stand with a chipped basin and a cracked jug, a small trunk with a broken lock. No fire in the hearth, not even a pile of wood for me to make one.

"Yes, here is where you will stay."

"Not you," I said.

He laughed. "By God, no." He turned to go, then turned back as if he just remembered. "Oh. There are no garderobes in the tower, except in my bedchamber of course, so you'll have to use the privies outside. In the yard."

I let him go down a few steps before it boiled out of me. "My dress. I'm soaking wet. I need clothes, and I need a maid to help me."

He pivoted on the stairs, one foot above the other. "My goodness, listen to you. 'I need, I need.' I have no female servants, you have no other clothes, and until I get your dowry from your father, we have no money for either. So very sorry, Your Highness." He sketched a very graceful, very mocking bow and went on down the stairs.

He didn't even duck when I threw the cracked pitcher at his head. How did he know I would miss?

Cold, wet, miserable.

A hostage to my dowry.

Shivering, I wrapped my arms around myself.

As contrary as Sir William had been when we had first met, he had not been like this. When I had called him moon-mad that night under my window, I had not truly meant it. I had thought merely that he was mad for courting me so determinedly when I was repelling him so fiercely. I still did not believe he was mad. Whatever had brought about this erratic behavior must surely have a cause. All I needed was a good meal and some rest. And to work out who the servants were and how they felt about this. Already I could see that Gregory was unhappy with his master. Perhaps I could win him over and make him my ally.

I had not escaped misery in my father's house only to suffer a worse fate in this one.

I looked around once more. There was not even a proper window in this wretched room, only two deep, narrow slits for shooting arrows. With no glass. It would be delightful in winter.

Winter? He wouldn't dare keep me in here, in this barren chamber, through the winter. His wife, his Kate. I was Lady Kathryn.

He wouldn't, would he?

Well, Lady Kathryn did not have to stay in this room, freezing.

I went out into the stairwell.

The sound of voices—harried, worried, outraged voices, all talking over one another—rose up from below. "I don't understand," said one, and another, "never like this," and "what's she done to him?"

Naturally, the servants blamed me.

I fled up the stairs.

There was only one door on the next landing, a thick, imposing door strapped in iron. I did not even attempt it.

At the very top, there was a tiny landing and an ordinary wooden door that opened freely to my hand. Daylight poured through. I was out. Free, for the moment.

From the top of this tower, the view stretched for miles and miles. To the west, I thought I might be able to see past the River Severn all the way to Wales, where everything melded into green mists and greener hills. To the east was a town that could have been Atherstone but might not. I had no way of knowing. Standing there, letting the sun soak into my sodden dress, I looked down over a world much larger than one I had ever known, one I had longed to see and yet, now that I was in it, was finding much harder to navigate than I had expected. Perhaps Sir William had been right to mock me for my small-town ignorance. What more he had seen, what more did he know of the world than I? Not by choice, but still.... I leaned against the wall and stared down into the vast valley below until, a short time later, I saw Sir William stride out of the keep with his dogs in a mob at his heels. The long curve of a bow stretched above one shoulder and a quiver of arrows bristled at the other. Water sprang into my mouth. Fresh meat. They set off across the fields and the hounds fanned out.

If he were hunting, he would be gone for some time. I would take advantage of his absence.

I hurried down to the hall, looking for Gregory. He and three of the other servants were just finishing the cleaning of the dais after the disaster that was breakfast. He looked up, saw me and, when I beckoned to him, came over to me with a wary look.

"How may I be of service, milady?"

"Gregory, I understand there will be no dinner today, but I did not have anything to eat this morning at breakfast. I would like the cook to make up a plate for me—something simple, no trouble to anyone, but I am very hungry."

Gregory looked stricken. "Milady, would that I could. But I dare not for my life."

"What do you mean?"

"My master has just now gone out, and he left very strict instructions that there was to be no food prepared today until supper."

I frowned. "But that is unreasonable and foolish. I am hungry and I need to eat."

I could hear Sir William's mocking voice in my head. *"I need, I need."* But I did!

"Milady, I can do anything else to give you comfort. Only not that. And my master is gone, so I cannot ask him to change his orders."

"Very well, Gregory," I said. "If you will not oblige me, I will go to the kitchen myself."

"Oh, milady, please don't!"

I strode off the dais and headed for the door through which the men had brought the covered dishes earlier. That door led to a corridor and faced another door. I opened that door and found myself in the courtyard outside.

In my father's house, the kitchen was at the back of the house. I knew where it was, and I knew Cook.

Here I could not even find my way to the kitchen.

I took a deep breath.

"Gregory," I said, my voice pinched and tight, "do be sure to let me know when your master returns. I wish to speak with him."

"Of course, milady," he said, bowing.

From the look on his face, I felt certain he would not.

It was not terribly difficult to run away.

Gregory was busy inside with the other servants, and while there was someone in the stables, he was heaving straw down from the loft in great, dusty chunks and could not see me.

I simply walked through the gates and made my way down the hill, ignoring the pain in my feet from tiny pebbles and sharp, dry grass.

There was a town to the east, so I headed that way.

My feet were screaming at me and I was sweating profusely by the time I made it to the little village. Weren't villages like this supposed to huddle at the feet of their protecting keeps? This one made me walk across some very unfriendly terrain before it made its appearance, and it was decidedly disappointing to boot.

My town—no, I must think of it as my father's town now— Whitelock, was a real town, with two roads going through it and a real green in the center for markets and gatherings. Our part of High Street was even cobbled with stone. We had a merchants' meeting hall, a pretty, old church with glass windows, a smithy, our own mill down on the river, plus a whole street of shops. We even had a lawyer.

This poor excuse for a village was merely a cluster of buildings huddled together like freezing men. Instead of solid stone or snug black-and-white, half-timbered houses like the one I had grown up in, these homes were made of rough-hewn logs and branches patched with mud and moss and topped with ragged thatch. Some had birds' nests at their peaks or under their eaves. Through their midst ran a strip of flattened mud, deep with ruts and the tracks of cattle hooves. There was no green, just an empty patch of dirt in the center of the houses where there stood a trough of stale water.

Walking into this, I slowed my pace and swallowed hard. The long years of prosperity under King Edward while I was growing up, which had so benefited my father and the town of Whitelock, had not reached this place.

What was I to do now? These folk could not help me. Clearly, they were hard pressed to help themselves.

I made my way to the trough. One look at the water, and the dead flies floating in it, convinced me I should not drink, but I splashed some on my wrists and neck nevertheless. Then I turned and sat on the edge, the stone sharp and unyielding beneath me. That was all right. It suited my mood entirely.

"You must be from the keep," a voice said behind me.

On another day I would have leaped to my feet and whirled around to face her. But the air was so hot and heavy, and I was so tired, I merely turned my head.

"So I am," I replied.

The girl, probably about my age or maybe a little younger, came around the trough to stand beside me. She was filthy—she probably had not bathed in weeks, perhaps not in months—and her hair hung in lank strands of an ashen color that was perhaps light brown when it was clean. Over it she wore a cap that was dirtier than her face, and her kirtle was gray with age and stains. She was too thin and careworn to be truly pretty, but she looked me over bold as could be and said, "We heard Sir William might be getting married. So I see he has."

Was this how she behaved to her lord's wife? Shocking! "Indeed he has," I replied, anger rising in my throat.

She settled on the trough beside me and shook her head. "Too bad she brought her own maids," she said, gesturing at me. "We was hoping—" Here she waved a hand at the houses around her. "We girls, that is, we was hoping there might be work up at the keep, once the lord took a wife."

I cleared my throat, choking down the anger. She thought I was a servant, not the lady. I ran a hand down the front of my dress. Well, why not? Look at my condition. My dress might be fine but it was filthy, my hair was a mess, I was sweaty and on foot.

Lady Kathryn. What a laugh!

"Well, there may be yet. They've only just arrived."

The girl's face brightened. "Oh, you think?" I could only imagine what working for Sir William might mean to her and her family. My cheeks went hot with shame. One veil in the trunk I had left behind at home cost enough to feed her for—how long? I did not even know. I had no idea how much it cost to feed a family. I had never shopped for anything of real value at the market, only sweets and vanities.

"What is your name?"

"Elizabeth," she said. "Named for the queen that was."

I nodded. Queen Elizabeth had been queen for as long as I'd been alive, married to King Edward and mother to his many children. There were lots of girls named Elizabeth all over England, including the queen's own eldest daughter.

"The lord just returned from Westminster, where he saw the king."

"He did?" Her eyes went even rounder, wonder and awe dancing there. "Is that where he met his lady?"

"No," I said, "he met her on the way back here. In a town called Whitelock."

"Oh." She seemed disappointed. "So she isn't a fine lady."

I bridled. "She's fine enough for *him*, that's certain."

A movement across the way caught my eye. Two women stood in the doorway of one of the houses, one with a grubby baby on her hip. They were looking at us without seeming to—I was well accustomed to the glance-and-look-away they were performing—and talking furtively, their heads close together, though there was no risk of being overheard by us.

What was so suspicious about me, then?

I glared back at them.

"If her ladyship does decide to take on some help, I'll put in a good word for you, Elizabeth," I said. "What can you do?"

"Oh, I'll do anything. Anything to work at the keep. Get away from this." She motioned with a helpless hand.

I glanced at this ragged girl sitting beside me, her stained clothes, her splintered fingernails. As many times as I had imagined escaping my little village and going to the royal court where I could be one of the glittering ladies dancing and singing and hunting and... whatever else ladies did at court—as much as I had longed for another life, how much more must this girl long for an escape? Could she even begin to frame what life at court would look like? Had she ever seen a gold necklace or a silver plate, or even a pewter cup?

If my father's money could do anything, it could give this girl work. It could give her hope.

I patted her knee. "I will do what I can for you. I promise."

Those women were still looking at me and whispering. What could I have done to make them stare so?

"Is there anything you'd like to say to me?" I yelled across at them.

The women disappeared into the darkness of the hut and slammed the rickety door shut behind them. Elizabeth grabbed at my arm, pulling me down. "Hush, now!" she said. "They mean no harm. None of us have ever seen anyone dressed as fine as you, is all."

I laughed, bitter and sharp. So fine, with mud and manure stains on the back, the fabric ruined with water, and the train torn.... Still, look at Elizabeth. One day of hardship and I was complaining. She lived like this all the time.

Something moved within me. This was important, I knew, but had no idea what to do with it. "Elizabeth," I said, not sure what more I meant to say, but I never did finish because suddenly, the pounding of horse hooves drowned any words we might have said to each other.

I sprang to my feet as two horses galloped into the square and skidded to a stop in front of the trough, raising a cloud of dust. I flung my hands up to cover my face. Elizabeth ran for the nearest tumble-down hut.

Gregory jumped down from his mount, the reins of both horses in his hands, relief on his face. "Oh, thank the Almighty I've found you," he said, bowing as he came toward me. "Please, milady, allow me to escort you home."

The dust was settling like face powder all over my dress and hair. Wonderful. "Home?" I asked. "What can you mean by that?"

He barely restrained himself from rolling his eyes, which made me want to laugh. "Back to the keep, milady. Please. Before my lord returns."

His hand was stretched out, half an invitation, half a command. Cheeky, for a servant.

I smiled and allowed myself to be helped into the saddle.

After all, what other choice did I have?

Back at Bitterbrook Keep, I slid from Conveyance's saddle without Gregory's help. Somehow, I did not thud on the ground like a sack of potatoes, yet I did not manage the landing with any grace at all. My rump was sore from hours on horseback, and my legs ached from walking farther than I had in my whole life, and that in flimsy little silk shoes, leaving my feet pricked all over like a pincushion. Gregory took hold of the horses' reins and led them off toward the stables.

I started for the wide stairs into the keep, ready for a good lie-down.

It was then that I spied the smoke.

Ah! Smoke, gray and sooty and a bit greasy, billowing forth from the chimney of one of the outbuildings.

Where there's smoke, there's fire, they say. And where there's fire, there's food, say I.

With a final glance at Gregory's retreating back, and keeping the horses between us as cover, I dashed across the courtyard as quickly as my protesting lower body would allow.

The building belching smoke was entirely made of stone with no wood except the doors and shutters, and no thatched roof. Perhaps if I had noticed that earlier, I might have had something to eat by now. Also, there was a fat brick oven squatting like a beehive just outside the door. Really, I ought to have been paying closer attention.

My mouth began to water as I took hold of the door handle. I imagined the feast I might order up for myself, something on the scale of what I had been denied yesterday when the beastly Sir William had failed to show up for our wedding. Apple-roasted pork, fresh bread, a bit of cheese, some fish fresh out of that stream outside the keep, baked and smothered in cream sauce with onions and herbs....

Inside, the kitchen was dim. Well, of course it was, its walls being thick stone and its windows being small and square. Orange light and thick heat from three massive cook-fires bled over everything and everyone so that I might have walked into the very pit of hell. And, as in hell, a devil reigned in the center—a man tall and strapping, all long limbs and booming voice, waving evil knives like extensions of his own hands, ordering about the other servants who scurried, heads down, to do his bidding. With one knife, he hacked something to pieces—a turnip, perhaps?—and with the other, he scooped it up and hurled it into the pot slung over the nearby fire, yelling all the while at the boy stirring it.

Mouth agape, I backed slowly out of the door.

No wonder Gregory had refused to ask for anything against orders. Not only would he cross his master, he risked the wrath of this knife-wielding madman.

Chastened and still hungry, I headed back to my room.

There came a time when I could no longer put off a visit to the privies. Suffice it to say that in my entire life, I had never had to use a hole in the ground surrounded by a patched-together wooden shed through which sun and wind penetrated. That helped with the stench, of course, but again, I couldn't help wondering what this would be like in winter.

Breathing through gritted teeth, I closed my eyes and balanced over the hole, my kirtle and train draped over one arm. I would not be subjected to this through the winter. I would *not*.

As I left, the door slammed shut behind me, an announcement. I cringed, scuttling away like a beetle, wiping my hands on the filthy hem of my chemise for lack of anything else to use. I kept up a stream of muttered complaints as I went, the litany of my grievances masking worries about my future, when a commotion ahead of me made me look up.

Sir William was returning, walking in through the deep entry surrounded by his dogs. Now that I was at eye level with him, I could see he was dressed differently than he had been last night, not as richly, wearing dark clothes splotched with mud and grass stains. I almost smiled. He looked like a boy who had been off romping about the countryside with his pets. Almost smiled, but stopped myself. They were hellhounds, and he a fiend.

I dropped the edge of my chemise and looked around, hoping to escape his notice, but most of the buildings in the courtyard were still a mystery to me, and after seeing what awaited inside the kitchen, I did not know where it would be safe to flee. I froze, watching him— and them—pour through the gate. Perhaps he would not notice me. Perhaps—

"Kate!" A broad smile spread across his face, and a dimple appeared in one cheek.

Damn him!

He crossed the distance between us in a trice, coming to stand before me with his feet planted wide, arms across his chest, still with that cheeky grin. Master of all he surveyed, including me, I supposed. Looking away from the impressive display—which he clearly intended—of his muscled arms and broad chest, my gaze fell on the dogs. Mistake. The beasts swarmed at his heels, their massive heads level with his hips, their attention pinned on me. One of them licked its chops. I shivered and resisted the urge to cross myself. He wouldn't let it eat me, would he?

"You look wary, Kate."

"Rightly so, I think."

"Have you never had a dog?"

I hesitated. In fact, I had. When I was eight and Blanche was five, Father brought home a pup. Not a hunting hound like these or a bruiser for guarding his wagons, but a house pet. A little lapdog. He was black and tan with a small head and big paws and just fit in my two hands together. In the first day, Blanche and I nearly loved the life out of him. We even slept in one bed together so we could cuddle with him. For one week, we were inseparable because of that dog.

But he had one flaw.

He preferred me to Blanche.

I do not know what became of him. My father is too much a man of means to have destroyed something he paid for. I believe—I have to believe—Father sold him to some other family on his next journey.

I also believe that was when I began to hate my sister.

"I—No. Never."

He twisted at the waist to gaze upon his monsters. "They look much worse than they are. There's nothing to be afraid of."

Tongues lolling. I could count their teeth. Long, sharp teeth. I gave him a dubious look.

"Ajax," he said, tapping his thigh. One dog moved forward and sat beside its master. "Say hello to my lady."

The beast tilted its head up at me, ears flopping. I had to admit, it was an endearing display. At a slight hand gesture from Sir William, the dog raised one paw toward me.

Uncertain, I looked at Sir William.

"Take it," he said.

I took the proffered paw.

The dog licked my hand.

"Ah. Courtly manners," I said, releasing its paw and wiping the spittle off on my dress. It was disgusting yet charming at the same time. "Very nice, Ajax."

"Pat his head."

"Pat his head?"

"Yes."

"He won't bite my hand off?"

"Nay."

"He looks like he will."

The softest breath of a chuckle. "Yes. Yes, he does."

"But he won't."

"Nay."

"Pat his head, you say."

"Yes."

I shook my fingers out a little. If this was the last time I was to use them, I wanted to be sure I felt them one last time. I took a deep breath.

"All right, Ajax," I murmured.

"Show him the back of your hand, not your palm," Sir William said, so I did.

Ajax sat quivering, leaning forward, sniffing, nose reaching for my hand.

Something hit me from the side—one of the other dogs, unable to restrain itself any longer. I staggered, wobbled, and collapsed. The pack surged forward, Ajax first in what I could only hope was a protective act, and I was soon submerged in dog legs, noses, faces, and tails. They stamped, gouged, licked, snorted, grunted, snapped. The smell of their breath and their bodies was suffocating.

Sir William was cursing. From between my fingers covering my face, I saw flashes of his hands darting into the sea of dogs, grabbing necks and torsos, hauling bodies away only to have them flood back in.

I took my hands off my face long enough to brace them underneath my body and push up, surging out of the swarm of dogs, forcing them off me like water in a tub. They eased back enough that I was able to get to my knees and then to my feet.

Shaking, I stood.

Sir William, gathering his dogs and scolding them, was laughing.

Had I ever been angry before? It seemed I had not.

"You are a demon," I said, my voice shaking as much as my knees, my hands. "You are a devil sent from hell to torment me. That is the only answer."

He shook his head, trying to stifle his laughter. "Oh, Kate, you should have seen— It was—Kate!"

He reached for me as I passed. I left a ragged strip of sleeve in his hand as I stormed into the keep and up to my room, my horrible, awful little room. This—this man, this marriage—this was my punishment for the life I had led.

The chipped basin followed the pitcher down the stairs. I was saving the table for later.

I debated whether I would even go down for supper, but in the end I was so hungry—weak with it, in fact—I made my way down the stairs and out into the hall.

The table on the dais was again set up with two chairs. The dogs were nowhere to be seen. One of the servants, Nicholas I thought was his name, was building up the fire in the hearth on the dais, and there were candles, too, to chase away gloom and shadows there. I took a breath and let it out. Perhaps, at last, a chance for quiet. And, God willing, a meal.

I walked into the hall and onto the dais. At the same time, from the opposite side of the hall, Sir William did the same. I stopped, surprised. He stopped too. I shook my head. Yet more odd behavior.

All right, I thought. *Try again.*

"Good evening, Sir William." I curtsied. My dress was so filthy, I didn't want to touch it. Oh, I hoped someone had gone back to my father's house for my clothes.

"Good evening, my Lady Kate." He bowed. He had changed clothes again. The deep blue of his doublet brought out the color of his eyes. Oh dear. I did not want to notice that.

I smiled. "I hope we can forget what happened earlier today and enjoy supper together."

He frowned. "Supper?"

Not again. "Yes. This morning, you said there would be no dinner today but that there would be supper. And since I haven't eaten since dinner on Saturday—"

He cut me off. "It is not time for supper."

I blinked. "It is not?"

"No. We ate supper hours ago."

"What can you mean? The sun is still in the sky." But in this ancient keep, a place built for defense, not beauty, there were only those narrow slits high up on the walls, and it was impossible to tell how much light remained in the sky. A fire burned, candles were lit. It might have been midnight, it might have been nearing dawn.

He looked at me.

I crossed my arms. "I think you are mad, sir. And if you are mad, there is no marriage and no dowry."

He crossed his arms too. "Nevertheless, you are mistaken. It is not time for supper. And I think you will not find any here who dispute me."

I went to the table and sat, putting my hands flat on the table. "Fine. Have something brought to me now. Nevertheless."

He just looked at me, a half smile on his face.

Mad.

"What? Now you will tell me that we do not eat in this house except when the lord and master so decrees? Then why was I not summoned? You call me the lady of this place and you treat me like one of those bloody dogs!"

"My falcon is now sharp and passing empty," he said with a wink.

"What?"

"My lady," he said, "do you know aught of hunting birds?"

My thoughts spun round my head. What had this to do with supper? "Nay, sir."

"Good," he said. "Come."

He grabbed hold of one of my hands.

"Nay!" I snatched my hand back. "What are you doing? Unhand me!"

He took hold of both hands and pulled. I dug in my heels and sat hard in the chair.

Far from getting angry, he smiled.

Using one booted foot, he turned my chair so I faced him directly and pulled again. How much use could my resistance be against him, strong as he was? I fairly flew out of the chair and into his arms. The collision knocked my breath away. I blinked up at that damn dimple.

He let go of my hands and slid his hands down to my waist. My heart began to race and I still could not breathe. Every inch of my skin was aware of that touch, and every bit of me was frozen, wondering what it meant, what would happen next.

He dumped me over his shoulder like a sack of flour.

I did not kick, and I did not scream—that would have been undignified, hanging upside down as I was—but I pounded his back with my elbows, and I think that could not have been pleasant. Judging by his grunts as he trudged up the stairs, it was not. So there was that.

He kicked open the door to my room and tossed me onto the bed. I sank into the itchy, poking straw mattress, panting and wide-eyed, my heart galloping at top speed, suddenly and for the first time in his presence truly frightened. He was strong, we were alone, and he had been given every right under God's law and man's to do whatever he wanted with me, body and soul. This marriage was not a game I could play until I won, because there was so much, too much, that I could lose.

But there was the dimple. There was that crooked, cocky smile.

"Kate," he said, looking down upon me, "you need a lesson all your many tutors never taught you."

My heart began to slow its pace. I blinked and breathed. I had not lost, not yet.

I waited. He said nothing more.

I raised my eyebrows, inviting him to speak. Still nothing.

He was silent so long I had to ask, against all good judgment: "What is that?"

His grin showed me that he had won. "Moderation, Kate."

He spoke for hours.

His knightly training gave him the stamina to stand and pace and lecture me. His knightly heart gave him the cruelty to continue long past the point that any decent person would have. An archbishop would not have lectured me so!

Tedium and exhaustion vied for possession of my wits, but he would not desist, and he would not let me sleep. He made me walk with him while he paced. He made me sit with him on the hard floor leaning against the bone-aching wall. He forced me to look at him all night, and if I closed my eyes—if I even blinked for too long—he tickled my ribs or cheek or the bottom of my foot to keep me awake.

As the sun rose pink and gold through the arrow slits, I realized that his lecture on moderation had been rather immoderate in tone and length. I found that rather amusing and it set me to laughing. Tired as I was, once I had begun, I found it impossible to stop.

Finally, he left. But not before he tore the bed apart, scattering the straw around the room so I could not lie down to sleep.

Chapter Eleven

If anything, I laughed harder, watching him destroy the bed. What matter if he pulled apart the mattress, since he was not going to let me sleep on it?

A tiny part of me began to wonder whether it was not Sir William who was mad, but I.

I lay among the straw on the floor for a long while, listening to the keep. It was entirely different from my room in Whitelock with its window overlooking the street. From there, I could hear the soft clop of horse hooves, the clattering of wagons on the cobbles, the voices of people on their way past the house going about their business, the splash of a bucket dumped into the street, and the honking of a gaggle of geese on its way to the butcher. All the hum and buzz of a busy town.

Here, there was the whisper of a breeze whistling in the narrow window-slits, the singing of birds, the groan of the stable door, the call of one servant to another. It was nearly silent in comparison to the town. An entirely different world.

If I could not eat and I could not sleep, at least I could become familiar with this place.

It took all of my strength—which by now was greatly diminished—to haul open one of the stable doors. It was quiet and warm within, the air thick with the smells of manure and straw, thin shafts of sunlight piercing like blades through cracks between the planks of the walls. I was greatly disappointed to find it entirely empty but chided myself that I should not be. No doubt the horses had been released into a pasture for the hottest part of the day.

Still, Conveyance was the only thing in this place that felt like mine. It would have been good to see him, to feel his breath, to rub behind his jaw and between his ears.

"Contemplating your next escape, milady?"

I turned swiftly to find Gregory behind me, his expression somewhere between concerned and amused.

I smiled. "Your master need have no fear on that account, Gregory. I lack the skill to equip a horse." Glancing back over my shoulder, I added, "And at the moment, it seems I lack even a horse."

Gregory chuckled and reached for the stable door. I backed out of the way and he dragged the door shut with considerably less effort than I had required.

"Gregory," I said. "All of these buildings here in the yard must have some purpose. Can you tell me?"

"Of course, milady." He came to a halt beside me. "That one there is the kitchen," he said, pointing to the long stone building I had visited the day before. "There is storage in those sheds, and there is the brew-house and still." His finger moved on as he spoke. "There's a small garden just over that little fence there, herbs and vegetables and such. On this side of the keep, just here, are the stables as you saw, and beside them the kennels. Over there—" We turned about. "We have our own smithy, but of course..." Gregory's face clouded and he frowned. "We haven't had our own smith here in many long years. There's just pigeons roosting in it now, but pigeons are good eating!" His face brightened again and he laughed. My stomach clenched, and my fists with them, at the mention of food. He must have seen something in my face for he hurried on. "Beyond that, there's the sheds for the pigs and chickens and such, but my lady will have no cause to concern herself with them."

My head reeled, and not just with lack of food and sleep. At my father's house we had bought nearly everything we needed. The brewery, the bakery, the smithy, the stables were all elsewhere, businesses run by other people with whom our family traded. This keep was, or could be, self-sufficient, given enough money and enough manpower. Truly, a different world.

"And what is that?" I asked to cover my astonishment, pointing to a tiny shed tucked between the stable and the hall.

"Oh, that be the mews," Gregory replied.

"Mews? You mean, Sir William keeps falcons?"

Gregory looked evasive. "I did not say that, my lady."

I planted my fists on my hips. "No, you didn't, but I am asking you. Does Sir William keep falcons?"

"Well, yes, but—"

"Then I must see them!" I set out across the courtyard. I had told Sir William that my father desired nothing in the world so much as a hawk, and that was true, but I had not told him that I wanted one as well. All my life, I had heard stories of wealthy men and women with their hawks and falcons, and had seen images of them in the tapestries that came through the house in my father's business, but I had never seen a falcon up close. They were said to be terrible, beautiful birds.

Gregory followed behind me, his footsteps quick with worry. "Milady, I think you ought not go in there."

I had reached the mews, my hand on the latch. "Why not?" I challenged him, lady to manservant.

He withered but replied, "Milord would not desire it."

That was all I need to hear. I jerked the door open.

"Gently, milady," Gregory implored in an urgent whisper. "They frighten so easily."

As he spoke I heard the rustle of nervous feathers and so slowed my steps. The shed was very small, just wide enough for the cages on their tables and a space down the middle for one person to walk. Most of the cages were empty, as the stalls in the stable had been, yet another reminder of this keep's fall from prosperity, but two were occupied, and I caught my breath, freezing, at the sight of them.

They were similar in looks but not the same, one being much smaller, about the size of my two fists resting on top of the other. The larger one had feathers of a bluish-gray on its wings and back while the smaller one was a plainer gray. Both had cream-colored breast feathers flecked with brown, cruel-looking yellow talons, and harsh, curved beaks. Both wore leather hoods so I could not see their eyes or the tops of their heads; from their claws dangled long ribbons with small silver bells that jingled when they moved.

Gregory spoke quietly at my shoulder. "The larger one is a lanner hawk, the smaller one a merlin."

"They are beautiful." I could barely frame the words, so lost in admiration was I. Then, "Why are their heads covered?"

"To keep them calm and help them rest during the day," Gregory replied. "But, milady, we really must go. We should not be in here."

"Why not?" My voice was petulant and over-loud even to my ears, and both the falcons bated, flapping their wings and keening in distress.

"Milord is still training them, and they should not be disturbed while he does so." Gregory hovered so close at my side, I thought he might dare to lay a hand on me and pull me out with him. With a regretful glance at the birds, I backed out of the mews and allowed him to shut the door. Only then did he breathe normally again.

"Is it possible, Gregory...." I was suddenly shy about asking the question. "Do you know if one of those falcons is for me?"

He would not raise his eyes from his boots. "Milady, I know it. The merlin is ever a lady's bird. That is why I did not want you to see. For now, milord keeps them here, isolated from all but him, hungry save when he works with them, so that they come to know and trust him and—" He stopped abruptly.

"And what, Gregory?"

"Nothing, milady." He avoided looking at me. In fact, his entire body was leaning away from me. "Nothing. It is only that I have thought of something I ought to be doing just now. I must not neglect my duties."

"No, you must not." I frowned. I did not think forgetting his duties would cause his face to flush pink as it did.

He started back toward the keep. I stared after him, puzzled at his sudden departure. Before he even made it up the stairs, I hurried after him.

"Gregory," I said, my feet stirring the dust. "Please."

The poor fellow turned, bit his lip. "Milady, you know I cannot."

"Even the beggars who come to my father's door need only ask and are given alms. Bread or soup or coin." I could see I was tearing at his heart, and I was sorry for it, but I had no choice. "I am starved for meat, giddy for lack of sleep, mightily abused, and for what cause, I know not. I have never wanted for anything in my life. I do not know what else to do."

Gregory looked around. "My lady, you ask me to lay my head upon the block to fetch so much as a crust for you."

I held out my hands to him. "But why?" I wailed.

"True and perfect love," said another voice from behind me.

Gregory bowed low and fled up the stairs as though the devil himself had just appeared. As far as I was concerned, he had.

"How dare you?" I said, turning to him. "How can you speak of love and behave in this manner?"

He said nothing.

"Have you sent to my father for my clothes yet?"

"Nay."

"When? It is a journey of many hours from here to there, and I cannot go on wearing this dress!"

He gestured vaguely. "It is on toward suppertime. If I send someone now, he will not be back until tomorrow."

I stamped my foot. "It is barely past breakfast. Oh, infuriating rogue! Will you now command the sun?"

"Will it do my bidding any more than you?" he retorted.

I wanted to tear my hair out. I wanted to tear *his* hair out. "Send someone to my father today."

I turned to storm away, intending to go into the keep.

"Don't forget," he said, "you have to clean up the straw in your room."

I spun and glared at him.

He raised his eyebrows. "You don't expect the servants to deal with that mess, do you?"

I swayed slightly. I could not even choose the best words to spit at him.

He walked away from me and then stopped and looked over his shoulder. "Oh, and Kate. Please stop breaking the crockery. I am not a rich man, you know."

I moped on the steps in the shade of the front door. I was not about to clean my room if that was what *he* wanted me to do. Picking at the mud spatters on my hideous dress with broken fingernails, I drowsed in the heat.

A door banged, jolting me out of my doze. I started to my feet, pressing against the wall behind me for support, but my knees wouldn't hold and I plopped back down on my bottom with a grunt. How ridiculous! Was I too weak to stand already?

The servant called Nathaniel came out of the mews carrying a wooden stand, which he carried to the far end of the courtyard. When he set it down, it was about the height of his waist. A few moments later, Sir William emerged wearing a thick leather glove on his left hand and one of the birds perched upon his fist. It was the larger, darker one, that Gregory had called a lanner hawk. It held itself alert and quivering, ready to take flight at any moment. Its bells chimed softly. Sir William set each foot with care as he walked to the perch Nathaniel had placed for the bird.

I leaned forward to see better, moving out of the shadow cast by the door. When that was not enough, I scooted on my bottom to the top step and let my feet drop down, wrapping my arms around my bent knees. It was hot in the direct sun, but I was better able to see. It did not occur to me at first that I could also be seen, and once I did realize it, I decided I did not care if it meant watching the hawk.

With a movement that was as graceful as a dance between them, Sir William swiped his fist next to the perch and the hawk stepped off his hand and onto the wooden stand. I could hear Sir William's voice as he spoke to the hawk, though I could not make out what he was saying. The hawk turned its head, listening but also looking around with bright, fierce eyes.

Sir William turned and walked slowly away from the bird for several long strides. A long, thin line trailed behind him, and I realized it was still attached to the hawk somehow. For its part, the bird watched him intently, its fierce gaze on his every move. When he had reached the length of the line, he turned to face the hawk again. He reached into the pouch at his waist with his right hand and removed something which he placed in his fisted left, the hawk watching carefully the whole time. He raised his fist and called to the bird. It sprang from the perch, flying swift and straight to his fist, where it landed and began to tear with its beak at whatever he held there.

Sir William ambled back to the perch and returned the hawk to the wooden stand. I watched, baking in the sun, as with infinite patience he repeated the action over and over. Every time the hawk left the perch, I was startled anew. It was utterly still, and then it was pure motion.

After a short while, Sir William went with the hawk to the perch and lingered there. I squinted against the sun, trying to ascertain what he was doing. He removed the heavy glove and passed it to Nathaniel, who moved only as close as necessary. His voice drifted toward me on the air, low and soothing, murmuring to the bird words I could not make out. The heat and soft sounds combined with my half-closed lids to lull me into a doze.

I snapped to myself when Nathaniel strode across the courtyard, a length of coiled line in his hands. Something dangled from the end of it, something bulky and fuzzy, about the size of a rat or a small bird.

My eyes darted to Sir William, who stood near the perch with the bird back on his gloved fist, still talking softly to it and stroking its breast feathers. I began to have an idea of what was about to happen.

When Nathaniel stopped and faced his master, I leaned forward, my arms gripping tighter around my shins. An anticipatory stillness settled over the courtyard. Even the hawk was tense, waiting.

Sir William nodded, and Nathaniel uncoiled his line and began to swing it in a long, slow circle. The hawk gathered itself even more tightly, its wings fluttering in anticipation. With a pump of Sir William's fist, the hawk erupted into flight, its tiny bells ringing, the long line trailing behind it as it flew, arrow-true, for the lure that spun around Nathaniel's head. Talons flashed, and as I blinked, bird and lure slammed into the ground in a puff of dust.

The hawk sat proudly atop the lure, glaring, then began to tear at it. Nathaniel took a step back. Sir William walked forward, gathering the line between him and the hawk carefully into his hands, and stood over his bird.

"Well done, my friend," he said, watching it eat. "Well done."

He stooped to take up the bird once more onto his glove. I was surprised that it did not protest, but then I saw it continue to eat from his hand and understood. A reward for a job well done.

"I think that's enough for today, Nathaniel," Sir William said, his voice low but carrying. The servant gathered up the lure, now even more ragged than before, hitched the perch over his shoulder, and headed back to the mews.

"Well, Kate, are you coming down from there or not?"

I blinked. He had not raised his voice at all, had not raised his eyes from the bird on his glove, but his words hit me with full force as though he were right beside me.

I had forgotten, in the joy of watching this beautiful predator, that I was completely exposed here on the steps.

Damn.

I rose with as much dignity as my filthy, ragged dress and state of exhaustion would allow and went slowly down into the courtyard.

"Come," he commanded.

This was unlike the hounds. I wanted so badly to go closer to the hawk, to touch its feathers. Were they silky? Were they soft? But I would not do what he ordered. I remained rooted to the spot.

"What's this, Kate?" he said, smiling, darting his eyes to me. "Afraid?"

I scowled. "Not at all."

"You should be."

Damn him. Damn him for the devil he was. I took a hesitant, sliding step closer.

The bird's head pivoted immediately, tracking my movement. My heart began to race. He was right, I should be afraid. Its beak was as thick as my thumb and looked fit to rip it off. And the talons, sharp as razors where it shifted on his hand. I swallowed thickly.

When I came no closer, Sir William took the three steps necessary to move alongside me, his right arm by my left so that the length of his body was between me and the hawk. I cursed my traitorous body for trembling so.

"He is beautiful," I said, my voice barely a whisper. I told myself it was because I was hot and thirsty.

"Thank you," he said, his voice also low so as not to upset the hawk. "But he is a she."

"Oh." Why did that make my cheeks flush? It must be the sun, the warmth of Sir William standing so close. "Have you had her long?"

"I bought her a few months ago, after my father's death," he said, stroking the feathers of her breast. I longed to do the same but feared to try.

I did not fear to confront him, however. "What of *my* bird?"

His glance flashed like lightning from the hawk to me and back again, but I could not read what I saw there. Was he annoyed? Surprised? Satisfied?

"Your bird is no more ready to be given than you are ready to receive her."

My cheeks heated. "Why?" I snapped. My tone made the lanner hawk restless, but I charged on. "Because her will is not broken? Because she is not as obedient as one of your dogs?"

He shook his head slowly, careful not to disturb the bird as I had. "I won't ever break her will, Kate. When she hunts free, she will hunt as my partner, not my servant. She will return because she wishes to do so. She is no hound following at my heels, hoping for my affection, doing all for my pleasure. She is still a wild thing at heart, and always will be."

Looking at her fierce, bright eyes, it was my turn to shake my head. "I don't believe it. I can't believe it."

"That is your choice."

"She will return," I said, "because you feed her." My stomach made an embarrassing rumble in reply. I watched him struggle against laughter.

Thoughts spun in my head too fast for me to pin down. Men and beasts, dogs and hawks, predators and prey.

In the dark center of the hawk's clear, blue eye, I saw the memory of its attack on the lure. The swift, sure, instant death it was capable of dealing out. Feathers and blood and talons.

"Excuse me, Sir William."

To my surprise, he made no parting comment as I staggered up the steps and into the keep.

When I had dragged myself up to the little chamber in the tower, I found a broom and some empty sacks waiting for me.

I could hear his mocking voice in the empty space. *"You don't expect the servants to deal with that mess, do you?"*

Moving slowly, I swept the straw into a rough pile in the center of the room, placed the sacks on top of it, and lay down. At least I slept for a little while before he was nudging me awake with his boot.

"Kate," he was saying, "come, come and see who is here." He hardly waited for me to open my eyes, hauling me up from the floor and brushing straw from my kirtle as though it were worth doing. I let him, not minding his hands.

"Who is here?" I repeated his words, hoping for an answer.

"You will see." Taking hold of my hand, he pulled me off down the stairs, ignoring my protests that my feet in their silken slippers could scarce find purchase on the worn stone.

As we emerged into the hall, I yanked my hand free and paused, hoping to regain some of my composure if not my dignity. I hoped, too, to see one of my father's men with a trunk of my clothes. Truly, I could imagine no sight more welcome. But I did not recognize the neatly dressed man standing in the center of the hall, his hands behind his back, nor the two younger men with him, surrounded by large boxes they had clearly just set down. Atop the boxes were bulky shapes that could only be kirtles wrapped in muslin.

The men, seeing Sir William enter, bowed low.

I hesitated, almost afraid to approach. Could it be that these were meant for me? At last, at long last....

Sir William said, "Now, Kate, it seems to me you have some objection to this kirtle you are wearing."

I tore my eyes from the tailor and his assistants. "Yes. Yes, of course I do."

He waved a hand at the men. "The tailor has arrived from Coventry and awaits your leisure."

I thought it best that I should not run. Instead, I took Sir William's proffered hand and allowed him to escort me to the tailor. The tailor bowed low again, first to Sir William and then to me.

"Your lordship," he said in a voice as crisp as the tailored pleats on his gown. "Your ladyship. I am speechless with the honor of having been sought out to fashion these *habillements* for you."

I glanced at Sir William, eyebrows raised, but he showed no reaction to the man's ridiculous speech.

"And I can well see that the lady is as glorious as the kirtles which you have ordered for her, my lord," the tailor went on, with a sly smile toward Sir William. This remark bought him only a frown, and he hurried to direct the apprentices to bring forth a long, flat box. "Firstly," he said, "here is the headdress your worship did bespeak."

With a flourish, the lads produced a headpiece such as one of the ladies at the king's court at Westminster might have worn. It was the very height of the latest fashion, and *height* was the very perfect word for it.

"Oh!" I said, unable to conceive of other words. "Oh!" The tall cone of the headdress was a deep russet silk embroidered with gold thread, shining like a maple tree in its autumnal glory. The point rose a foot or more from the crown, and from its tip cascaded a length of gossamer gold veil that seemed to move with a life of its own. My hands went out for it.

I had never been offered something so beautiful in my life. And consequently, I had never wanted anything so badly in my life.

"Nay, it is all wrong," Sir William said. "It's like a silken sword. Fie, away with it."

"No!" I cried, lunging at the apprentice holding the headpiece, grabbing his arm. "Its fashion suits, and many great ladies and gentlewomen wear caps such as these."

"When you are *gentle*," Sir William said, "you may have one too, and not till then."

None too gently, he removed my hand from the apprentice's arm and waved him away. "Where is the dress, tailor?"

The two apprentices unwrapped one of the muslin bundles. I was wary now. After being denied the headdress, I had no certainty of gaining this kirtle. But surely, even if he disliked it, he would let me have it if only to get me out of the ruins of my wedding dress?

I almost could not bear to look.

The kirtle was the same russet silk as the headdress, trimmed with a wide, gold braid and, Lord help me, were those pearls? The square, plunging neckline would show a lovely chemise underneath. Once this wedding chemise had been washed, it would look very well. Scarcely daring to breathe, I took a step closer. It also had a stomacher, that insert of stiffened fabric that flattened one's torso and made one's bosom appear fuller and more rounded. It had false sleeves, long swathes of extra fabric draped from the shoulders like a partial cape that would sway beautifully when I danced. The kirtle was cut to the highest fashion and made of the finest materials. I could have been presented without shame to King Richard himself.

"Oh, God 'a mercy," Sir William cried. "What is this here? Fit for a vulgar masque, not a true lady, not for my wife! What is this? What is this?" He jabbed his finger accusingly at the garment, stabbing at the depth of the neckline, the stomacher, the extra fabric around the sleeves.

"You bade me make the dress properly and well, sir, and so I did," the tailor said, wringing his hands. "I have made it to suit the fashion and what would best suit your gracious lady."

"Speak not so," Sir William replied, yanking the dress from the apprentices and flinging it to the floor. "I did bid you make it, but I did not bid you ruin it."

"Sir," I said, scooping the precious thing into my arms and moving away from him, "I never saw a better-fashioned kirtle, nor one more elegant, more pleasing, more commendable."

"It is none such," he insisted, grabbing at the dress.

"Nay!" I yelled. "For once, you will listen to me! Why won't you listen to me? Why doesn't anyone ever care what *I* want?" My heart was racing, flying, fast as a striking hawk. The tailor fled, cowering with his apprentices near their boxes like soldiers behind battlements. My voice shook as much as my hands, but I forced it out. "I will speak what is in my heart lest it break."

Sir William stared but I could not read his expression. "It seems to me you have never had trouble speaking your mind," he said at last. "Whether that is the truth of your heart is another matter entirely."

He was so smug. He thought he knew everything. He thought he knew *me*. I had never been so angry. I could scarce see.

He took hold of the kirtle with both hands. I would not relinquish it. The tailor, his handiwork in peril, grew bold. "Sir! My lady! Please!"

He hovered between us, his hands fluttering over the precious kirtle.

Sir William jerked and I felt the fabric give. "No!" I screamed and "No!" again as, with another yank and a loud rip, the dress came apart in my hands. I sank to my knees, the ruined gown in my arms.

The tailor leaned down to take the pieces of the kirtle from me. "It was not finished fine," he said gently, as though to a child. "It was only half-stitched so as to be fit to your ladyship. It may yet be mended."

"What does it matter?" I murmured, my words lost in the whisper of silk sliding out of my hands.

Tailor, apprentices, dress, headpiece—all rushed out. I did not move.

In the sudden silence, Sir William crouched before me. He looked at me for a long time before he spoke. "Come now, Kate. This matters not. It is the mind that makes the body rich, and as the sun breaks through the darkest clouds, so honor peers through the meanest clothes. Do you see, Kate?"

His words poured over me, but I felt nothing. I made no reaction.

"Is the jay more precious than the lark because his feathers are more beautiful?"

More birds.

"Of course not, Kate, and neither are you the worse for your dress."

I shook my head, not disagreeing. "Leave me."

He remained.

"Leave me, I say."

"I will have you understand."

"I understand your cruelty. Go away."

At last he rose and left me.

If I had needed escape in the morning, I needed it a thousand times more after that. One of the lads directed me to the west of the keep, to the pasture where the horses grazed. The wide expanse was lush with grass and flowers. The hand-laid wall of native stone that bordered it began not far from the wall of the castle and ran away from me toward the river that formed the moat. It was so long that I could not see where it ended. Moss spotted the rough stones, and along the top, puddles lingered in little hollows where birds came to bathe and splash. Their songs and chirps filled the air. The three horses grazed, a little apart from each other but in company together. The serenity of the scene imbued me with an immediate sense of peace. It was exactly what I needed.

The fellow must have trusted my word that I could not saddle a horse and assumed I was even less likely to ride one bareback. The wall was chest-high on any ordinary horse, though Sir William's charger probably could have walked over it. I smiled to myself. Perhaps not. I sized him up honestly, in the clear light of day. He was big but not that big, and in any event, he seemed disinclined to flee.

I plucked a bunch of daisies from the base of the wall and clambered up. What use caring for my dress now? For a time, I sat on the wall and watched the horses move slowly about the pasture, my hands idly twisting the daisies into a chain. The fresh air, the quiet of the place were good for me, and I felt much of the anger and confusion of the last few days sliding away.

I have no idea how long it was before Conveyance took notice of my presence and ambled over to greet me. He put his muzzle in my hands and tore away the daisy chain, then snuffled my palms looking for a real treat. "Are you seeking an apple, sir?" I asked, laughing, and rubbed behind his jawbone. "I have none, alas, for if I had one, I would have eaten it myself."

He pushed against me, whickering, and I continued to scratch his face and ears. "I have never had a horse of my own, you know," I told him. "You are my very first, and I intend to spoil you greatly."

He blew a breath out at me.

"Well, yes, I am not beginning very well if I neglect you now. But you see, I am not being treated very well myself at present and, therefore, I cannot spoil you yet. There will come a time, I promise you. I will sort this out."

I wanted to laugh at myself. I was talking to a horse! But I was friendless here, and there was something so easy, so comforting in speaking my thoughts out loud and in knowing he would not judge, would not say something sharp or witty or combative. Conveyance was the one creature here I did not have to fight with. "How did I get into this predicament?" I traced the blaze of white on his face. "In fact, it is not so different from the manner in which you arrived here. Bought and paid for, and that's the truth. That's the way of marriage for wealthy maids, Conveyance."

The horse snorted into my skirt, his breath hot and wet in my lap. "Well, I suppose you can't make it any worse," I said, laughing. Indeed, I was as lighthearted as I had felt in days.

"And yet Sir William's behavior is unaccountable. I do not understand him at all. When we met, he seemed determined to think the best of me, despite knowing that everyone in Whitelock thought me the worst sort of woman. And now, any show of kindness is gone. He seems a very devil himself, and even his servants fear him. If he is not mad, and I cannot believe that he is, then I cannot see any purpose in his actions!

"But what if my father won't see his error and take me back?" I paused, searching Conveyance's eyes for a reply. "You are right. Why would I want to go back to my father? Is it any better there? Perhaps. Oh, I don't know! At least I understand my father. I understand Blanche." I combed my fingers through the long, coarse hairs of Conveyance's mane. He leaned against me, heavy and warm. Only his steady, soothing presence could have mellowed me enough to speak so calmly of my family. "All my father ever wanted was a son, you see. What else does a wealthy merchant want but a son to bring into the business, to leave all of his wealth to? Thus, you see, I was a dreadful disappointment. Not only was I a girl, but in bringing about my mother's death, I delayed his getting a son that much longer, what with the mourning time and then marrying again. And then Blanche arrived, and my shortcomings were only that much more glaring. She was mild where I was wild, sweet where I was sharp, content where I was demanding, easy where I was clever, fair where I was ordinary...." My voice trailed off, the familiar litany too painful to continue. Instead of my wonted hot anger, it only opened an aching wound of loss, of unfairness, of bitterness. I never indulged these feelings. They were hallmarks of weakness. Shuddering, I sighed into Conveyance's neck, hugging him close. From the slow cadence of his breathing, he might have been sleeping. I sighed again, trapped under a dozing horse. "'Why can't you be more like your sister?'" I murmured, twining my fingers tightly in his mane. "They all wanted me to be like her. And there were times, my friend, I wanted that too."

A footstep ground on a patch of dirt and pebbles behind me, and I twitched in my place. Conveyance jerked his head up and flung it over my other shoulder to see who was there. I turned at the waist.

"Sir William," I said.

"My lady," he said. He had an apple in one hand, half-eaten. He seemed to be out for a stroll, or perhaps he was looking for me. Maybe it was one disguised as the other.

Conveyance had his eyes on the apple, the treat I had not been able to bring him. He gave a little whinny and moved closer to Sir William, ears and nose forward, pressing his chest against the wall. I tried to ignore the fact that my hunger urged a similar response.

"How long have you been there?" I demanded, falling back on anger.

Sir William looked around. "Here? On my own land, observing what passes? Ah, well, to be precise, I was not here whilst I served as page and squire—"

If I had been standing, I would have stamped my foot. As it was, I cut him off. "I mean, how long have you been there, just now, while I have been *here*?"

"Oh, that. A few minutes, I should say. Why? Is your conversation with your horse terribly secret?"

His tone, his smile, invited me to laugh. I would not allow myself to. "As a matter of fact, it is." Even as I said it, I realized how ridiculous that sounded.

"Well then, I shall leave you to it." He tossed the apple in the air, caught it, and turned to go. Then he looked back over his shoulder. "I do have one question though. Perhaps Conveyance has the answer."

"What?" I snapped, in no mood to be mocked.

He turned fully to face me. "I have been wondering why you care."

"Why I—?"

"Aye. All these people who scorn and revile you, you expend so much effort to scorn and revile them in turn. And yet it appears to me that you consider all of God's creation, including poor Conveyance here and my humble self, to be entirely beneath you, and so I have been wondering why it matters at all what such lowly creatures think of you?" He took a bite of the apple. "My lady."

"You are one to speak of scorn, sir!" I swung my legs over the wall and jumped down. "I have only to look at the way you treat your servants—nay! I need only look at the way you behave to me! You are high-handed as a king! You care nothing for my feelings, my comfort, my health…. You would starve me to death—"

"You will not starve, Kate," he said calmly.

"—you will not let me sleep, you keep me in this awful, filthy dress—"

"Yes," he agreed, "it is quite an awful dress."

"—but you deny me a new one! You do not treat me as a proper wife!"

"Why should I? You do not act as one."

"And why should I? You did not properly marry me! You left me there, waiting at the church for the whole village to mock!"

"And I ask again, why do you care what those folk think?"

I stopped, breathing hard. "You gave them what they wanted—a figure of fun. Kathryn abandoned. It was what they expected all along. No one would marry Kathryn the shrew, not for any price." I had to be careful or I might cry, and I would not cry, not in front of him.

He frowned down at the apple in his hand. "You may be right about that, and I am sorry to have caused you that pain. But I ask you this: how many times have *you* given them what they expected, Kathryn? And when were you going to stop?"

He walked over to the wall. Conveyance leaned eagerly across, reaching for the hoped-for treat. Sir William held out the apple, and my horse, the traitor, took it, crunching away happily, slobbering on the wall as Sir William rubbed between his ears.

He did not look at me again before walking away. I was glad of it.

That night, alone in my room, I undid all of Margaret's carefully braided plaits. I had never done my own hair—such a pampered life I had led!—and so with meticulous fingers, I inspected how she had done them and practiced until I learned how to do them myself. As a married woman—ha!—my hair should properly be under a headdress as well as done up, but since I did not even have a decent kirtle to my name, a headdress seemed to be too much to ask.

Still, I had never been so proud of myself. And at least my hair was neat and tidy again.

Next, I set about to remove the tattered train and useless angel sleeves from my kirtle.

Not an easy thing to do without a knife or any other tool. Even more difficult without removing the kirtle from my body, which I was not going to do in case Sir William happened to walk into my room unannounced as he had done before.

But he did not, that night.

Exhausted as I was by dawn, I felt a little better. I had accomplished something all on my own. And I had calmed enough to consider that, if nothing else, Sir William had to keep me alive for my dowry. If I died of starvation, I was certain my father would never hand over the gold.

He was too good a merchant to carry through on a broken contract.

Chapter Twelve

The sun was hot and high when I woke with a cramp in my neck and a crease in my temple from leaning against the edge of the table. The straw ruins of my bed had been swept up and taken away, though the bed frame remained, taunting me. As I staggered to my feet, the objects on the table rattled against one another and I put up my hands to keep them from falling. In my sleepy state, it took me a moment to realize that the serving pieces— the ones I had been tossing down the stairs in the general direction of my husband's head—had been replaced. Beside a small, deep bowl for washing up, there was a pitcher full of fresh water and a small, plain cup.

There was even a towel. Rough, and homespun, but clean.

I washed and drank, and then decided I'd stay in my room. If he wanted to fight, let him come to me.

Hours passed before he popped his head in through the door. "There you are," he said, cheerful as could be. "I was wondering where you'd got to."

I gestured, a small circle of my hand as the heat and lack of food made me drowsy. "Where could I go?"

He tipped his head. "Run home to your father, perhaps?"

I grimaced. "You know I wouldn't. That's why you can treat me as you do."

He grinned. "I don't know what you mean," he said, walking into the room and holding out his hand. "Come, let's go for a ride."

I stared at his hand, then looked up at his grinning face. "Oh, why not?" I said and took his hand, letting him pull me to my feet.

We emerged from the keep into the softening light of the late afternoon and waited on the steps for the horses to be readied. I could not find a place to put my hands where I did not have to touch my rumpled, filthy, ruined wedding kirtle. It was a constant reminder of my situation and I could not bear to wear it any longer, but what choice did I have? Go about in my chemise? Might as well walk about in naught but my skin. I closed my eyes and pictured myself in the glorious russet kirtle the tailor had brought with him. I imagined the feel of the silk on my skin, the soft rustle of the skirts as I moved, the swish of the false sleeves trailing behind me....

Hooves striking hollow on the ground and the squeaky rub of leather saddles and straps alerted me and made me open my eyes. My Conveyance was led forth first, his coat gleaming like velvet in the sun. The lightness of his step, the arch of his neck, the fineness of his features all marked him as a steed of quality, but more than his worth in gold, there was this: Sir William had said he was my wedding present, back before he had turned my life into this sleepless nightmare. This beautiful, dancing, joyful creature belonged to me.

Sir William stepped down toward the grooms and I was glad of it because my eyes had filled with tears. God, what a weak thing I had become after being denied comforts for a couple of days.

But as my hand came up to wipe at my foolish eyes, Sir William was suddenly there in front of me, lifting my chin with his fingers so I could not avoid him. With the other hand, he touched, very gently, the single tear that was coursing down my cheek. "Kate," he said quietly, "why do you weep?"

I could not answer. I knew if I spoke, I would burst into real tears. I gulped a breath and looked back at my horse. My Conveyance. What an awful thing to call him. The joke calmed me. I found I could speak.

"That he—that such beauty should be mine," I said.

I expected some quick mocking remark, but Sir William just looked at me for a long moment, saying nothing. Then he dropped his hands from my face and moved back, just a bit. He took my hand and raised it, but instead of leaving a courtly kiss on the back of my hand as I anticipated, he turned my hand over and pressed a kiss into my palm, then folded my hand closed around it.

Before I could fathom this unaccountable act, he had turned away

to give the horses bits of apple. He seemed to have forgotten all
about me.

Had I not been tired beyond exhaustion, hungry beyond
faintness, and confused beyond words, I would have enjoyed that ride
very much.

We were alone in the world, Sir William and I and our horses,
alone in a green, sloping countryside bathed in golden light that
promised to linger for many hours yet. At times we rode side by side,
at times one after the other, but as much as I could make my poor
tired mind focus on anything besides staying in the saddle, I struggled
to understand why Sir William was treating me so.

After a long, invigorating gallop, we came to a stop beside a swift-
flowing stream and dismounted to allow the horses to rest and drink.
Sir William took my horse's reins from me, surely to keep me from
leaping back into the saddle and running away. The thought made me
laugh to myself, for while I could tell very well which direction we
had come from, where would I run to? Did he truly think I would flee
back to my father? Even under these circumstances, I knew I would
not.

When the horses had finished at the water, I crept to the edge
myself. Golden light danced on the water, dazzling my eyes, so I
closed them and listened to the voice of the river instead. Behind me,
leather straps creaked and eased as Sir William loosened the girths on
the horse's saddles, speaking to them in low tones. I was soothed. I
was light-headed. I sat quickly on the rock beneath me.

"What are you doing?"

His voice was like a chill draft in a warm room, or a scratchy burr
you can't locate in your clothes. I opened my eyes. "I am—Nothing. I
am going to get a drink of water myself."

I leaned forward, but the rock on which I sat was at least a foot
over the river. I would have to lie flat upon it and scoop dripping
handfuls up to my mouth to get a drink here. Not far away, a chain of
rocks led out into the current, where I could squat beside a slight fall
of water. Perfect for drinking.

"Kate...."

I took pleasure in ignoring him. Besides, I had to concentrate on where to place my feet in their silk slippers on the water-slick rocks. How many new things had this proper, town-bred girl done in the two days since leaving home?

Two days? Was it three? It was hard to say as I'd neither slept properly nor eaten since then.

But water. Water would fill my empty belly for a while and cool my skin and help me to face him....

The stone beneath my foot wobbled as I shifted my weight forward, tipping enough to slosh water over its surface and soak my shoe with freezing water coming straight down from the Welsh mountains. Gasping, I tried to pull my foot back—a mistake, I realized even as I was doing it, but too late. There was no room on the angled stone where my left foot rested for both feet to safely reside, and I perched, waving my arms, searching for a place to land my flailing foot.

The only place was in the riverbed.

Down went my foot, calf-deep in the frigid current. I cried out in shock and again as my foot slid on the slick river bed. My legs split like the limbs of a draughtsman's compass, and I tumbled into the water, drenched up to my shoulders. The river pulled at me with cold fingers, tugging at my dress, my hair, my skin, urging me to come along with it to wherever it was going.

"Kate!"

Sir William had bounded across the stones lining the riverbed and was leaning over me, concern writ all over his face. "Are you all right?"

Fighting the water and the multitude of stones and pebbles under my legs, I managed to pull my legs together. I was not hurt, not even bruised as far as I could tell. No, just sitting in the middle of a cold river on a hot day. And I still hadn't had a drink.

I had thought it couldn't get worse.

Helplessly, I burst out laughing.

Sir William scooped me out of the water, his arms tight around my waist—I was too weak with laughter and exhaustion to help much—and dragged me to the riverbank. When he dropped me down in a patch of sunlight, I rolled onto my back and squinted up at him, still giggling. "At least now my dress is washed," I said.

Without a word, he crossed to where the horses were grazing in the thick grass, shaking the wet off his sleeves. In a moment, he came back with a waterskin from his horse's gear.

"You might have asked," he said.

"Sorry," I said, taking the skin from him.

He walked away to sit on a large rock by the river, leaving me in my warm, sunny patch. He sat watching me thoughtfully as I sat watching him. I pulled my knees up to my chest and wrapped my arms around them, a tight, defensive ball like a hedgehog. Except a hedgehog puts the spines on his back out to the enemy. I sat facing out. Facing him.

The horses pulled grass and chewed. Around us, a thousand invisible insects went about their noisy living.

"What were you thinking, running away?"

So he knew. Gregory must have told him, even at the risk to his own skin for letting me slip away. More fool me, for thinking I had an ally in the fellow, compassionate though he seemed.

I made a face. "Didn't get very far, did I, so what does it matter?"

"You think you're safe? Do you know where you are?"

I blinked, not quite understanding the question. "I believe I am in England. Although I think I saw Wales from the top of your tower."

"Exactly," he said, as though that were all that needed to be said.

"Exactly what?" I demanded.

Sir William turned his eyes upon the distant hills when he spoke. "Henry Tudor will return, bringing war. When he does, he will come through Wales, the land of his forebears."

"Henry Tudor is in Brittany," I scoffed. Not everyone had been happy when King Richard put his nephew aside with that claim of illegitimacy, and those who sought his downfall—and sought to rise to power with a different king—supported Henry Tudor's claim.

"France," he said. "He was finally convinced it was time to leave Brittany, and he is now in France. Things are moving quickly, and not all in King Richard's favor." He dropped his eyes to me, that sharp, blue gaze that sent sparks through my unwilling skin. "Tudor attempted a landing the year before last, in October, or had you not heard, immured in your quiet little town?"

I decided to ignore his disparaging tone. After all, he was the one who had plucked me out of that quiet little town. "I heard. It was during the awful rains that fall, and he never did land. The Duke of Buckingham was executed for rebelling against King Richard in Tudor's name."

"And what if he does succeed in landing this summer? Or what if he already has? What would become of you, a woman alone walking about the countryside?"

I hadn't thought about that. Still.

"So I should stay with you regardless of what you do to me rather than risk being accosted by a rebel army passing through your lands?"

"That, or brigands. Yes."

I wanted so badly to think. There had to be an answer to what he was saying. Sadly, my exhausted mind would not work properly.

But armies and brigands would do worse to a woman than quarrel with her and refuse her food. He was right about that.

His horse took a step forward, the strike of its hoof like a stone dropping from height. The drone of insects sang like a lullaby. I did not want to engage him in conversation. I did hate him, after all. If only I could have ignored him, I could have slept peacefully, letting the sun bake the damp out of my sodden dress. But there was something about him, that burr-hidden-in-your-clothes quality that demanded my attention. "How is it that you know so much about Tudor and his rebels?"

"I learned a great deal while I was at court. Naturally, everyone there is quite concerned about what Tudor is planning, when he might land and where and who might join him. And one hears rumors...."

He looked off toward the Welsh border again and grew silent. My eyes drifted closed, and I watched the play of dark and red shadows on the back of my lids, not quite asleep but not quite awake, waiting for him to prod me back to the world.

"My demesne, this keep and these lands," he said, "this is all very old."

I opened my eyes with a sigh and looked over at him. Was I supposed to respond to something so manifest?

"There have been improvements, of course. But parts of the keep were erected when the first King Edward conquered Wales and gave it to his son."

A very long time ago. Yet Wales remained restive and rebellious, a captured principality, not a conquered one. Henry Tudor claimed the blood of the Welsh as well as the English royal families, though there hadn't been a true king in Wales in hundreds of years.

"My family received it from King Henry the Fourth," he continued.

"You are for Lancaster, then." That was why he knew so much about Henry Tudor, the last scion of the House of Lancaster.

He grinned. "No one is openly for Lancaster now, if they are wise. And I just returned from doing fealty to King Richard of the House of York."

I waited, stretching out my legs at last, unfolding from my defensive hedgehog posture. Not that I trusted him more, but the cold damp had pooled in my lap and I was starting to shiver.

"But my father always said, 'We are men of Lancaster,' and said it with pride," he went on. "You are for York, I suppose."

"Of course," I said. "Why wouldn't I be? My father prospered in the peaceful years of King Edward's reign, and a York king wears the crown at this moment, so why would I not?"

"Your name, Kathryn, and your sister's, Blanche. Both were wives of the Duke of Lancaster, years ago."

I looked down at the water rushing past, at the white shapes it made where it leaped over a stone. I opened my mouth, then shut it. He had no right to know my story. Still. "I was named for my mother, who died in birthing me." I swallowed past a lump in my throat that felt like a peach stone. I never spoke, rarely even thought, of her, the unknown woman whose death had altered my history. "Blanche is an old family name on her mother's side, going back to a woman who had been a maid in the Duchess of Lancaster's service. But we do not move in noble circles. We are—we were—safe enough in our little town where no one cared for York or Lancaster so long as there was peace."

Sir William plucked a tall weed and twirled it through his fingers, staring at the tufted top. "When York defeated Henry the Sixth, back in '61, my father did not get involved in the fight. He had much to lose, and King Edward was young and strong, so much better than the weak old king. My father hoped, like so many, that the new king would bring peace to the realm. But ten years later, my father joined the plot to restore Lancaster to the throne. I told him...." He began shredding the top of the weed, tiny seeds falling to the ground. "I told him it was a mistake. I asked him not to. But I was only a boy, why would he listen to me? And for a time, he was right. For a time, they succeeded. King Edward was put to flight and my father had a share in the victory and the spoils, such as he'd never had."

"But King Edward always won," I whispered, not expecting to be heard.

"Yes, I told him that." He threw the weed, now stripped of its head, and brushed his hands together, wiping away the seeds, wiping away the past. "I told him the old king was mad, not fit to rule. I told him that having the queen and the prince ruling in his place would just lead to more fighting among the great lords, and that King Edward would return...." He smiled briefly, bitterly. "Yes, well. I had little satisfaction in being proved right. He lost everything then. King Edward stripped him of his lands and all his money. We had nothing."

I frowned. "But...."

"One good thing about a usurper is that he needs allies. When King Richard pushed Edward's son aside and stole his crown, he returned my father's lands to him. And upon his death, confirmed it in me. Contingent on my support in the region, naturally."

"Naturally?" I repeated, not really understanding.

"Tudor," he said. "I told you. Henry Tudor is above all a Welshman. When he returns from exile to make another attempt at the throne—and he will, and it will be soon—he will land in Wales to gather support and he will march through these lands toward London. Richard expects men like me to help stop him."

I held that thought in my mind, turning it. Then I asked, "What will you do?"

Again, that bitter smile. "I do not know."

It was nearly dark when we trotted back through the gates into the courtyard. Two of the servants came out with torches to see to the horses.

Sir William dismounted first and came to stand beside my horse, waiting to help me down. After my last experience, I hesitated. I had no desire to be dumped on the ground like so much baggage once more. Yet I was exhausted and weak, and he was standing right there. How could I refuse? I kicked my feet free of the stirrups and suddenly I was sliding down into his arms. For the space of two breaths, I sank into him. I allowed myself to be glad of his strength. I leaned into his chest, my head tucked under his chin. His heart beat slow and steady beneath my cheek. I remembered his words to Gregory, in explanation of his behavior: *true and perfect love*. For a moment, I was comforted. For a moment, I felt safe.

Only for a moment.

I pushed away from him and went into the keep without a word.

The heat of the day clung to my room. I tried to lie down on the ropes of the bed frame, but that was like an instrument of torture, cutting and binding and threatening to throw me over. I sat up against the cool stone wall as I had the night before, but I was so worried that *he* would come in and disturb me that I couldn't rest. Every whisper, every footfall below, had me jerking alert.

At last, he had me so tired I could no longer sleep. A victory for him indeed.

So I sat awake, listening instead for any sounds in the courtyard that would tell me a horseman had been sent to my father, or was returning.

I listened to my heart beating in silence for a very long time.

Some space of time later—I could not tell how long—voices drifted up the turns of the stairs like ancient ghosts, and I followed them down. At home, in my father's house, I had become accustomed to avoiding the squeaky wooden boards of steps and landings. Here, I needed to be cautious of patches of stone worn smooth as ice or rounded deep as cups. Thus, creeping quietly was not an issue, but staying upright was.

I paused in the archway of the main hall, letting its shadow conceal me. Sir William sat at the table on the dais, facing the other door from which Gregory and a couple of the other lads were bringing food.

My mouth filled and my stomach clenched. Food. From where I stood, I could not smell it or even see it clearly, but plates piled with something set on a table were enough to put my innards into turmoil.

Sir William took up a small brown sphere and tore it in two—oh, bread!—and set half of it down. The other half, he spread with something soft and pale, butter or cheese.

I bent over, squeezing my arms into my gut to halt the pangs.

When I straightened again, he was alone. Eating.

I plotted a mad dash into the room, pondering how much I could grab and cram into my mouth before he could stop me.

Putting the bread down on the plate, he shifted in his chair. His entire posture was alert, listening.

I froze. Had I made a sound? Had he noticed my presence? What would he do this time?

When he turned his head to look around the hall, I caught a glimpse of his arrow-sharp nose, his angular cheek, his piercing eyes, all topped by that tousled hair. Just as when I had first seen him leaning on his horse in the courtyard of the inn, the sight of him gave me a shiver. I jumped back, pressing up against the cold stone. Yes, he was handsome. Yes, he made my heart skip. But he was maddening, infuriating, horrible! And he wouldn't let me eat!

The chair creaked. I peeked around the corner again. He had settled back to his meal.

I drew an unsteady breath, watching him. All right, then, he was too alert. A mad dash for food was not going to work.

I lingered in the archway, unable to tear myself away from the sight of food although it was torment to watch him eat.

He lifted the bread to his mouth, opened his lips—how I watched every movement he made, like a hawk sighting a vole for its dinner— but then he paused, looked at the bread, and set it back down on the plate.

Why?

I almost screamed the word and had to clamp a hand over my mouth. If only one of us might eat, then eat he should. He must!

He covered his mouth with one hand, staring at the plates before him, shaking his head so slightly I wondered if he was even aware of the motion. Then he leaned back in the chair, pressing the heels of both hands into his eyes and letting out a sigh.

Perhaps he was tired? If he was, it was his own fault. Riding through the night, keeping me up with no sleep, tormenting me all the day long....

He muttered something, so faint I could not hear it. Only a few words reached me. "Who knows...." He shook his head again. "I wish he'd tell me."

What? He wished someone would tell him what?

"Gregory," he called, his hands still over his eyes.

I froze. Straining to hear what he was saying to himself, I had crept forward out of my hiding place and was out in the hall, exposed.

As Gregory hurried into the room, I scampered back into the dim archway.

"Take this away."

"But, sir," Gregory protested, "you've hardly eaten anything. Are you certain?"

"Yes. I've no stomach this evening."

Gregory bowed and began stacking the dishes in his arms. "Yes, sir," he said, backing away. "Very well, sir."

I watched as my only chance at food disappeared through the other archway.

Sir William dropped his hands to the arms of his chair with another huge sigh.

I frowned, not comprehending. What reason did *he* have to be so despondent? He had food at his beck and call, and a bed to sleep in if he chose, and no one tormenting him every moment of the day.

I slunk back up to my room and curled up in my little hedgehog ball on the far side of the room, staring at the door, waiting for the next assault.

Under cover of midnight darkness, I made my way back to the kitchen. Though the cook might be a demon in the service of the devil, that demon had to sleep sometime.

My greatest fear was that, suspecting I might try this, Sir William might have ordered the kitchen locked up at night. But when I tried the latch, it lifted with ease. The room was scarcely any less bright, for the fires had only been banked, not extinguished, but it was positively serene by comparison. All the pots and kettles had been washed and were neatly stowed below the tables or on shelves lining the walls. Knives lay in rows on a table, gleaming and freshly sharpened. Fat loaves of tomorrow's bread rested under cloths near the window, casting a faintly yeasty smell over everything.

I knew well enough that there would be at least one boy sleeping in here, tasked with minding the fires and preparing the morning's porridge during the night, so I moved as silently as I could toward the back of the kitchen and the large opening I was sure signaled the pantry and food.

Food.

I'd take anything at this point, even slops out of the pig's bucket.

Hadn't Gregory said something about a pig?

I was nearly there—I could see the shadowy shapes of jars and canisters and sacks and barrels—when I tripped and went down, hard, on one knee.

Biting my lip to keep from cursing, I rolled onto my back, clutching at my right knee, eyes squeezed shut against sudden tears. Pulling a deep breath in through my nose, I collected myself and sat up.

My kirtle had a lovely new rip and my knee was bleeding. Wonderful.

Worse, though, a rattling snort told me the kitchen boy was stirring.

Panicked, I scooted toward the pantry opening. I had not come this far to leave with nothing. On a low shelf just inside the entry was a bowl of apples and one of pears. I grabbed blindly and scrambled, half bent over, back to the kitchen door.

I gulped down the pear core and all—Oh sweet! Oh soft!—and started working on the apple as I headed back to the keep.

Head down, satisfied with my little victory and checking on my scraped and bloodied knee, I walked right into Sir William.

Naturally.

He caught me by the arms as I staggered backward and kept me upright. In the half-light cast by the knife-blade moon and the stars, his eyes and teeth were bright, his features shadowed. Heat from his hands traveled up my arms straight to my core, unsettling me more than stumbling had.

"Aren't you up and about early this morning?" he said.

"Morning?" I stammered around a mouthful of apple. "It's the middle of the night."

"Maybe so, maybe not. Looks like full day to me."

I tried to back away from him. "As you say, sir. If you'll please let me pass...."

"By all means, if you'll tell me where you've been."

I gritted my teeth, sifting through a dozen sharp replies. "I've been for a walk."

"A walk."

"Yes."

"By yourself."

"Yes. I've done it before, you know."

"Oh yes, I do know. I just can't imagine where—"

"Why? Because it's the *middle of the night?*"

He smiled and shook a finger at me. "Oh, good. Oh, very good." He released my arms and stepped aside. I was suddenly cold without his touch and tucked my hands inside the long sleeves of my dress. Nodding an abrupt courtesy, I went past him toward the keep.

I don't know what made me turn around. Maybe it was the moonlight, the safety of darkness. But before I could think the better of it, I said, "Why didn't you come to the church?"

He stood silent, staring down at the dusty ground. I took a step closer, wanting to confront him, wanting to make him look at me. "You said you were sorry you caused me that pain, so why did you do it?"

He moved closer to me as well but slowly, like a man approaching a skittish horse. "Do you remember what it was like... of course you do. Shut your eyes. Think back to that day. Think of your father. Think of the priest. The people there, waiting."

Against my will, my eyes drifted closed and I did what he urged. I went back to that day in my mind. My father, fairly twitching with his eagerness to be rid of me. Master Greenwood and Master Lawry, eyeing each other like roosters ready to fight. The crowd pressing near outside the church, smirking behind their hands, all gloating because the fool knight had been tricked into taking me for money.

My breathing quickened and my face heated up. My hands balled into fists, ragged nails cutting into my palms. My shoulders rose up to my ears. I wanted to strike someone, anyone. I wanted to—

"There, you see?"

My eyes flew open to see Sir William before me, close enough to punch... close enough to kiss. He put his hands on my tense shoulders and squeezed gently, soothingly. "Had I been there, you would have had no choice. With all of those eyes watching, with all of the demands of family and church, there would have been no question of not going forward." His hands stilled, their weight heavy on me, pressing me down, rooting me in the earth. "If you were going to come with me, I wanted it to be on account of your own will."

His words were as heavy as his hands. I tried to make light of it. "A woman will have her will," I joked, but my voice was feeble and shaky.

He gave my shoulders a final squeeze and slid his hands down my arms. Where our fingers met, they held and seemed not to want to part. The rest of me longed to follow, melting toward him as he drew away. "You should get some rest," he said.

Simple words, yet sufficient to flare my temper once again. "You may have forgotten, sir, but I have no bed!"

He spun on his heel, and while still walking backward, spread his arms as wide as his grin. "All that has happened since you have been here is within your power to change."

I watched him dash up the steps and into the keep, mouth agape. *Get some rest.* The man was impossible!

Chapter Thirteen

When I went down into the hall that morning, I found Sir William alone in a chair on the dais. There was food on the table. The fruit I had devoured at midnight might never have been from the way my body reacted to the sight of food.

Looking up, he saw me. A smile lit his face, and my traitorous body glowed in response. Oh, stop it! Yes, yes, he was handsome, but....

"How fares my Kate?" he called, rising to hurry across the hall to me.

Gone was any hint of the distress I had observed in him at the table last night. Gone too was the sober man who confided in me his conflicted loyalties. No, this was the fellow who had come courting and claimed me for his wife: loud, cheerful, confident.

Perhaps I had only imagined the others.

I moved forward to meet him and was shocked when my legs swayed under me.

He was at my side in an instant, his arm wrapped tight around my waist, holding me close, holding me up. I did not want to admit it, but I was glad of his strength. Again.

"You are not well, by the look of it," he said, leading me toward the dais with great, almost exaggerated care.

"How else should I be?" I snapped as he helped me into the chair he had just vacated. "You have starved me for three days."

"Three days?" he said, seating himself on the table. "That cannot be! You have only been with me for a day and a night."

I squinted up at him. Surely that could not be right. Surely not....

But with so little sleep, how could I really be sure? These damned thick walls blocked out the sun.

He handed me a goblet. Without even lifting it, I could feel the alcohol in it pricking at my nose and my tongue. I could not drink wine in this state. I set it down.

"Here, Kate, look how diligent I have been in your care," he said, reaching for the plate in the middle of the table. "I have prepared your meal myself."

He removed the napkin covering it to reveal what, to me, was a dream of a meal: a slice of ham, the skin crisped with honey, a heel of white bread made from finely milled wheat, a piece of fragrant, mottled cheese, a handful of bright red strawberries. Dizzied by the sight, I gripped the edge of the table.

"Would you like something to eat?" he asked.

I couldn't take my eyes off the food. I was too weak, too flustered to say anything. I nodded.

He dragged the plate across the table. The sound was impossibly loud in the empty hall.

My hand moved out to snatch up the ham off the plate. My mouth was already full of juices in anticipation. Oh joy!

Fast as a striking snake, he grabbed my wrist, my bones like twigs in his fingers. I froze. Men had a right to "correct" their wives—God and law gave them that—yet for all our battles, he had never hurt me. His hand holding my wrist, so large, capable, and strong, was a clear reminder that he could.

Very softly, not quite threatening, he said, "Even the worst servant is repaid with thanks."

I could scarcely believe it. After everything I had been through, he was going to stand on ceremony?

My tongue itched with scathing words. I wanted to unleash them, to pour them over his head like a bucket of ice water.

I could feel my heartbeat racing in my veins under his fingers.

I drew in a shuddering breath.

"I thank you."

He released his grasp one finger at a time and moved away. I scooped up the ham and the bread with one hand but shoved a strawberry in my mouth first. The explosion of sweetness almost made me cry. I couldn't bear to look at him, watching me grab at food like an animal, but I couldn't help it. I glanced up. The only way I could describe it was that he was studying me. There was no mockery in his face, no gloating over my shame, no disgust or shock or any of the things I expected.

I put the food down.

"Done, then?"

I swallowed. My stomach felt like the cavernous inside of a cathedral, the food like the first trickle of pilgrims on a saint's festival day. Nay, my gut screamed. There must be more!

"Yes, thank you. I'm fine."

He whisked the plate away, replacing the napkin. I had to press my fist into my stomach to keep from begging.

He sat on the edge of the table and picked up a strawberry. I watched him—how could I not?—as he raised it to his mouth and ate it, savoring the sweetness.

"Kate," he said, and I tore my eyes from his lips.

"What, Sir William?"

"We will travel to your father's house today and collect your dowry."

This statement unleashed a torrent of emotion in my breast. "Must I go?"

His lips quirked up on one side. "Of course you must. What would you have your father think? That I made off with his daughter in the night and then trapped her in a tower? No, you will come with me and show him how satisfied you are with your lot."

"Satisfied?" I wanted to scream the word, but I had no breath for it.

He got up from the table, ignoring me. "Let's see, we have just had dinner, so if we leave now, we should be at your father's by suppertime."

I pointed up at the high window-slits, admitting thin streamers of what was clearly the pale, clear gold of first light. "Look you, sir, it is morning. If we leave now—and I do not know how far it is to my father's house, but I know that we rode through the night—we will surely not be there until dinnertime."

He spun around, his face suffused with anger. "Whatever I say, or do, or think about doing, you are determined to cross me. It is midday, I say, and we will leave now, and be at your father's at suppertime."

With that, he strode out of the hall, calling out for the servants to saddle the horses.

I managed to devour the bread and ham before a boy came to collect the plate.

Had the midnight journey from my father's house to Bitterbrook Keep been difficult? Had it been vexatious? Had I been unhappy and uncomfortable?

It was nothing, *nothing*, to the journey back.

I should say, the half-journey back, because we never got there.

We started, and started again, and started again, Gregory in front on his patient white pony and Sir William behind on his fiend from hell. But if I said anything, if I dared to contradict the all-knowing knight, if I allowed Conveyance to set one foot off the path, with a shout—"Crossed, crossed, ever crossed by this woman! Come, Gregory, turn about now!"—Sir William would order us to return to the keep.

The looks Gregory shot me every time he had to pass me to take the lead heading back west were not fit for a servant to give his mistress, but I no longer cared. I no longer cared about anything.

We would proceed westward for a while, long enough for me to doze a bit, and then Sir William would decide that I was docile enough to try again. After all, there was quite a bit of money at stake. So we would turn again and head for Whitelock.

Until some stray remark or wrong footfall doomed us to another tantrum by my lord....

We made it as far as the deep river by noon. I remembered crossing the river at night, the water up to Conveyance's belly, almost wetting my feet, the rush of it frightening in the darkness.

Gregory led the way.

"At this rate," I muttered, waiting, watching his pony pick its careful way across the slippery ford, "we will arrive at suppertime, just as he predicted."

Behind me, Sir William said, "What's that?"

"Nothing, sir. I said nothing."

"Move along, then," he said. "Gregory's almost across. No reason to just sit here wasting time."

I glared over my shoulder at him and nudged Conveyance into the water. He clearly remembered the night crossing as well as I did. Every muscle in his body communicated his reluctance to move forward, but at my urging he did, slowly and carefully.

When he was belly-deep in the river, when Gregory's pony was splashing and clattering out on the other side and Sir William's beast was snorting on Conveyance's heels, they attacked.

I never saw where they came from. I was looking down, watching as Conveyance placed his feet in the stony bed of the river, hoping he would not stumble.

I only looked up because someone shouted.

Gregory was suddenly surrounded by three men on foot with long, sharpened sticks they wielded like polearms and clubs, some jabbing at him and the horse, some striking at him.

He had drawn a sword I didn't know he had and was slashing down at them.

I pivoted in my saddle to look behind me.

A man on horseback, dressed in a stiffened leather breastplate, had charged into the water on a shabby horse to challenge Sir William. The two of them were hacking at each other with swords, the clang of steel ringing in my ears.

I was frozen in place.

Never, never in my life had such a thing happened. Never had I been so close to swords. Fighting. Brigands.

Conveyance surged forward, leaping for dry ground, angling away from the fighting men. I struggled with the reins. Although I did not want to be near the fighting, neither did I want him to bolt in a panic and get us both hopelessly lost.

Sir William's warnings about being alone suddenly made desperate sense.

As Conveyance's hooves struck the pebbly shore, someone

leaped up from a group of boulders, making my horse shy and dart sideways. While I fought to stay in the saddle, grabbing fistfuls of mane, the lad grabbed for the headstall. Conveyance jerked away from him, nearly pitching me off, but he got a hand on the reins and hung on. Instinct screamed at me to fight back, so I swung out a foot to kick the boy away, but I succeeded only in nearly tossing myself out of the saddle again while the boy got both hands on the reins. Using all his strength, he hauled Conveyance's head around and dragged him forward out of the water.

"'Ere," he called out, shifting sideways, and suddenly there was a knife pressed into my ribs. "Everyone quiet now!"

Suddenly, it was still. I dared not move. Sliding my eyes to the right, I could see Sir William in the middle of the river, his attention split between his opponent, who was bleeding from several wounds, and me. I could sense the tension in his body, his yearning to charge across and strike down the boy beside me. To my left, Gregory was also frozen, his face a mask of horror that it had come to this.

I trembled. My hands on the reins shook. I was ashamed of my fear, but I could not help it. I could not think what to do. Try to make Conveyance kick? But he was not battle trained. Try to knock the blade away with my hand? I'd most likely slice myself, and that thing was pitted and rusty....

While these thoughts flitted around my head like panicked birds, banging into one another and knocking themselves senseless, Sir William and Gregory stared. At me. At the lad and his knife. At one another.

I noticed the tiniest of movements, the slightest lift of Sir William's head.

Gregory's hand flew.

And the lad was face down on the ground, his knife-hand dangling in the water, with Gregory's dagger protruding from his back.

Conveyance squealed and danced away from the body, stumbling on the slippery rocks. I struggled to soothe him and to keep my seat, wishing all the while for Sir William to come to my aid.

The swordsman was dead before Conveyance was calm enough to stand still.

His shabby horse bolted downstream, leaping over the fallen body of its rider. The water around him turned red, then pink, the blood flowing like a cloud before a brisk wind.

Sir William charged the bank, bloody sword uplifted like some image of vengeance in a morality play. The men with the staves scattered, but he and Gregory pursued them into the underbrush lining the riverbank.

Shaking, I slid from Conveyance's back and ended on my knees on the pebbled shore. My knees and palms would surely be cut, but I hardly noted it at the time, so dazed was I. My stomach clenched and heaved, threatening to expel what little food I had enjoyed that morning. I closed my eyes and fought it back down, fought it down along with the gasping sobs that pressed at my throat, aching to be expelled.

Sir William emerged from the undergrowth, wiping his sword on a broad leaf. I turned my face away.

He was at my side in an instant, his heels grinding the pebbles underfoot. "Kate," he said, his voice full of urgency, "are you hurt?"

I could not force my tongue to form an answer, so I shook my head.

He slid a hand under my arm and lifted me. I might have weighed nothing I was so limp and boneless in his grasp.

With a sigh, he brought me back to Conveyance. Gregory bent to retrieve his dagger from the back of the boy who had accosted me.

To my utter humiliation, that was the moment that undid me, and I lost my breakfast on Sir William's boots.

He said nothing.

He lifted me, gently, into the saddle.

"Come," he said. "Let's go home."

When we returned to the keep, Conveyance stumbled into the courtyard with his head down, perfectly reflecting how I felt—off-balance, exhausted, spent. I did not wait for Sir William to help me off his back but slid off as I had by the river, somehow keeping my feet. There was a tingling in my fingers and tiny, bright stars danced at the very edges of my vision.

Dear God, I thought, *this is killing me.*

I made my way up the stairs into the keep. As I went, I had to put one hand down on each step in front of me so I did not fall.

Inside, the cool darkness engulfed me so suddenly I nearly swooned.

Sir William caught me.

I could not see, but I felt his strength enfold my weakness, and inhaled his scent: leather, sweat, and blood.

I gripped his arms and straightened, blinking up into his face. In the dimness, I could scarce see, even so close. His eyes were dark, shadowed, hidden beneath long lashes. His face was still, unreadable. I wanted—what?

I wanted to understand.

I wanted to know what he wanted from me. I wanted to know why he had freed me from my unhappy situation only to bring me here and make me just as unhappy. I had had no illusions of love, but nevertheless....

I pushed away from him and moved into the hall.

My eyes were adjusting to the lack of light indoors. I saw the hall again as I had the day I arrived, what was it, two days ago? Three? More? I could hardly say. The large space lacked the grace of my father's hall, lacked the ornaments and trappings of wealth. Its hearths yawned empty, its walls barren. Even the dining table and chairs on the dais that ought to have been grand were plain and undecorated, the table scarred with burn marks I could see now that the cloth had been removed in between meals. A title was no guarantee of anything. Certainly not peace for me.

I went to the dais and slumped in a chair. I was too spent to face climbing the stairs to the miserable little room that was mine. My head drooped and I let it fall, catching it in my hands, reminding myself fiercely all the while that I must not cry.

"Is she asleep or awake?"

"I don't know."

Was I? If I was asleep, I would not be able to hear the whispered voices, and I would not be aware of the numbness in my legs from sitting still so long. So I was fairly certain I was awake.

"Poor child, to fall asleep like that. I want to bring her a pillow. And feed her too."

"You wouldn't dare!"

"Nay, nay, of course not. But I've never seen the master like this. I don't know what's gotten into him. I feel sorry for her, poor thing."

"As do I. But the master knows what he's doing." My senses were returning to me; that was Gregory's voice.

"He does? What's he doing, then?"

"He does but mirror her own actions. She was a notorious shrew in her home town."

"Huh," the other voice said, considering. "But to what end?"

"To make a change, of course."

"Ah." A pause. "Do you think it be working?"

"I cannot tell, Curtis. I cannot tell. Come along, it's time to fetch supper."

"I don't know, Gregory. Is it to be supper or dinner now?"

Laughing, their voices faded away.

My eyes opened slowly.

The vast emptiness of the hall stretched before me. No tables in a room meant for feasting. Cold stone walls unadorned by even threadbare tapestries. Servants cursed for failing in their duties. I recalled Sir William's words: *"I am not a rich man."*

And yet the clothes offered by the tailor were of the finest quality, fit for great lady. The tailor himself bowed and scraped before Sir William as before a great and magnanimous lord, not an impecunious one. The food was fine and the servants clean and well kept, and clearly they were as confounded by his behavior as I.

All but Gregory, who thought he had the answer.

"He but mirrors her own actions."

I colored at the thought. Was I as impossible, as horrible as Sir William had been to me? If I had been, did I not have cause to be? I hated what I had become, what years of living with my sister and my father had made of me, but I knew no other way to be. If I was not the shrew, who was I?

"Good morrow, Kate."

Sir William's boots stood before me. I had been so wrapped in my thoughts I had not noticed his approach. I let my eyes travel up to his face, unreadable as ever. I tried to stand so as not to be disadvantaged, but my numb legs refused to support me and I crumpled to the floor. He made no move to help me. I gripped one arm of the chair and the edge of the table for support. From where I knelt on the floor, I could see out through one of the high, narrow window-slits. The sky was evening-dark, deep blue shading to purple, and the widening face of the moon was just sliding into the frame.

"You greet me amiss, sir. Though I may have slept here for a time, yet I know it is night."

He crossed his arms. "How so?"

I pointed over his head. "Look you where the moon shines."

He craned his neck up, looked back at me. "It is not the moon that shines so bright but the sun. It is near midday and time for dinner."

I rose unsteadily to my feet. The room tilted dangerously and I put both hands on the table to balance myself. "It matters not what meal will be served since you will not let me eat it, but the truth of your eyes you must acknowledge. I say it is the moon that shines bright."

"And I say it is the sun."

I stamped my foot, sending tingling needles up through my numb leg. "This is outrageous! A fool knows, a babe knows it is the moon!"

With great patience he said, "The sun, a star, a rock, a tree. It shall be what I say in my house."

Instinct raged in me to fly at him, claws out, futile as that would be. My heart was racing, my breath coming faster. My body wanted to fight. I closed my eyes and clenched my fists, pressing my nails into my palms, directing the pain into myself instead. Lashing out in a rage had always been my response. Harsh words and contradiction were my instant reply. Only a few days ago I had looked forward to this marriage as a chance to escape from my home and from the way I was forced to live there. Yet here I was, living exactly the same way, doing exactly the same things. Not unprovoked, surely, but nevertheless....

Nevertheless, what would change if I did not change? It had to start somewhere. His words of the other day by the pasture came back to me: *"How many times have you given them what they expected, Kathryn? And when were you going to stop?"*

If he expected me to fight, then that was what I needed *not* to do. I would surrender, instead.

God knew, I was too tired to do anything else.

I faded back to my knees. "Moon or sun or candle, it is whatever you say it is. Henceforth, I swear it will be so for me."

He took a step closer to me. "I say it is the sun."

I didn't look up. "I know it is the sun."

"Nay," he said. "You lie. For it is the moon."

I almost laughed. "Of course, husband. It is the blessed moon. For it is the sun when you say it is the sun and the moon when you say it is the moon, and the moon changes even as you change your mind. Whatever you call it, that it is, and so it shall be for Kathryn."

He came closer, then closer again, so slowly I thought I was imagining it. I felt something—I thought I felt something touch the crown of my head—but perhaps I had fallen asleep again in my little heap on the floor, for I jerked alert when he said, "Kate. My dear. Off to bed now."

I struggled up the stairs as quickly as my weakness and my dignity would allow. I felt his eyes on me until the first turning where I was swallowed up in the blessed darkness.

The door of my room was locked and would not open no matter how I rattled it. I was too troubled, too tired to puzzle it out. I turned to the only other door on that floor. It too was barred to me. I had to bite my fist to keep the tears from starting. What was happening? Was it not enough that I was broken, that I had given up? Was his victory not sufficient? Did I have to sleep on the floor before his bedroom door like a servant, like a dog?

Turning back to the stairs, I continued on my way. My feet seemed to fasten to each step so that I could not pull them away from the stone to force them upward. But at last I reached the top and drew a breath.

There was only the one door, and it stood slightly open, inviting me in. I was beyond trying to understand. I entered.

The room was spacious, taking up the whole of the upper floor, its walls curving in the shape of the tower like embracing arms. A slow, warm fire burned in one of the three hearths, casting an amber glow over the rich furnishings, apparently the only wealth that remained to Sir William. Carved armchairs with embossed leather seats. Thick woven rugs that could only have come from adventures on Crusade in Outremer. A huge, curtained bed deep with feather mattresses and fine linens. Folded neatly atop the bed lay a nightgown, and even from here I could see the quality of the fabric and the beauty of the lace at the neck.

A vase full of dried lavender stood on a table in the far corner next to a basin and a graceful silver pitcher. I imagined it full of clean water and looked down at my filthy dress. Tired as I was, I had to get it off, I needed to wash. I began to move across the room, my feet sinking deep into the impossible softness of those silk carpets.

As I poured water into the basin, the truth of what had just happened began to unfold itself in its fullness—I had given in.

"Moon or sun or candle, it is whatever you say it is." Had I truly said that?

Cold water sloshed onto my feet. I had been staring at nothing, blindly tipping the pitcher until it overflowed the basin. Cursing, I set the thing down and took up a towel to dab at the front of my dress.

My finger caught on a loose thread, sending tiny beads scattering. In fact, strands of beadwork hung loose all over the bodice. The once-dainty bows at the waist drooped, limp and sad. One sleeve was torn up the inner seam, revealing the pale skin of my forearm. The silk wedding slippers that peeked out from the muddied, tattered hem of my dress were ruined, spotted with mud and water and worn through in places. Hours of handiwork destroyed.

Never mind the towel, then. I couldn't bear to be near this horrific thing any longer, to have it on my body. First I yanked the sleeves off at the shoulders—they pulled free of the bodice with distressing ease—then grabbed hold of the bodice itself, disregarding the laces I couldn't reach anyway.

I shredded that kirtle as though I could take back what I had done.

Shivering in my chemise, the dress a heap of green silk at my feet, I wavered between rage and tears. How had I been reduced to such weakness that I had surrendered my own will to his? Had he starved and abused me into obedience?

Was there another creature on earth as miserable as I?

In my memory, tiny bells jangled.

The hawks. *They* were as miserable as I, trapped and blinded and starved until they complied.

Rage swelled. I should run out and set them free. I should release all of us from his tyranny, brigands be damned. A quick death by rusty knife would be preferable to losing myself here.

If only I could move.

The carpet was so soft under my feet, and the deep featherbed beckoned.

And there was something else, a thought flitting just beyond my reach.

Something Sir William had said.

What was it? Something about a falcon....

"My falcon is now sharp and passing empty...."

Yes, he had equated me with one of his captured birds, to be tamed and tied down!

No, that wasn't quite right.

I closed my eyes and remembered heat and sunlight. I remembered drowsing and waking, and the bright eye of the hawk on his fist.

He had called his hawk a partner. A wild thing at heart who would never be tamed. Was I like a hawk? Wild? Free? Never to be tamed? Was his intent through all of this madness not to crush my spirit, but to preserve it?

I sank down on the bed, my strength ebbing out of me with my indignation. Memories streamed through my mind, tripping over one another in their eagerness to be seen, touched, reexamined. Sir William's words, his actions—from the first time he leaned against the doorframe of my father's house to prevent me from escaping my lessons until this very night and our quarrel over the sun and the moon—were a challenge to me to stop fighting. He was showing me how awful it really was, and he was offering me an alternative.

And after all, was it so bad to agree with someone for a change? If he said the moon was the sun and I knew—I *knew*—he was wrong, what did I really lose by conceding the point?

I stood up. Because maybe he saw things that I didn't. Maybe what I thought was the moon wasn't the moon after all. Maybe dinnertime truly was suppertime. Maybe what I had believed all my life was simply flat-out wrong, and he was trying to show me.

"Kate is slender as the hazel branch." Sir William had said that the night he came to my window.

Blanche always said I was unattractively skinny. But Sir William called me slender. Maybe he liked that about me. Maybe he had liked me from the beginning.

Blanche always told me I wasn't pretty. She said my eyes were dull and brown as a cow's, and my nose short and snubbed like a pig's. And I had no reason not to believe her. Everyone knew she was the beauty in the family. I had looked upon her every day. I knew the truth. I *knew*.

But what if I was wrong?

What if she told me those things to make me doubt myself? What if she pushed me down because it lifted her up?

Without Blanche, I might have been pretty.

Maybe I was pretty.

My hands drifted up to my face. For the first time in my life, I wished for a mirror.

Maybe Sir William thought I was pretty. Maybe he had been trying to tell me, but I wouldn't listen. I couldn't.

The moon is the sun and the sun is the moon. I had to see what he saw. He had to *make* me see what he saw.

Me.

Kate, not Kathryn.

PART THREE

Whitelock Town, Again

Chapter Fourteen

Thursday, or perhaps Friday

"Good morrow." The words fell on my skin like rain. I hardly knew I was hearing them. All around me, the room still glowed but no longer amber-gold with firelight. It was the pink-yellow of a summer sunrise bringing with it a damp heat. My body was enfolded in softness, such a bed as I had never imagined, and for a moment I stretched and rolled in it. Then I remembered the voice and I jerked awake, up onto my elbows.

Sir William stood beside the bed—the opposite side—finishing the lacings of a crisp, white shirt. He chuckled.

"Are you awake?"

I narrowed my eyes at him slightly. "Am I?"

He nodded. "I thought," he said, stringing the words out in an amused, lilting tone, "that we might attempt a return to Whitelock today. Retrieve your dowry and your belongings. Prove to them all that you are married." He paused to fix a cuff. "Happily married," he amended.

"Of course," I agreed, even though the last thing I wanted at that moment was to return home, to see Blanche. My realization was so fresh, I wanted to savor it, to try it out safely here, away from her. If I went back, everything would be the same, and I was afraid I would fail the test. How could I be any different around her, around my family?

"Good. I'm glad you agree. Now make yourself ready so we can go." The slightest movement of his hand drew my eyes to the wall nearest my side of the bed.

There hung the kirtle, or its twin. The very kirtle he had mocked and destroyed before my eyes. When was that? It felt like a lifetime ago, though I knew it was but a few days. Had so very much changed in so little time?

I felt the smile start somewhere around my heart. "Thank you, Sir William."

He inclined his head, hiding a smile of his own. "You are welcome, Kate."

I don't think my feet touched the steps as I went down to the hall that morning. In part, this was because I felt like royalty in that dress, and, in part, because after days without eating the heavy fabric was the only thing anchoring me to the ground.

There was only one problem, and I hesitated at the archway leading into the hall.

Sir William caught sight of me and rose from his seat on the dais to join me in the shadows. "Don't you look lovely," he said, reaching for my hands.

I pulled back, holding tightly to the skirt, shoulders rigid. I could hardly blame him for his puzzled look. "The dress," I said, trying to explain. "I need—" His taunting came back to me, but I thrust it away. "I need your help."

His eyebrows went up. "You do?"

"I'm certainly not going to ask Gregory," I snapped, then bit my lip. "I don't have a maid, remember?"

A slow smile, thick and sweet as honey, spread across his lips. I watched them. I could not help myself. "You want me to play the part of your maid?"

I could not answer, caught between sharp words and fair ones. Oh, this change of heart was not an easy thing! I spun around to reveal the long open back of the dress, ribbons dangling low on my waist. The false sleeves swished as I moved, making me smile. I did adore them so.

I felt him freeze behind me. "Kate," he said, his voice gruff, close in my ear. "You are not wearing a chemise."

My heart slipped into my stomach and quivered there. I glanced down at my hands, still fisted in the kirtle's voluminous skirts and forced them to unclench. "I only had the one I brought from home, and it was filthy. Everything I was wearing was ruined...." I trailed off, suddenly aware of nothing but his presence at my back, his hands on my waist, his breath on my naked shoulders.

He slid one finger into the loop at the bottom of the bodice and drew it snug. One loop at a time, he worked his way up, pulling the ribbons tighter, and it seemed to take an eternity to accomplish. Because I wore no chemise, his fingertips brushed against my back again and again, sending whispers of fire along my skin. My breath caught as the dress pulled tighter and tighter against me, holding me as close as I suddenly longed for Sir William to hold me.

His fingers brushed the fine hairs at the nape of my neck. "Finished," he said.

I leaned back, just a breath farther, barely touching my body to his. He pressed forward, his nose just behind my ear, his fingers splayed along my collarbone.

I drew an unsteady breath and dragged myself away. "Thank you," I whispered and turned. He was facing away from me and I could not tell what he was thinking. Ah, well, when could I ever?

Dizzy as I was with more than hunger now, the table on the dais seemed farther away than ever. I had to ask for his help once more.

"Please?"

He offered me his arm and escorted me to the dais. "My lady? You are all politeness this morning."

"I have learned my lesson well, my lord."

"What lesson is that?"

"It is an ill tutor that knows not what he is teaching."

"The way you insisted that the tutors had nothing to offer, well, you were just asking for me to teach you something."

I could picture him standing in the doorway of my father's house, blocking my way. It was only a handful of days ago, less than a fortnight, but it felt as far away as a year or more. As if it had happened to another person.

A grin tugged at my lips. "This was hardly what I expected when I ran away from my lessons that first day."

He pulled out a chair for me, then took a seat across the corner from me. "Are you so very disappointed?"

"No, but...." Watching his face, his beautiful eyes, I almost couldn't do it. I couldn't bear to hear the answer if it was as I feared it was. "I know you came to Whitelock with a purpose," I said. "Did you come.... Did you come for us, for me and Blanche?"

He paused, frowning a little. "I told you, but perhaps you were so busy refusing my proposal that you have forgotten. Whenever your father visited my father over the years, he spoke of the two of you with the obvious intent of connecting his family to mine."

I stiffened. It felt good in the tight bodice of my new kirtle, all that pressure inside pushing out, outside pushing in. "And that idea appealed to you."

"Surely you know—" He leaned forward across the table, his eyes intent on my face. "Surely you must know that your father wanted me for Blanche."

I leaned away, pressing against the hard back of the chair. "Of course I know that."

"But do you know the rest? Do you know why you are here and she is not?"

"I assume it is because my father offered an amount of money that a man in your position could not refuse." Even to my own ears, my voice sounded strained and distant.

His hand hit the table with a resounding slap that echoed in that strangely empty hall. "No. There is no amount of money that would have been enough to induce me to take Blanche, and no amount of money that would have turned me from you. Can you understand that?"

I stared at him. Was he truly saying that he had rejected my beautiful sister? That he had not taken me solely for my dowry? "I don't—"

"The way your father spoke of you both, I knew there had to be more to the story than perfect Blanche and squabbling Kathryn. From the moment you interrupted us with a problem with your father's accounts, I understood what your life was like. What was it he said? 'Why in the name of heaven would a man want a clever daughter?' And everyone in town took his scorn for you as permission to treat you just the same."

I had no response to this. He had known, all along. He had indeed.

My face went hot, then cold, then hot again. Tears started in my eyes and I couldn't think what to do with my hands.

Then my stomach, unable to bear being surrounded by good food any longer, unleashed an outraged growl.

Sir William sat back and pulled my trencher toward him, quietly filling it with food while I collected myself. "Eat, Kate," he said. "We have a long ride ahead of us. You'll need your strength."

When I did not move, he took a bit of ham—oh yes, the ham!—and used his knife to cut a tiny sliver. "Here. Eat." With careful fingers, he brought it to my lips.

I watched him while I chewed and swallowed. My body rejoiced and demanded more.

Sir William chuckled. "At least you did not bite me," he said. "There is that to be thankful for."

I laughed too and began to eat, trying not to mimic a beast in the barnyard.

When I had eaten enough to quiet my stomach's sharpest demands, I sat back in my chair and picked at my plate. "How long do you plan on staying at my father's house?" I asked.

"Only long enough to get my coins," he said. "Why? I did not think you would want a longer visit."

"Nay, indeed not," I replied. "I would not go back at all if not for the dowry. In fact…" I looked at him. "I don't know if you will allow me to insist, but I will not stay under his roof."

"I would not ask you to. If we need to stay the night, we will stay at the inn."

"Thank you."

"Of course."

I dropped a berry uneaten onto my plate, suddenly no longer hungry. "I still don't understand. Could you not have found a wealthy wife who did not argue with you every minute of the day?"

"Of course I could," he said, smiling. "Think of all the trouble it would have spared us both. But a patient wife, a quiet wife, a dutiful wife, that is not what I need."

He gazed on me intently, urging my understanding, but it would not come. I shook my head slightly.

"Think back to what we talked about the other day. About Lancaster and York, and choosing sides, and what happened to my father."

"Yes," I said, drawing the word out as I considered his words. Another confrontation between the two great families was inevitable, and when that day came, Sir William would be in the thick of it. "I understand that if, or rather *when* Tudor marches an army through your lands and clashes with King Richard's army, all peaceful occupations will be disrupted. Your crops will be destroyed, trampled underfoot or cut down and eaten by the soldiers. And you need my gold to build up your defenses here and pay for the military service you will be required to provide to the king."

"Yes."

I threw up my hands. "But I still do not understand why you would not want a sweet, docile wife waiting for you at home in the midst of all this."

He hesitated, even shifted uncomfortably in his seat. I sensed he had never spoken these thoughts out loud before. "Because I may not be able to leave her waiting patiently at home. There may be—" He knocked his knuckles on the table. I had never seen him so ill at ease. "Look, Kate. Think of the alternative. I have a wife whose dowry is in gold. I have no children to protect, no other family to worry about. The worst that could happen, if I throw in my lot with Tudor and he fails, is that I lose this keep and my title, and truth to tell, that has happened before. I survived."

I found I could hardly swallow. "Nay. The worst that could happen is that you could die."

His laugh was sharp, bitter. "Then you would be a very wealthy widow. I hardly think your father would want you back again. You would open up a bookshop somewhere or marry a man of your own choosing. Don't tell me you would grieve."

Would I not grieve? I couldn't look at him. I hardly knew what to say. Instead, I pushed the question aside. "What about your people?"

I said. "The peasants and villagers who depend upon you for their livelihood?"

He frowned down at his clasped hands. "You've been to the village. You've seen how they live. It's no better in any of my demesne. When King Edward stripped my father of his title and lands, he put no one here in his place. Bitterbrook was empty for years. There was no one to protect them from raids by the Welsh, stealing their sheep and their cattle. No one to protect them from marauders or brigands or even from merchants taking advantage." Here he glanced at me, but if he expected me to defend my father's business practices, he was mistaken. "There are so few left now, so many have gone off to live with relations elsewhere, that it has been a struggle to seed the fields this spring. I don't know what the harvest will bring. I may have to hire workers to bring it in, but whether the yield will bring enough at market to pay them is anyone's guess." I began to say, but decided not to, that he had more than enough money to hire workers now that he had married me. His point, it seemed, was not about the gold.

"So my people? What do they care?" He gave another bitter laugh. "If I die in battle, the king gives them a new overlord. Little difference it will make in their daily lives. Or he leaves it vacant, and they continue on in their misery. Again, little difference to them."

I thought of Elizabeth, the girl in the village, whom I had promised to help. If William was gone, and I with him, then her hope went with us. But for the others? Maybe he was right. Maybe it made no difference which lord ruled.

He leaned forward in his chair, pushing the plates out of the way. His eyes on me were bright, blazing like a flame. I could almost feel the vehemence of his emotion burning into my skin. "I don't need this," he said.

I shook my head slightly, bemused. "What?"

"I mean, I don't have to have this. All this. I lived without it all those years. I can do it again. I don't have to be Sir William, Lord of Bitterbrook Keep. I can be William Pendaran, Nobody from Nowhere. If I sided with Henry Tudor and he failed, and if I survived, we could go anywhere. Take your money and do anything we want."

For a moment—for a long moment—his words frightened me. Terrified me. To be homeless, landless, adrift.... But if I closed my eyes, I could picture the Frankfurt book market. A bustling Flemish port. The wonders of Paris. Even the heretic unknown of Al-Andalus, all open to us to explore.

I leaned forward in my chair, reaching out but not quite touching his hand. I smiled at him instead. "Sir William Pendaran, still and always. From everywhere, not nowhere. And we'd be together. That's something."

He finished the gesture I could not, covering my hand with his. "Yes. That is something indeed."

Yes. Now my cheeks were flaming, the rest of my skin singing along with it, all from the simple touch of his hand on mine. I looked down, suddenly shy. He sat back, relieving me of the joyful pain of that contact, leaving me yearning for more.

Still, it had to be said, the hard truth at the center of our talk. "But it would be treason. To take up arms for Henry Tudor against King Richard, Sir William, it would be treason."

He took up the knife that lay on the table and held it up between us. The sharp edge glinted in the dim light that reached us through the high windows. With great skill, he spun the knife in his hands. "Not if he won."

Standing on the steps before the hall, waiting beside Sir William for our horses to be led forth, I was contented enough to allow myself to feel my place as the lady of the manor. In the days I had been here, I had not yet looked at these walls, this earth, as connected to me in any way. Now I tried to envision them as the home in which I would spend the rest of my days. It was both comforting and frightening, and I shivered a little despite the growing warmth of the sun and the weight of my kirtle. The beautiful kirtle that I could not keep myself from touching.

Two of the servants, Curtis and James, led the horses forward, one by one, the huge destrier in the lead. I couldn't help but remember the last time we went for a ride. How much had changed in me since then. I only hoped I could hold tight to that fragile knowledge, to keep it strong and vibrant when faced with Blanche once again.

Sir William offered me his hand to walk down the stairs. I took it. As we approached the horses, he started to chuckle.

"Why are you laughing?" I asked.

"Eleven days," he said.

"Eleven days?"

"Eleven days ago, I went to your village and met your father. Eleven days ago, I first saw you. And now here we are."

"And you find this amusing?" I heard the old sharpness in my voice. How easy it was to fall back into that old habit, to be the old Kathryn.

He lifted me into my horse's saddle. "Not at all."

I kicked his hands away from the stirrups and settled my feet in place. But I was laughing too.

The sun, climbing toward noon, was quite hot, and my face was beaded with sweat. Birds clamored and sang in every tree and thicket as we rode, and flying insects went about their work. The unmistakable scent of honeysuckle hung in the air. Tiny rustlings in the grass hinted at small creatures escaping our horses' hooves. The morning was alive.

I turned my head. "Sir William."

"Will, if you will," he replied.

Memories swirled like seeds borne on a puff of wind. A touch of Kathryn's old anger flared.

"Have you bent me to your will, then, sir? Are you now satisfied that I have no will but yours and I am thoroughly subdued?"

"Is that what you imagine this to be?" He seemed surprised.

"That is what you said."

"That may be what you heard, but it is not what I said."

I closed my eyes and went back to the tavern's common room in my memory. "I will be her only will and she will be mine." I opened my eyes. "Is that not what you said?"

"Am I not your Will, Kate, or do you have another? Shall I release you from this bondage so you may go to him?" He clutched dramatically at his heart. "Oh, Kate, you wound me! I thought you were mine and I yours!"

I burst out laughing. "I find I can trust neither my eyes nor my ears in your company."

"Nay, Kathryn was deceived. My Kate sees true."

"True enough," I said. "But you did nearly kill your wife with your 'kindness.' Surely there was some other way."

He looked down at his hands on the destrier's reins before looking at me. "Though words are your favorite weapon and you seemed to enjoy sparring with me, I could not make any progress against your armor. You never seemed to believe anything I said. And even after I told you to stop doing what is expected of you, you went on defying me, did you not? It needed time, and it needed you to open your eyes."

And my heart, I thought, but did not—could not—say. Fighting sudden tears, I blinked at my horse's mane, at the flowers dotting the grass, at the clouds high in the blue vault overhead.

"Still," I said, relying on words to protect me as always; he was right about that. "Still, you must know that I will have my revenge for the unspeakable manner in which you treated me."

"Oh, most unfair! I did only what was needful!"

"True. Nevertheless."

"Nevertheless?"

"I am devising diabolical torments for you."

He grinned. "I shudder to consider it."

"As well you should, sir."

"William, if it please you. Or Will."

"William," I said, enjoying the feel of his name on my tongue, "have you noted how the moon pours its gentle light over this meadow like milk, making the world pallid and white. One can hardly distinguish one plant from another. The evening air is so cool and fresh, don't you think?"

"Do you mock me now?" he said. "Enough, Kate, you know it is the sun."

I shook my head. "You cannot command me here, sir, for I

remember well what you said: that it shall be as you say in your house. And this most certainly is not your house."

He grimaced. "Ah, Kate, you are too clever by half."

"'Tis your doing, sir."

"How so?"

"You married me. I have always had too much will, and now I have married Will so I have an excess, a plenitude, nay, a surfeit of will."

William grinned and reached his hand toward me. I held out my hand, and he took it, pulling me closer. My horse grunted in protest but complied. Standing in his stirrups, William leaned toward me.

"Kiss me, Kate," he said.

So I did.

I don't recommend horseback for a first kiss. The unsteadiness of swaying back and forth in the saddle, the grunts and sudden, jerky movements horses make, the missed step dropping out from under you resulting in smashed noses or crunched teeth. These are not the joys you hope for.

Still, his lips—strong, warm, tender—the long-awaited touch, the welling up of your spirit as you feel this, *this*, at last, the resolution of so many questions, and the opening up of new, delightful ones.

Would it be entirely too dull to say that the day seemed brighter, the birdsongs seemed more joyful, the flowers smelled sweeter after that? Well, either you have been kissed or you haven't. If you have, you'll know what I mean, and if you haven't yet, you will. The nighttime journey from my town had been a blur of darkness and anger. This daytime journey is no clearer in my recollection because of its brightness. The sun illuminated not just the trees and meadows and tilled fields along our way, but shone its light within me. When we were not speaking to each other, I was content to let the birds speak for me. Everything, that day, was as new as the first day of spring.

As we approached within a few miles of Whitelock, we espied another entourage approaching from the north. Sir William took us off the road at once until he could be sure they were neither brigands as before nor the advance guard of a war party, whether royalists or Tudor's men. It was, we soon discovered, a company much like our own. A wealthy man traveling with his servants and, because he himself was not trained in arms, his hired guards.

After some deliberation, Sir William decided to approach them. There was more security in greater numbers, he said. We trotted our horses over to meet the man who was, like my father, a wealthy merchant, and I immediately recognized his name.

"Oh, Master Lawry," I exclaimed. "Your son—for it must be your son—has been a frequent visitor in my father's house and has been paying court to my sister, Blanche. The only barrier to their wedding is that the young man requires your approval."

Beside me, William muttered, "That was not the *only* barrier."

I prodded him with the toe of my boot, and he subsided, chuckling.

The elder Master Lawry, however, did not look at all pleased at the mention of courtship and marriage arrangements. "I cannot let that boy out of my sight," he said. "Forgive me, but do you mind if we proceed at a more determined pace?"

"Not at all," William said. "We are as anxious as you to get to Whitelock."

The man gathered up his reins, jerking his horse's head and making the animal fret. "With respect, sir, I think not."

We rode into the town square not an hour later. I will never in my life be able to do sufficient penance for the pride I felt in our arrival. I know how I must have looked, gleaming in that spectacular kirtle, with the headdress a foot tall and the veil brushing my waist, riding a magnificent horse who was fairly dancing at all the attention. And then there was Sir William with the breastplate of his knightly armor shining in the sun with his sword and shield strapped to the back of his blood-red destrier. Add to that, the parade of servants and guard all mingled together and the grand-looking Master Lawry adding his air of dignity to the procession. No amount of penance will ever be enough, for I shall never, ever feel sorry for it.

The citizens were gathered all agape by the time we had stopped before the inn, and Sir William and Master Lawry were debating whether Master Lawry should accompany us to my father's house or retire within the inn where young Master Lawry was staying. The dictates of hospitality were not entirely clear, as neither of the men lived in town. I allowed myself to look down just once and saw Ellen, awestruck, peeking out of one of the inn's windows. I flashed her a "can you believe this?" smile and she waved in bemused agreement.

All the good-natured disputation was beginning to grate on me. I wanted to get past the meeting with my family, obtain my dowry, and go back to Bitterbrook Keep—go home, I realized with surprise—as soon as possible. As I contemplated this shift in perspective, I saw my sister and her tutor, Cameron, hurrying across the street. His posture toward her was at once familiar and protective, and it all came crashing back into my memory. In everything that had happened to me since leaving, I had overlooked the revelation of Blanche's last "lessons" with Lucas and Cameron, that they were both imposters. The former, of course, being the real Master Horton, and the latter, the real Master Lawry, this elder Master Lawry's son. That the man who had been meeting with my father as Master Lawry was actually a servant and the tutor was the master. What I had reported to our traveling companion was not incorrect, but it was not nearly correct either.

As all of these thoughts tumbled through my head, I blurted out her name, pointing: "Blanche!"

The men fell silent, looking where I indicated. Blanche stopped. Her companion drew back from her, and I sensed he had been holding her hand or her arm. What had happened in the days I had been gone? She looked toward me, right at me, through me, and away. They continued moving up High Street toward my father's house.

"What the devil?" Master Lawry exclaimed. "That was my son!"

"As my wife told you," William said, "he has been courting her sister."

"I will get to the bottom of this!" Master Lawry said, pulling his horse's head around and setting off High Street after them. Most of the crowd, sensing a confrontation, followed at a respectful distance.

It seemed the decision had been made.

William, our servants, and I were the only ones left in the square.

"Are we not going to my father's house?" I asked.

"Soon," William said. "There is one thing we need to do first."

William dismounted in front of St. Bernard's church and tossed the reins of his horse to Gregory, then turned to help me down from the saddle. How many times before had we been in this position, with me waiting to come down from my horse's back, and how many different ways had that moment ended? All of them flitted through my mind, wrapped up in this one slice of time as I slid my feet from the stirrups and let myself fall into his hands, floating, light as the air around me, light as a leaf on the wind, so that I might never touch the ground again.

He set me down—in actuality, it took no longer than usual for my feet to reach the earth—and drew me close to him, but it is hard to comfortably embrace a man wearing a steel breastplate. He muttered an oath that should have made me blush but instead made me laugh. Taking my hand, he led me inside the church.

The nave was blessedly cool, its walls so thick that the heat of summer never truly penetrated. It being not even midday, only one candle burned, the red candle high above the altar, indicating the presence of God in the church. No ceremonies were going on, and the place was deserted. William went ahead to look for the priest, and I stood in a square of sunlight with my eyes closed, enjoying the sensation of being cool and yet bathed in sunlight at the same time.

It was only a few moments before they returned, the sound of William's long strides echoing off the rafters overhead, the priest's humble sandals a shuffling counterpoint. They were speaking as they approached, their voices melding with their footsteps so that I could not hear their words until they were nearly upon me.

"But have you not lived as husband and wife?" Father Edmund was saying, looking very worried.

"Nay, nay, Father, we have been chaste."

The priest cast a dubious eye on William, turned a hopeful look upon me. I gave him a wide, honest smile.

"You can hear our confessions first, if you wish, Father," William said.

"Nay, nay," Father Edmund said, a small echo of William's big voice.

"We want the church's blessing, Father," I said.

"There must not be any questions about our marriage," William added.

Father Edmund nodded vigorously. "Oh indeed, I take your meaning, sir." He collected himself. "Shall we step outside, then?"

Weddings took place in front of a church's doors to show that the partners had nothing to hide and to allow passersby to object if necessary. I must have paled. After Sunday's embarrassment, I had no desire to be seen getting married here, no matter what William said.

"Just *inside*, if you please, Father," William said, giving the purse at his belt a slight jingle.

"Indeed, sir," Father Edmund said, still nodding. Priests made a good living from such clandestine weddings.

He made us to face each other and clasp hands. Laying his stole over our hands, he said a prayer or two in Latin, the words of which flowed over me like so much Arabic for all I perceived their meaning in that moment. Then he was saying something to William, and William answered him. Then he turned to me.

"Do you take this man to be your husband?"

Oh. That simple. "I do."

Turning back to William, he said, "Do you promise to love, honor, and protect Kathryn your wife whatsoever may come, be it sickness or health, sorrow or joy, riches or poverty, until God our heavenly father does see fit to take you from this earth?"

"I do." Under the fine linen of the priest's stole, William—my true husband now—gave my hands a squeeze.

I knew what was coming. "And you, Kathryn, do you promise to love, honor, and obey William your husband...." When he said "obey," I tilted my head slightly, raising my eyebrows at William.

The priest finished speaking. "Kathryn?"

William winked.

"I do. Yes, of course, I do."

William laughed, loud and echoing in that sacred space. He pulled me close and dipped me back in his arms, kissing me thoroughly. I went hot and cold all over, all at once, my legs weak beneath me. Father Edmund leaped backward, jerking his stole away as though touching us might have sullied it.

"Have you a ring, sir?" Father Edmund asked when William set me back to rights. I was grateful for his arm about my waist, for I was as unsteady as I had been at any time in the last few days, only now it was not for lack of food or sleep. The look on the priest's face seemed to say that nothing could apologize fully for William's behavior.

"Oh, yes. That I do."

William produced a ring from his belt pouch and handed it over to Father Edmund, who blessed it with holy water from the font nearby, his back to us, and returned it to William. As William slid it on my finger, fumbling to get it over my knuckle, he said, "With this ring, I thee wed. With my body, I thee worship. With all my worldly goods, I thee endow." I had heard the words many times before, but never had they had such meaning. His hands on mine spoke volumes. We might have been alone in the church.

It was probably a good thing that we were not.

Father Edmund cleared his throat and made a fluttering motion with his hands. "Yes, well…."

"Thank you, Father," William said, handing him the entire purse from his belt. Father Edmund's eyes widened. I imagined William was thus forgiven for the kiss.

We burst out through the doors of the church. The ring on my finger sparkled in the sunlight, and I took a moment to examine it more closely. It was a simple gold band, with no ornamentation or jewels, and with a wry smile I recalled his words so oft repeated, *"I am not a rich man."* My sister had a dozen rings that were far more ornate, but not a single one so precious as this.

William, with a firm grip on my hand, pulled me in the direction of High Street. Surprised, I pulled back. "What is the hurry?"

"Your father owes you a wedding feast, does he not?"

I grinned. "That he does."

I should have known Blanche would ruin it.

Why did my father seem bent on playing out the folly of our lives in the streets around our house? Why had Father Edmund said nothing about secretly marrying my sister that very morning? Almost that very moment? And why, why, *why* could I never have a joy of my own without Blanche taking it for hers?

As we came up to the house, all I wanted was to speak to my father, to collect the coins he owed us for my dowry now that we were, in fact, married, and leave. That, and force him to acknowledge that I had a better life without him. And if he did that, maybe I could even say thank you for this marriage that had opened my eyes.

Instead, we found my father and Master Lawry the elder on the step at the front of my house. Before them were Blanche and the younger Master Lawry, kneeling and half cowering as both fathers poured their disapproval over the heads of their children. I listened, stunned, as Father said such harsh words to Blanche as he had never said to her in her life. Words like "ungrateful" and "disrespectful" and "unworthy of my favor."

We forced our way forward through the crowd of eager onlookers. I found myself clinging to William's arm for support. "Why did she not wait for approval?" I whispered.

"Hush," he whispered back, but nodded at the same time to let me know he agreed.

At last, their tirade spent, Father and Master Lawry drew back into the doorway and spoke quietly together. Then Master Lawry announced, "We are going to decide what is to be done about your dowry and your marriage portion"—here he pinned young Matthew Lawry with a sharp look—"of *my* lands and goods. But what's done is done and, as the priests say, what God has joined.... Well."

Blanche and Matthew, kneeling, dared to raise their heads, and I noted some of Blanche's old confidence in her face again as the elder Master Lawry came forward to lay his hands on their heads and bestow his blessing. All eyes were on them. I may have been the only person who saw the look on my father's face as he noticed me in the crowd and looked between his two daughters. His eyes moved from Blanche, who had deceived him, to Kathryn, who had done exactly as she was asked. I might have pitied his confusion, his clear sense of betrayal, had I not a lifetime of grudges piled up. As Master Lawry backed away, Father visibly shook himself and stepped forward to bless them, and I knew the moment had passed forever.

"Come," Father said, "come inside my house. I will have a wedding dinner prepared for this young couple."

Blanche and her husband rose, beaming, amid sounds of general merriment and approval. My hands clenched into fists, nails driving into my palms, except that where my hand grasped William's arm, they drove into his sleeve. "A second time?" I said through gritted teeth. "She has had my wedding feast and now her own, and still I have none!"

William gently loosened my grip on his arm. I had left marks on the fabric. "Gently, my dear," he said. "Remember why we are here, and it is not for a feast."

"Indeed not." But I was still shaking. How quickly it descended upon me, the old rage, the old injustice....

"Kate." William slid his arms around me, clasping his hands at my waist, just tight enough to comfort and not bind. He murmured in my ear, "Kiss me, Kate."

I squirmed in his arms, trying to face him. "Here? In the street?" The crowd that had gathered for the spectacle was now departing, some invited in for the feast, some heading back to the green to spread the gossip. Still, there were so many people about.

"Why not? You're a married woman. Are you embarrassed?"

"Well, nay, but...."

He moved his lips a little, pressed a kiss behind my ear, sending a shiver down my spine. "Should we leave instead?"

I was still shaking, but for an entirely different reason now.

"Wait." He loosened his hold enough for me to twist around to face him.

Will. Who had seen me, seen *me*, from the moment we met. Who hadn't slept or eaten either, to help me see myself.

In the middle of the street, in the middle of the day, I went up on my toes and lifted my lips to his.

It was better than the one on horseback, and hinted at more. Warmer, hotter, deeper. His hands tightened on my waist, pressing me close.

Damned armor, crushing the breath out of me.

Releasing me, he began to fumble with the straps at his shoulders, muttering under his breath, "Where is Gregory now that I need him?"

I glanced down the street, and sure enough, Gregory was coming, leading the horses from the church at a leisurely pace. "He comes. Let him help you with that, and then we will go in. You have not yet spoken to my father about the dowry." I stepped back, clasping my hands to still their trembling. "Besides," I added, "I have to see what happens at my horrible sister's wedding party."

William took my hands in his and kissed them, one then the other. "I would not deny you, if you wish it."

Chapter Fifteen

Friday

Blanche sat at the head of the hastily erected table in the courtyard with her new husband on display beside her like the Queen of England with a valuable new prize. Father beamed proudly, and the Mountain, roused from her bed yet again, gloated while she stuffed herself on the excellent dinner. I never once met her glance, but I could tell what she was thinking: both girls married in less than a fortnight, both with surprisingly little effort, both to prominent, important men.

I was surprised to see that Master Horton, seated near us at the table, also had a new wife by his side. Apparently, having seen something of my sister's true nature, or at least having tired of being her plaything, he had married that widow in his cousin's household. She was a stocky woman who, frankly, looked a great deal like him, right down to the dark hairs sprouting from her chin.

At the far end of the long table, Father raised his glass. "I bid you all, drink the health of the new-married couples, Blanche and Matthew, as well as Kathryn and William."

A rousing cry of "The new-married couples" went up. I shook my head, fuming silently. Had they all forgotten that less than a week ago, William had failed to appear at the church? That he had taken me from this very house under cover of night? No one questioned whether I had wanted to go or not. No one cared whether we had ever had a church ceremony. No one wondered whether I was happy or well cared for. No one was asking any questions because there had been an agreement. And besides, it was only Kathryn. Blanche was the one who mattered, and Blanche was happy.

William covered my fisted hand with his. "Peace," he said. "They don't see you."

I blew a long breath out of my mouth. He was right.

I smiled, unfurled my hand beneath his, and took a huge swallow of wine.

Old Master Greenwood, who of all the men had come up empty-handed in this matrimonial contest, said in a loud voice, "You gentlemen both seem to have done quite well for yourselves coming here to our town."

Matthew, the young Master Lawry and now my brother, seemed at a loss. William raised his glass toward my father. "Whitelock, and matrimony, have been nothing but kind."

Master Horton, already a little drunk, murmured across the table to William, "For both our sakes, I hope your words are true." I glanced at his wife, sitting beside him, who could not have missed his comment. I realized I did not even know her name.

William smiled at him and said to me, "Why, I do believe my friend Horton fears his bride!"

The woman frowned at William. "I am not afraid of him."

"You mistake my meaning, mistress," William said. "I mean to say, *he* is afraid of *you*."

"He that is giddy thinks the world turns round," she muttered, looking pointedly at me.

"Roundly replied," William said, clearly dismissing her, but I would not let it rest.

I leaned forward, planting my elbows on the table. "'He that is giddy thinks the world turns round,'" I repeated. "I pray you, tell me what you mean by that."

Of course, I knew exactly what she meant.

Master Horton put a hand on his wife's arm and laughed nervously. "Now, now, my dear. It is a wedding party, after all."

His wife drew herself up and looked over at me. "Your husband," she said, "being burdened by a shrew for a wife, thinks my husband to be in the same situation. Which, of course, he isn't." She smiled, a singularly unpleasant thing. "And now you know my meaning."

I turned to William, whose eyes were bright with restrained mirth.

"I still cannot make out her meaning, husband."

Master Horton shook his head and groaned. "Sir William, please...."

William rested a hand on my arm and leaned in close. "Don't give her what she wants," he whispered. "Don't be who she expects."

I settled back in my chair and smiled across the table at Master Horton's wife. "Oh, all right. But surely she knows that by any proper measure, she falls well within the mean."

I was watching her puzzling through my words, trying to make out whether she should take offense—*oh, yes, yes, you should*—when Blanche stood up at the head of the table. "I need my sister's help in preparing for my departure to my husband's home."

William took my hand as I started to get up from my seat beside him, tugging gently until I bent to him. He whispered a single word in my ear, his breath stirring my hair, warm on my skin. "Peace" was all he said, a reminder, but his touch had the opposite effect.

The Mountain struggled up from her chair. "Can't do it without me," she insisted, and I found that awful woman, Dame Horton, behind me as I made my way inside. I suppose she took our departure as a signal for a general withdrawal of the ladies from the head table.

The sound of merrymaking in the courtyard below drifted up through Blanche's window. I picked my way across the room, avoiding the clothes strewn on the floor, and looked out. Some of the guests had begun to dance on the small lawn, laughing as they tried to avoid the fountain and flower beds. The men still at the head table grew more raucous, jesting and clinking their glasses together. I turned back to survey the room and sighed. Of course she asked for me. She didn't want to have to clean up all by herself.

The Mountain lumbered in, supported by Margaret, and deposited herself on the bed. She picked halfheartedly at a linen chemise, perfect for summer. I wished I had one under this silk kirtle, which by now was clinging to my skin in interesting ways. "This'll do for now," she grunted, "but you must make your husband buy you new things. Fine things."

"Naturally," Blanche replied, tossing a blue chemise at me to fold. "He will do whatever I ask of him."

I took the gown by the shoulders and gave it a firm shake to get out the wrinkles. Blanche scowled at me. "Have a care, Kathryn."

I did not even look at her, folding the chemise shoulder to shoulder. *"He will do whatever I ask of him."* Blanche knew nothing.

Dame Horton picked up another item of clothing and rumpled it into something resembling a folded mass. "My Master Horton has promised me a new kirtle of brocade and one of velvet, once his latest shipments have arrived."

Blanche smirked. "How nice for you."

"Now, Blanche," said the Mountain, "you know what is expected of you as a wife, in your husband's house."

Dame Horton smiled wickedly. "Aye, and in his bed?"

I cringed. Oh, surely not this.

From outside came the pounding of fists on the table and shouts of laughter. "A hundred," someone shouted, and "No halves" someone else called. What was going on out there? It sounded like wagers. Could I possibly escape this dreadful conversation and join whatever game the men were playing?

Dropping the folded chemise into a small trunk, I shut my ears to words like "the staff of his manhood" and picked up another one. I tried to ignore the Mountain's rumbling voice, Dame Horton's cackle, Blanche's high, almost nervous laugh. The door opened suddenly. I looked up, immensely grateful.

Benton, a servant of Matthew Lawry's father, stood in the doorway. He made a pretty bow in Blanche's direction. "Mistress, my master your husband sends me to bid you come to him."

The women fell silent. I kept my hands in the trunk, not moving. This was going to be interesting.

Blanche looked at him as if she had never seen his like before. "Your master says what?"

To his credit, the fellow did not flinch. "My master Lawry, your new-wedded husband, sends me to bid you come to him."

Blanche waved a scarf in the air. "My husband bids me come to him."

He looked relieved. "Yes, mistress."

Blanche smiled. I knew that smile. Poor fellow. "Please, do tell your master I am busy—" she gestured at the messy room about her "—and I cannot come."

"This…" Poor Benton looked around the room. I busied myself with the clothes in the trunk. "This is your answer, mistress?"

"Indeed. Now leave us."

He bowed again, not quite as prettily as before, and left, closing the door softly behind him. The other women erupted in shouts of laughter.

Dame Horton slapped Blanche on the shoulder. "Now let's see how he takes it."

They rushed to the window, falling to their knees so they would not be seen. The Mountain, perhaps knowing she could not so conceal herself, perhaps not really caring what was going on now that we girls were married and no longer under her charge, settled herself deeper into the pillows. I hesitated, but I had to know what was going on in the courtyard. I scurried over behind Blanche and leaned against the side of the window.

"Indeed?" my husband was saying. "She is busy and cannot come? This is her answer?" His voice was huge with astonishment. I wanted to laugh out loud but dared not.

Young Matthew was downcast, shaking his head as the other men laughed at him. "It is fine for you to say so, Sir William," Master Greenwood chided. "You had best pray that your wife does not send you a worse reply."

"Indeed, Master Greenwood, I do hope for better."

Master Horton gestured to Benton. "All right, Benton. Go and entreat my wife to come here to me at once."

William laughed. "Oh, *entreat* her. Oh, well, then surely she will come."

Master Horton frowned at him. "Say what you will, sir. *Your* wife will never come."

We all scrambled away from the window, expecting Benton at any moment. "They're up to something," Dame Horton said. "I'll have none of it."

I went back to folding my sister's clothes. The others didn't bother with the pretense and stood staring at the door, awaiting Benton.

When he swept into the room and bowed, he seemed to notice right away that something was wrong. His smile faltered. "Mistress

Horton, if it please you, your good husband sends me to *entreat* you come join him. At once." He swallowed loudly and repeated, "If it please you."

Dame Horton crossed her arms over her broad bosom, frowning down upon the boy. "Nay, it does not please me. I am not a dog to be summoned or a toy to be used in such a manner. Let my husband come to me."

Benton did not stay for further abuse but bowed while backing out the door. Blanche congratulated Dame Horton on her reply, shaking her hand.

We returned to the window. Benton had arrived in the courtyard to make his report. Master Horton was now the butt of laughter.

"Oh, this is terrible," William said. "Worse and worse. This is intolerable. This is not to be endured! Gregory, go to your mistress and say I command her to come to me."

Master Horton snorted. "I have known her longer than you, sir. I know what her answer will be."

We rearranged ourselves once again. Gregory came to the door. His bow, though not as pretty as Benton's, was perfectly respectful. "Milady," he said. I did like the way that sounded, here, in this room, with these people. "My master, your husband, commands that you attend him."

I could hear Blanche giggling. Dame Horton, like her husband, snorted. The Mountain rumbled.

I stood up from Blanche's traveling trunk. "And so I come."

The women fell silent.

I followed Gregory down the stairs. He glanced back at me once, only once, and there was satisfaction on his face. I smiled at him as he passed out into the courtyard. I paused in the wide archway, making sure they all marked me. "What is your will, husband, that you send for me?"

My father swore an oath for which he would have to do penance.

William had his back to the door, as though he cared little for my arrival. With great indifference, he turned to face me. "Why, where is your sister? Where is Master Horton's wife?"

I tossed my head up at the window. "They are upstairs, chatting in Blanche's room."

"Bring them down here. If they refuse to come, beat them until they relent. Go now, and bring them here at once."

I dropped a neat curtsy and went.

The sound of the men's voices followed me up the stairs. "A wonder," and "a marvel," they said.

Not so. Just not what you expected. I smiled to myself.

Blanche and Dame Horton were staring at me, gape-mouthed when I entered the room.

"Well?" I said. "Are you coming, or do I have to beat you until you relent?"

Blanche scuttled across the room.

Dame Horton narrowed her already squinty eyes at me. "You wouldn't dare...."

I charged toward her, my hand reaching for her ear. "I'll drag you, woman, don't think I won't."

"Don't think she won't," the Mountain rumbled.

Her hands up to protect her ears, Dame Horton yelped, ran forward, and hurried out the door. Blanche followed after her. I went behind, a sheepdog with my little flock.

It is hard to describe the shock on the faces of the men when we returned to the courtyard. There was a nervous, uncomfortable edge to their laughter, unsure as they were whether this was just some elaborate joke William and I were playing at their expense. Blanche and Dame Horton were sullen and pouty, Blanche much more attractively of course, and they moved apart, as far from me as they could while still avoiding their husbands. Dame Horton crossed her arms and glared at me.

I dipped a pretty curtsy toward the table, to my husband, and waited.

William took a few strutting steps, looking me over. "Kathryn," he said, tilting his head to the side. "That headdress you are wearing becomes you not. Off with it, throw it underfoot."

Oh, a blow to my heart! But I let none of that show. We were partners now. I reached up and loosened the pins, letting it drop as though it were a leaf or a bit of thread, a thing of no consequence.

The gathered guests gasped as one.

"Lord, I pray I never be brought to such a silly pass," Dame

Horton said to my left. I did not spare her a glance, keeping my attention on William.

"Kathryn!" Blanche said, running forward to snatch up the headdress, waving it under my nose. "What foolish duty do you call this?"

Matthew Lawry stood up. "I would that your duty were as foolish, too, my dear wife! The wisdom of *your* duty has cost me a hundred crowns since dinnertime."

All the men roared with laughter. So they *had* wagered on our obedience.

Blanche stamped her foot and shook the headdress at him. Inwardly, I cringed. The damage to my beautiful ornament! "The more fool you for wagering on my obedience!" she retorted.

"Kathryn," William said. Whenever he said that name, it caught at me like a knife on my skin. "I command you, tell these headstrong women what duty they owe to their lords and husbands."

Dame Horton snorted in derision. "Come, come, you are mocking. We will hear no such thing."

"Oh yes, I say, and first begin with her," he said, pointing to Dame Horton.

"She shall not," Dame Horton said, frowning.

"I say she shall," William said, moving toward her, towering over her, suddenly the man who had killed brigands without hesitation.

Dame Horton subsided.

I took a breath, looking around. Everyone waited to hear what I would say.

And then I realized, they *weren't* waiting to hear what I would say. They thought they knew what I would say. They were leaning forward in expectation, waiting for the shrew to emerge, to say harsh, devastating things. To show Sir William how very wrong he was to trust in my appearance of obedience, to believe in me. They knew me, you see. They knew Kathryn Mulleyn since she was born, and Kathryn Mulleyn was a bitter, angry shrew.

They wanted Kathryn. I gave them Kate.

As directed, I focused on Dame Horton with a smile. "Smooth your brow, and do not glare with scornful glances to wound your lord, your king, your governor." I took a step toward her, letting my hand sweep back toward the table where our husbands sat. "It harms your beauty"—I thought I heard a snicker or two—"as frosts do bite meadows, and is in no sense good or amiable. Your husband is your lord, your life, your keeper...." What more could I add? This was fun, now that I was deep in it. "He is your sovereign. The one who cares for you and for your maintenance. He commits his body to painful labor, both by sea and land. To watch the night in storms, the day in cold, while you remain safe at home, warm and secure." I could sense the men, merchants all, nodding at this description of their labors. Meanwhile, I knew a timid wife sitting at home was the furthest thing from what *my* husband wanted. He wanted a woman brave enough to take risks at his side. The glow of that knowledge filled me as I continued.

"He craves no other tribute from you but love, kindness, and obedience. Too little payment for so great a debt." It struck me at this moment that, having been married for only a few days—in reality, less than a few hours—I had absolutely no authority on which to base these statements. Yet the men approved as though I were reading from scripture, and the women looked sufficiently guilty that they were not protesting. I allowed myself to look at William, standing under the low-hanging branches of the apple tree. He was biting his lower lip to keep from smiling and nodded, just once, to let me know I was doing well.

Looking straight at him, I said, "Such duty as the subject owes the prince, a woman owes to her husband, and when she is peevish, sullen, sour, and disobedient to his honest will, what is she but a foul contending rebel, and a graceless traitor to her loving lord?" I paused. We had, that very day, solemnly discussed rebellion against our anointed king. He knew exactly how much weight to give my words.

He nodded again, just once.

Warming to my theme, I dropped to my knees, the sharp gravel of the path grinding into the many scrapes and sores there. But I refused to flinch. "I am ashamed that women are so unwise as to offer war where they should kneel for peace..." Here I looked toward Dame Horton again, "...Or seek for rule, supremacy, and sway when they are bound to serve, love, and obey."

I looked down at my hands, and brought them together on my

belly as I had seen women with child do. "Why are our bodies soft and weak and smooth, unmade to toil and trouble in the world, except that our temperaments and our hearts should match them?" *What folly my words are*, I thought, *as though childbirth were not more painful labor than any of these men had ever known.* As though women did not have to be strong in that labor, as though they did not give their own lives to bring forth new life. As my own mother had. I swallowed hard. This was becoming more difficult.

I stood and turned away from the table, facing Blanche directly for the first time. Her face was full of dismay and a kind of horror, seeing me transformed into something unrecognizable. I reached my hands toward her, and she shrank away.

"Come, come," I said. "I have been as arrogant as you, as willful, as determined to bandy word for word and frown for frown, but now I see that our lances are but straws. I see it now. The more we fight, the more we fail. Swallow your pride. There is no help for it."

I knelt again, more carefully this time, and placed my hands, palms up, flat on the ground. "Put your hands beneath your husband's foot, as I do, in token of your duty. My hand is ready, if it please him, to do him ease."

The silence in the courtyard was complete. Not a breeze ruffled the bushes along the walk. No one breathed or scraped a plate or cleared a throat. Finally, William walked forward and stood before me, but I kept my eyes on the toes of his boots. This felt uncomfortably, almost painfully, familiar. How many times had I been in this posture of surrender in the past few days?

I did not move, did not look up until he said, so softly that only I heard him, "Kate."

His eyes sparkled. He leaned down and took my hands and very slowly raised me up, just as a sovereign raises a subject. I stood tall, holding his hands tightly, aware of all eyes on us. I smiled, just a little.

William went down on one knee, still holding my hands. I heard a gasp. Blanche, I thought. "Now, that's my girl," he said, to me alone. "Come on and kiss me, Kate."

Stone by stone, the courtyard fell away. The wedding party disappeared. Sunlight, shadow, music, the scent of spices and sugar, all faded as I took a dreamlike step toward him. He pulled me down to sit upon his knee. Quivering, I recalled the day he'd proposed, when I'd called him no better than a stool, easily overlooked. How wrong I'd been. My fingers traced the line of his jaw, his cheek, his neck, discovering the feel of his skin. So warm, so alive, just a hint of roughness where Gregory's blade had missed in shaving him. Had I truly never touched his face before? Nay, only to strike him.

I bent my head, touched my lips to his, and my heart ignited. Something hard, stone and steel, as unmovable as armor around it, cracked, slipped, and fell away. My hand found its way into his hair— at last!—and discovered thick, silky, luxuriant bliss. I forgot entirely where I was.

His fingers touching my chin, William pulled away. "We... should go."

I nodded, not trusting myself to speak.

We stood, somehow not parting. I looked around at the company. Blanche was staring at me. I could not read her expression.

"We must away," William announced. "Thank you, Father, for your hospitality, and blessings upon you other happy couples. I am taking my wife home."

Father hurried over. Blanche called out, "But there's the dancing. You must dance at my wedding. You must!"

Ah, Blanche. Poor Blanche. To be so outdone.

Father shook William's hand and embraced him, whispering in his ear. He did not mean for me to hear him, but I did. "Another dowry for another daughter. I'm giving you another twenty thousand crowns, my boy. I don't know what you've done, but you've changed her. By God, she's a new woman."

William shook his head and tried to demur, but Father would hear none of it. I looked away—anywhere but at my father who was selling me yet again—and my eye caught a movement at the door. Margaret hovered there, and when she saw me looking at her, she fluttered a hand at me in a hesitant wave. I stepped away from William, sliding into the shade of the apple tree and beckoning to her. She came out to meet me, looking distressed and even a little frightened.

"Margaret?"

"Please, Mistress Kathryn, milady." She grabbed my hands and curtsied so rapidly I was afraid she'd fall. "Please take me away with you."

Looking at her troubled face, I realized I had not considered how this house might have changed in my absence. I would have thought that serving two women instead of three would be easier, but perhaps not if those two women were Blanche and her mother. Poor Margaret.

I squeezed her hands. "Of course. Of course. Get your things. Quickly."

She ran off. William was walking toward me, so I went to him.

"What was that?" he asked.

"My maid."

"Your maid?"

"Yes. If you recall, my husband did not provide me with one, so I have remedied that failure."

"And with no trouble at all to your husband. Excellent."

"I thought you'd agree." I glanced at my father, who had rejoined his guests. "Where do we stand on my dowry?"

William jingled a purse at his belt. "I have collected my wagers from this day's entertainment," he said, a laugh in his voice. "The rest, on the morrow. We'll need to hire a mule or two, perhaps a wagon and some of Master Lawry's guards. Now that the dowry amount is double, you clever girl."

I made a face. I had not done what I had done for money. Would my father ever understand anything in terms other than gold?

I sensed Margaret behind me, eager to go.

"The inn?" William prompted. Yes. He had promised we would not stay in this house. But it did not feel right just to walk away. Some last thing needed to be....

I caught sight of Blanche, embroiled in a quarrel with her new husband. In her hand, she still held my headdress.

"One moment," I said.

As I approached them, Matthew Lawry fell silent. Blanche, sensing victory, berated him a moment longer. I heard an ominous warning about who would be obedient to whom before she, too, noticed me and stopped talking.

We looked each other over for a long moment.

"My headdress, if you please."

She considered, then handed it to me as if it were a dirty rag. She shook her head. "I do not understand you, Kathryn. You have completely surrendered yourself. I would never have believed it had I not seen it with my own eyes. The Kathryn I know—"

I cut her off. "You do not know me. You never did."

Her eyes widened. "But this submission. This isn't you."

I wanted to look at William, but I knew she would see it as weakness rather than the gathering of strength that it was. She could only see love in her own terms, what she could get from someone, how she could control him. She would never understand. It was pointless to try.

And yet, years of pain cried out to be expressed.

"All my life, I've had to show the world a false face to make my life bearable. Why do you think that what you saw today was any more real?" I turned to leave, then realized there was one last thing I wanted to say.

"You once asked me which of your suitors I wanted. None of them. I envy you nothing. I don't envy you your suitors or your husband, handsome as he is. I don't envy you having to live in your father-in-law's house at his sufferance, obliged to justify every penny to him."

I looked at Matthew. "And I don't envy you, finding out who you really married. Good luck to you both."

"Kate?" William called from across the courtyard. In his voice, I heard his concern for me.

"I am ready," I said, and I walked away forever from Blanche, from my father, and from that house.

Chapter Sixteen

Friday

William opened the door to the inn and strode in without a thought. I balked at the threshold like a horse at the edge of rickety bridge, quivers of instability running up through its legs.

When a long moment passed and I did not enter, William stuck his head back out the door. "Kate, what's the matter?"

I twisted my hands together. "I know I must go in, but… William, the last time we were here, the things I said, and you…."

He chuckled at the thought. "Do you think anyone will remember?"

"Of course they will remember. They always remember. I am the shrew."

He walked deliberately down the four steps and stood before me, arms folded. "You are not the shrew," he said sternly. "You are Kate. My Kate. Have you forgotten your triumph so quickly?"

I shook my head.

"Must I sweep you up and carry you within?"

I gasped a laugh and discovered I was breathing again.

"Good." With a reassuring smile, William reached out his hand. I took it, and we went in together.

The common room of the inn was, thankfully, rather empty that evening. A small cluster of local men gathered around a table at the far side of the room. Several travelers ate or talked over their pints at the tables by the open windows. Master Miller perched on a high stool at the bar, talking Master Brewer's ear off.

Master Brewer looked up as we walked in, and he hurried over to greet us. William spoke to him quietly, the innkeeper nodding and agreeing to everything. As we settled onto a pair of stools at the bar near the stairs leading up to the guest rooms, William said, "Now, you see. It's not so bad. Master Brewer greeted us kindly, and no one else has taken note of you."

I gave a little snort. "Master Brewer is only glad to see you return with gold in your purse."

"That may be. Nevertheless, all is well, is it not?"

"Yes," I had to admit. "For now, all is well."

The man who had been posing as Matthew Lawry appeared in the shadows of the stairway beside the bar. He was dressed in the ordinary clothes of a serving man, drab and plain, and they suited him far better than the fine garb he had been wearing when he called at my father's house. Before, he had been constrained both by their too-small fit and by their improper style for his station. Now, he moved with ease in his loose shirt, dark blue tunic, hose of nubby, dull fabric, and soft leather shoes. He had piled several trunks in one corner of the common room, and a storm sat on his brow as he went about his work.

"Do you suppose he is moving his master's things to my father's house?" I nodded in his direction.

William pivoted on one leg to see. "I suppose so, yes. Why?"

I narrowed my eyes, taking a sip from the mug of Master Brewer's excellent cider that had appeared before me. "I cannot imagine he is very happy about the way fortune's wheel has turned. It is all very well for his master, for he has got what he wanted, but what of this fellow? He was put at great risk, and do you suppose he will be greatly rewarded for it? No, for young Matthew Lawry has no money of his own, and his father does not approve of what he did to secure my sister's hand."

William swung back around, a smile quirking his lips. "What are you saying, my dear? I have already given you a horse and a dress and a maid. Am I to hire a man I don't need away from your sister's husband on your whim?"

I leaned closer and whispered in his ear, "It is my will."

He groaned, rolling his eyes, and pushed away from the bar. In the dark quiet at the base of the stairs, he stopped the young man as he set a lute case on top of the stack of trunks. I looked into my cup of golden liquid to wipe away the vision of another lute destroyed, made to ring the neck of Master Horton by my own hands. Sighing, I took a deep draught of the cider. I could not regret what I had done, precisely, but I could wish I had shown a bit more restraint. Kate would be more circumspect, I vowed.

Ellen Brewer emerged from the kitchen and worked her way down the bar, wiping with a rag. Shame colored my skin at the sight of her. Not only had I wrongfully abused her over her suspicion of Master Cameron and Master Lawry, I had treated her badly the last time I was in this inn, expecting—nay, demanding—her sympathy and abandoning her when she didn't react in the way I wanted her to.

Kathryn had been a terrible friend.

Kate, I vowed, would be a better one, even if this was the last time I saw Ellen Brewer.

"Ellen," I said.

She gave me a sidelong glance from under her cap and approached me slowly, not pausing in her tending to the bar's cleanliness. Gripping the cider mug tight in my hands, I forced myself to look at her, forced myself to say the words, "Ellen, I'm sorry."

She looked startled, like she had never expected to hear those words from me. For which I could not blame her, as I had never said them before.

"Sorry?"

She was going to make me explain. She was going to get the most out of this apology. I drew in a breath. That was all right. She deserved it.

"I am so sorry for the way I treated you in the last fortnight. I'm sorry I doubted you about Master Lawry. You were completely right, and I should have believed you. I should have trusted you. I should have—" My voice was accelerating, my words tripping over one another.

Ellen rested a hand on mine, smiling slightly. "Kathryn. It's all right. Just to hear you say—it's all right. Apology accepted."

I heaved a sigh and returned her smile. "Thank you. When I saw you, I was afraid.... I was afraid you wouldn't talk to me."

She gave a rueful laugh. "Hardly. You're still my only friend in this bloody town." She twisted the rag in her hands. "And not even that any longer. You've gone far away now."

"Not so far...." But I trailed off. The half-day's ride to Bitterbrook might as well be a Crusade to the Holy Land for Ellen.

"Would you—?" She cut herself off, her eyes finding her father, who was still deep in conversation with the miller. "Could you possibly take me with you?"

I was startled into silence. For once, I had no idea how to answer her. "Ellen, I would if I could," I said at length, "but I don't know what I could offer you. We are friends. How could you work for me? It would be...."

"Strange, I know," she finished for me, her defeat showing in the slump of her shoulders. "I just want to leave, too, now that you're gone. There's nothing for me here."

"You'll inherit the inn, won't you?"

"I don't want the inn."

"But surely you don't want to be my servant either!"

She sighed. "I don't know what I want. But I see you." She gestured vaguely at my dress, meaning everything. "And I want something more."

"Shall I catch a knight for you as well?"

She flicked the rag at me, as she had that day on the green, and this time I laughed and let her hit me.

"I promise you, Ellen, I will find you a way out. I don't know what that will be just yet, but I will come up with something. I'll find you a prospect for marriage or work that will make you happy."

She touched my hand again. "Thank you, Kathryn."

"It's less than I owe you for your friendship all these years. And call me Kate. Please."

She gave me a quizzical look but agreed. "All right, Kate." She paused. "I thought you hated when he called you that."

I shook my head. "Changed my mind."

"Hmmm." She poured more cider into my mug. "Whatever you say, *milady*."

I groaned. "Oh, don't mock."

"My one friend in the world is a fine lady now and I can't tease her about it?"

"I am no fine lady," I retorted. "I don't even have a chemise under my kirtle."

"Lady Kathryn!" She feigned shock.

We both burst out laughing. She leaned in closer. "Mother's making up the best bedroom for you right now," she said, a sly suggestion in her voice. "She's up there now putting more straw in the mattress. Making sure it's nice and soft for you." My cheeks went red, and it wasn't from the cider or the heat in the room.

Ellen peered at my face. "Wait. What is it, Kate?"

Again, I could not speak.

"Have you not—?"

I shook my head. At the look on her face, I shrugged. "You know my sharp tongue, Ellen. We argued for a day and a night. And then some."

"And yet you seem quite content with each other now...." Her voice trailed off and up suggestively.

"Indeed," I said, looking down at my now-empty mug of cider.

Ellen glanced around, making sure her father was still well occupied, and reached under the bar. She came up with a tiny cup and filled it from a short brown bottle. My eyes began to water from the strength of the spirits as she poured. I couldn't help but laugh. "Ellen, what are you doing?"

"Mother always says, whiskey loosens the bones. Go on. All at once now."

Ellen's eyes were both eager and teasing. I knew if I held the tiny cup under my nose for too long, the bitter smell would vanquish me. It was only growing worse. I took a breath, opened my mouth, and poured it in. Fire exploded on my tongue as I swallowed, and Ellen laughed as I gasped for air. She hid the bottle back under the bar and whisked the cup off to the washing tub while I struggled to regain my composure. The warmth flooding my limbs felt remarkably like the heat of kissing Will earlier in the courtyard. My ears tingled. I glanced at him without turning my head, fighting the urge to smile.

Ellen refilled my cider. "Loosens the bones," she whispered with a wink.

Indeed.

From his place by the stairs, William spoke, raising his voice to address the room at large. In a moment, conversation stilled and all eyes fell upon him. The power of a title and a purse full of gold.

"I have a pence for any man who takes upon himself the office of this man, Adam, here, and delivers safely to the house of Master Mulleyn all of these goods here by the stairs. And a cup of Master Brewer's good ale upon your return."

All of the local men in the tavern and half of the travelers leaped up from their seats, and while there were more men for the work than needed, William gave each of them the promised coin and sent them off to my father's house.

He returned to stand beside me, watching the fellows scramble to do his bidding. His hand settled lightly, possessively, on the small of my back, and the thrill of it shot through me, settling, like the whiskey, in my belly, but then sinking lower.

Lovely. Intriguing.

Ellen, with a smirk, moved away, wiping the bar unnecessarily.

"William," I said, fighting through the sensation, "you have given them a week's wages for a walk down the street."

"That's all right," he said. "Today, I am a rich man with a pretty, young wife. I can afford to be generous."

Warm, glowing. Could everyone see my feelings? This wasn't just the whiskey, I was fairly certain of that.

I will be her only Will....

Here, in this very room, he had announced his intentions to the whole town.

His hand on my back. Oh, I had no clear sense of what I wanted, but I knew that standing here talking was not going to accomplish it. I wanted to be swept up in his arms, carried up the stairs, set down on that overstuffed bed....

My imagination failed. Failed, but wanted to know the rest.

Meanwhile, Will was still talking. I took a sip of cider and forced my wandering wits to attend to his words.

"...many a lady in my time, but you! You were resplendent today! The way you had them hanging on your every word—I knew you were clever, but that, my dear, was pure poetry."

I blushed at the flattery even as I bristled at the mention of others. "Many a lady?" I queried in my old, teasing voice.

He swallowed the rest of his cider. "Oh, don't be jealous now. Mayhap this one was clever, or that one had a beguiling singing voice, or another moved with grace—" He waved a hand around as though we were in the market together and he was showing me items for sale.

All my heat turned to ice and I jerked away from him, nearly oversetting the stool behind me. "How many, sir? How many were these numerous ladies with their numerous virtues?"

For a moment, he blinked and stared, stunned.

Then—woe unto him!—he laughed.

I lunged for him with a growl. He caught my wrists and pinned them close to my sides. Spinning me into the near-darkness of the stairwell, he held me while I hissed and spat, a wildcat in his embrace.

At some risk to his face, he held me tight, speaking low and soft in my ear. "You," he said, the word shivering along my bones. I stilled and dropped my hands, though he did not release my wrists. "You," he repeated. "So perfect, so peerless. What creature could ever compare to you?" His lips were so close to my ear they almost touched it; then suddenly they were tracing a path along my neck. I could hardly breathe. "All other women have their virtues," he went on, kissing his way to my collarbone, "but those are matched by their equal vices." Then he lifted his head, looking into my eyes with truth, with desire. "Only you, Kate, are worth more than everything else— more than the gold your father gave for you, more than your sweet face or your skill with a lute." He kissed the tip of my nose. "Or with the thumbscrews."

I had to laugh, though my breath caught in my throat, right where the trail of his kisses had stopped. Suddenly, everything I had been through in the past few days came bubbling up in my chest and that tightness in my neck threatened to turn into tears.

"I'm sorry," I said, leaning my forehead on his chest. I had to strive to keep my voice steady. "I have only just learned to be Kate. I'm sorry if I lose her sometimes."

He wrapped his arms around me, tucking my head under his chin with one hand and cradling me close with the other. His heart beat slow and strong beneath my ear. I closed my eyes and allowed myself to savor this entirely unfamiliar, entirely welcome sensation.

"If ever you lose Kate," he said, "come to me and I will help you find her again."

THE END

Thank you for reading! For more from Maryanne Fantalis, check out mfantaliswrites.wordpress.com and join her mailing list.

Please sign up for the City Owl Press newsletter for chances to win special subscriber-only contests and giveaways as well as receiving information on upcoming releases and special excerpts.

mfantaliswrites.wordpress.com

www.facebook.com/mfantaliswrites

twitter.com/mfantaliswrites

All reviews are welcome and appreciated. Please consider leaving one on your favorite social media and book buying sites.

For books in the world of romance and speculative fiction that embody Innovation, Creativity, and Affordability, check out City Owl Press at www.cityowlpress.com.

ACKNOWLEDGMENTS

On a summer evening in 2010, I sat in the Mary Rippon Theater at the University of Colorado in Boulder watching Shakespeare's "The Taming of the Shrew." I didn't know it at the time, but the path of my writing career was about to change.

When I went home, I couldn't stop thinking about the play. Instead of seeing a woman abused into obedience – which was what I had dreaded going in – I had experienced something entirely different. I started jotting down notes about what I had seen and felt, hoping to get it out of my system and get back to my "real" work.

Three months later, I had the first draft of what would become *Finding Kate*.

Thus, I have to begin with a heartfelt thank you to the Colorado Shakespeare Festival for their consistently excellent work, and specifically to the director and actors of that production of "The Taming of the Shrew" for their inspirational performance.

This book would not exist without the dedication and talent of the editors and staff at City Owl Press. Amanda and Tina, you took my manuscript and made my dreams come true in a beautiful way. Thanks also to Lisa of LisaBooks for the gorgeous cover design. The authors of City Owl are a loud, boisterous group – laughing, sharing highs and lows, and always there for you when you need them. I am so glad I chose City Owl as my publishing home.

There aren't words to express my appreciation to my Louisville writing group. We've been meeting every week for the past seven or eight years, and you've kept me going when it would have been so much easier to quit. You have each played a special role in my writing life: Trudy, my project manager and problem solver, keeping me on track from week to week and year to year; Stephanie, a fellow dreamer who always looks for deeper meanings; Lisa, who had the courage to try NaNoWriMo and showed me how wonderful writing without inhibitions and perfectionism could be; and Jack, the most recent member, who has been like an athletic training partner, demanding that I keep striving, achieving, and honing my craft. Without the four of you, I don't think I could have kept going through these waiting years… and it certainly wouldn't have been as much fun.

One of the best things about living in the Boulder/Denver area of Colorado is the vibrant and supportive community of writers here. Specifically, thank you to Tara Dairman, Jeannie Mobley, Jennifer Chambliss Bertman, and Emily France who have shared chai and advice about the business as they blazed the path to publication ahead of me.

I have to thank Katharine Owens and Courtney Mckinney-Whitaker for their long-distance friendship and honest feedback on my work. Kat and Courtney, you always make me think, and you always make me laugh. Thank you for sharing your lives and your writing journeys with me.

Special thanks to Cedric Pereira, who agreed to take my author photo even though he knows how much I hate photos of myself and then managed to make me look good, and thank you to Tami Westen, who made the photo shoot so much fun; to Chris Fravil and Becky Karch, for always reading my earliest (and ugliest) drafts and telling me to keep going; to J. Anderson Coats, who always knows where to find the most obscure medieval reference materials; and to Anne Sandoe, whose Shakespeare acting class taught me a whole new kind of courage.

My parents instilled in me a love of history, literature, and all things British. My mother, in particular, taught me to love reading and would have been incredibly proud of this achievement. My father, at 80, still works hard and learns something new every day. Without their example, I would not be the person I am today.

My husband's parents have always made me feel like one of their beloved children. Their love and support have been unwavering, and I am immensely grateful.

My kids have tolerated more than a little benign neglect throughout their childhood in my pursuit of publication. They've turned out well in spite of it. In fact, they astonish me.

Finally, a writer of romantic fiction has to have a good imagination, but she also needs a solid grounding in the reality of "happily ever after." I am lucky enough to be living my happily ever after, every single day. Jeff, I couldn't do any of this without you.

ABOUT THE AUTHOR

MARYANNE FANTALIS lives in the foothills of the Rocky Mountains with her husband and two kids, and it's the only place outside of England she'd ever want to live. Her fiction combines her two favorite subjects – medieval England and Shakespeare's plays – and she'll talk your ear off about either of them if given the opportunity. In addition to writing novels, Maryanne teaches writing at the University of Colorado at Boulder. Look for her in one of her favorite spots: playing in a racing mountain stream, browsing at the local public library, or getting inspired at the Colorado Shakespeare Festival.

mfantaliswrites.wordpress.com

ABOUT THE PUBLISHER

CITY OWL PRESS is a cutting edge indie publishing company, bringing the world of romance and speculative fiction to discerning readers.

www.cityowlpress.com

Made in the USA
Lexington, KY
19 April 2017